Thug Mansion

Mz. Lady P

Thug Mansion

www.shanpresents.com

I would like to dedicate this book to my READERS. You guys are the best hands down. Never in a million years did I ever think that this series would be so successful. With each book that I dropped in this series you guys wanted more and that's what kept me writing and coming up with dope plots for you guys. The Love and Support you guys showed this series has made Thug and Tahari Kenneth very popular in the Urban Fiction Genre. Not to mention you guys made them they epitome of that Hood Love you guys like to read about.

After eight books I wanted to give them a happy ending. As you know the whole crew has been through so much. The timing was perfect so that I could set the scene for a new generation in the Thug Legacy. This journey has been absolutely amazing and it's because of you guys. You all get the highest honor and recognition. It's your world. I just live in it. Thank you all so much for the love and support that I receive on a daily basis. Without you guys I'm nothing. Stay Tuned for more dope reads!!!!!!

With Love
Mz. Lady P

Table of Contents

Chapter 1- That Thug Life

Thug

As I sit in my man cave watching *Paid in Full* for the hundredth time, I can't help but think about my life and how far I've come. I have a beautiful, sexy wife and we now have eight beautiful children. We have officially adopted Monae and Nico's daughter, Nicaria. She's very much our daughter and we treat her as if she came from us. Monae wanted us to change her name because she wanted her to have no parts of Nico. We've renamed her Kylie Kenneth. It's taken some time, but she's grown used to her new surroundings and family.

I have more money than I know what to do with, and most importantly I have my freedom. After all of these years of running a successful drug operation and laying niggas down who felt the need to cross me, I'm blessed to be in the land of living and able to enjoy the fruits of my labor. My wife and my kids want for nothing. Over the years I've gone hard in the paint to give them the life that they deserve. I put my blood, sweat, and tears into building my empire so that I could one day pass it on to my sons. I know that I shouldn't want that for them, but it's a part of their genetic makeup. It's in the Kenneth blood to run drug empires. At the same time, being able to flip that shit into something positive. We might break the law, but we're smart enough to get rich in the process.

One thing for sure and two for certain, Tahari and I are raising the next breed of street royalty and they will not be fucked with on any level. Right now, I just want them to be kids and enjoy life like all kids should. However, I'm aware that they don't live like other kids. They have a rich, spoiled life. Not to mention their parents are the King and Queen of the Chi. Who the hell am I kidding? Tahari and I are legends in these streets and we aren't done with creating history. We've done a lot of epic shit over the years that has a lot of motherfuckers in relationships thinking they're the next Thug and Tahari.

I'm gone keep it one hundred, my baby and I are cut from a different type of cloth. We're flattered that we've had such an impact on couples. However, at the end of the day, we didn't choose this "Thug Life," it chose us. That's what makes us a cut above the rest. We embrace this shit because we had to fight from the moment we met to get where we are today. So, as I sit back and face this blunt and take another shot of this Remy, I embrace being in retirement and being a family man.

Not to get it fucked up, I'm still that nigga that has the ability to dismantle armies and make the streets bleed until I'm satisfied. Let's not forget, if I'm not satisfied Tahari will make sure I am. Fuck Bonnie and Clyde. It's Thug and Tahari these people looking up to these days.

*****

I laid my head back in my theater seat as I guided Tahari's head up and down on my dick. After all these years, she still has that million dollar mouth and pussy. That shit still right and tight after eight kids. After all these years of marriage, she makes each time feel like the first time. I'm more in love with her now than I ever was.

When shit was looking impossible, she made it possible. I was able to take leaps of faith in life because she was there to believe in me, regardless of whether my decisions were wrong or right. We've both made decisions that had the possibility to break us, but the shit made us stronger than ever. I'd do the shit all over again if it meant my wife would be along for the journey. No matter how hardcore of a nigga I am, Tahari Lashay Monroe- Kenneth makes me weak as fuck.

Tahari sped up the pace and started going crazy all on my dick. That made me cum full force, spraying my seeds down her throat. She looked up at me with those sexy, but devilish ass eyes, and smiled as she swallowed my seeds.

"Fuck you smiling for?" I asked her as she stood up and began to remove her pajama bottoms.

"'Cause I just did that motherfucker the right way. I had you speaking in tongues and shit."

We both laughed as she sat on my lap and got ready to put my dick inside of her. That shit was short-lived when we heard the sounds of someone banging on the theater door.

"You already know who that is," Tahari said. She stood up and placed her pajama bottoms back on and I put my dick away. I got up opened the door to see a eight year old Ka'Jaiyah standing there with her thumb in her mouth and her hand on her hip.

"What do you want, little girl?"

"Can I come in here with you and mommy? Kaine and Kash locked me out of their room, KJ said I can't come in his room because I can't keep my hands off of his things, Ka'Jairea is on the phone with Lil' Hassan, and Kylie, Kaia and Kahari are sleeping."

"Well go in your own room. Me and mommy are talking right now."

"All y'all do is talk with the door closed all the time. Why y'all can't talk with it open?"

"Ka'Jaiyah go to your room, right now. I done told your grown ass about questioning us when we say something. Do like your Daddy said!" Tahari said as she walked towards the door full speed ahead. Ka'Jaiyah stomped off and rolled eyes.

"If I hear one door slam or you tearing that room up, I'm whooping your ass!"

Ka'Jaiyah has anger issues like me. When she gets mad she tears shit up. I've lost count on how many tablets and phones of hers I've had to replace due to her breaking them when she's gotten mad.

"Why you got to be so hard on her, Ta-Baby?"

"That's her fuckin' problem. You let her get away with way too much. I have to be like that with her because she's out of control. She's eight, not eighteen. You need to start chastising her, not rewarding her. You're creating a problem that will be hard to break when she gets older. I'll fuck her up before I let her think it's okay to be disrespectful to us."

"She won't be like that. Stop exaggerating all the damn time Ta-baby. Ka'Jaiyah just happens to be our spoiled child and she requires more attention. She's just like you, Bae. Beautiful, feisty, and spoiled rotten by Daddy," I hit Tahari on her ass and grabbed another blunt to flame up.

"Daddy definitely spoils me," Tahari said as she sat on my lap and began to rub her hand over the waves in my hair. I handed her the blunt and she looked like she had drifted off into deep thought.

"What are you thinking about?"

"I was just wondering how Python was doing."

"Well you don't need to worry about what the fuck he doing. Leave that nigga where he at. Now we both agreed that we're out of the game and we're focused on our legit businesses and our family. Every motherfucking thing else is irrelevant. I don't want to hear that shit again Ta-Baby. Do you understand me?"

"Yes. I understand you, Ka'Jaire. You don't have to yell at me like I'm a child. I've told your ass about that shit."

Tahari jumped off of my lap and stormed out of the theater room, making sure to slam the door behind her. I couldn't do shit but laugh because she had just shown the same behavior our daughter does when she can't get her away. At the same time, I felt bad about raising my voice at her. Of course I hate for her to be mad at me, so I needed to smooth things over. A happy wife is a happy life. I'm not even trying to be in this bitch getting blue balls fucking with Tahari. When she gets mad, she holds out on the pussy and a nigga need that shit like I need air. I'm gone have to take one for the team this time around. I'm gone have to suck on that pussy real good tonight.

After I faced the entire blunt, I went upstairs to find Tahari. She was in the kitchen making dinner. I couldn't help but fallback and watch her ass cheeks jiggle with each step as she moved. I slid behind her as she stood over the stove. I placed soft kisses on the back of her neck.

"I'm sorry I raised my voice. I just don't want you getting any ideas about that nigga Python. We're retired and focused on our businesses and family right now. Don't it feel good to just relax and not worry about being shot at or the police coming for us?"

Tahari turned around and wrapped her arms around my neck. We engaged in a passionate kiss and gazed in each other's eyes.

"Yes, Bae. It feels great. I didn't mean to make you upset. He just crossed my mind, that's all. I'm happy and content with where we are in life. There's no need for you to get all upset and getting to acting crazy just because I thought about my grandfather. It's an adjustment to go from killing and drug dealing to just chilling, but I'm handling it. I love lying in bed and you're there with me every night. I sleep comfortable knowing you're safe from all the dangers the street has to offer. I love you, Ka'Jaire."

"I love you more. Now hurry up, a nigga hungry and I don't want no food."

I flicked my tongue out letting her know what I really was hungry for.

"You so nasty. Let me hurry up though so I can feed you."

"That a girl," I said as I tapped her on the ass and walked out of the kitchen.

As I sat in my recliner and turned on the TV, I wondered if I was really as retired as I wanted to believe. I still ran the streets silently. King, Dutch, and Nasir were doing all the footwork because my original crew was also retired and enjoying the fruits of our labor. Killing and drug dealing had been our life. Retirement has been good to us, but truthfully, I could always feel when something was on the horizon. I had a bad ass feeling I couldn't shake and I wasn't ready for any of it. I just want to live life and be great doing it.

Chapter 2- Life of a Thug's Wife

Tahari

I laid in bed next to Ka'Jaire, staring at the ceiling in deep thought. After all of these years of riding shotgun next to him in the streets, I was having a hard time dealing with retirement. As for Thug, he's so content and doesn't have a care in the world about the shit. These days, he's chilling, smoking, and drinking Remy. Enjoying the shit out of being retired. Sometimes he makes me mad at how relaxed and nonchalant he is. I know that I should embrace him being in the comforts of our home, because we never had a moment's peace when he was in the streets.

The kids are enjoying having their Daddy at home to take them to school, cook for them, and allow them to do whatever the fuck they want to do. He's a regular ole Mr. Mom, but I'm the one who does all the cleaning after they fuck up.

Don't get me wrong, I love him being home and spending more time with the kids and me. It's just that my house was a helluva lot less chaotic when his ass was in the streets. I'm just being honest.

That's still my baby after all these years. He still looks at me like I'm the most beautiful girl in the world. He makes me feel special. He still spoils me rotten, and he still fucks me like each time is the first time. In other words, he still and we still.

After all of our trials and tribulations, we still have so much to smile about and be thankful for. At the end of the day, and after all that we've been through, we're a strong united front as husband and wife.

Our life is a fairytale and most women would kill to be in my shoes. But like I've said before, these bitches couldn't walk a mile in my Louboutin's.

*****

Since Ka'Jaire was sleeping peacefully, I decided to get up and cook breakfast for my family. Marta was still living with us, but these days she's retired as well and living the good life right along with us. Marta definitely deserves to put her feet up and relax after raising our damn kids.

As I walked past Ka'Jaiyah's room, I could hear her talking. I swear this little girl was a damn night owl. She be up watching TV and sneaking on the phone with Heaven's grown ass. I get sick and tired of her teacher calling me damn near everyday because she always falls asleep in class. I'm tired of whooping her because Thug allows her to get away with murder. I'm going to fuck around and murder both of them if they don't stop testing my gangsta. I opened up her bedroom door, and just I expected, she was on the phone.

"Give me that phone, right now!"

"I can't Ma. I'm talking to Heaven and she's really sad."

"I don't give a damn if she is sad. Y'all have no business on the phone at five in the morning."

"Please Ma, don't take my phone! I was trying to make her feel better. Heaven was crying because Auntie Rosé and Uncle Remy were fighting. Uncle Remy was bleeding."

"Give me that phone," I snatched it out of her hand and put it up to my ear, but all I could hear were the boys crying.

The sound of Remy and Rosé arguing in the background made me shake my head in disbelief. Remy has been on some other shit since finding out that Thug was really his brother, and Rosé has been getting the brunt of all his anger. I felt bad for her because Remy is the gentleman out of the crew. So for him to be acting out of character is really hurting her. After listening for what seemed like forever, I had to hurry up and hang up. Thug and Remy were pissing me the fuck off being stubborn with one another, but this was the final straw. Thug was about to get up and we were about to go and see what the fuck was going on over there, whether he wanted to or not.

"Thug, you need to wake up!" I said as I shook him, trying to wake him up.

"What the fuck Ta-Baby?"

"You need to get up right now. Remy and Rosé are over there in that house fighting in front of those kids. Heaven and the boys are over there screaming and crying."

"Mind your business, Tahari. I'm not about to be getting in another niggas business with regards to the way he handles his wife."

"He ain't just another nigga, he's family and so is Rosé. I thought family is everything to you? I bet if that was Malik you would have hauled ass getting over there."

Thug was pissing me the fuck off acting like he didn't give a fuck about Remy, but deep inside I knew he loved him. Thug prides himself on being the big brother and the one who makes sure everybody is okay. So for Remy to be rejecting him has him feeling a certain type of way.

"Last time I checked, the nigga didn't fuck with me. So I don't fuck with him."

"You and him really getting on my fucking nerves being childish. Life is too fucking short for y'all too be acting like this. You can sit around and not do nothing but I'm going over there."

"It's too early in the morning for this shit, Ta-Baby. I'm not about to argue or fight with you because your hardheaded ass going to do whatever the fuck you want to do anyway. Just leave me out of the shit."

Thug pulled the covers off him and walked his naked ass into the bathroom. I followed him and stood in the doorway, with my arms folded across my chest, watching him as he pissed. He was doing too much right now.

"Why you got to say all that?"

"Look, I'm done talking about this bullshit. As you can see, I'm using the washroom. So either you're going to hold this dick while I'm pissing or shake it when I'm finished, and if you not then you can get away from this door, Tahari."

He slammed the door in my face like I wasn't even standing there. I was worried about Rosé, so I threw on some clothes and headed over to their house.

I used my key and went inside to find Remy trying to stop himself from bleeding and Rosé sitting on the stairs, smoking a blunt like it wasn't shit. For a minute, I just stood frozen, trying to see if I should snatch Rosé's ass up and get her out of the house, or if I should call a damn ambulance for Remy who was bleeding all over the place.

"You need to get to the hospital quick, Remy," I said as I tried walking towards him.

"I'm good, sis," Remy said as he walked out of the door. I turned and looked at Rosé, who was still smoking the blunt in silence. I went and sat down on the stairs next to her and she handed me the blunt.

"Would you help me pack some stuff for me and the kids. I have to leave this house. I can't stay in here another night with him acting like this. We need to give each other some much needed space. We've never been the type of couple that physically hurt one another, so this is too much. I lost control, Tahari. I stabbed him in front of our kids and now Heaven is mad at me."

Rosé put her head down on my shoulder and I felt so bad for her. I pulled her in for a hug and we just sat there, smoking blunt after blunt until she got ready to pack. For a minute I thought she was just in her feelings about packing and leaving, but she proved me wrong when she actually did. She threw me for a loop when she took her ring off and sat it on the coffee table, along with a note.

Shit had just got real, and I could only imagine what Remy was going to do when he came home to find his family gone. If he's anything like his older brother, shit was going to get worse before it got better.

"I don't think you should take your ring off. Right now you're just mad. Don't act on impulse, sis. Remy's going to go ballistic when he comes home and finds that ring here and you gone."

I was talking but I could tell Rosé wasn't trying to hear shit.

"I took it off and I'm not putting it back on until he starts acting like the man I married. I've been through so much being his wife at the hands of his family. Not one time did I get discouraged and feel the need to lash out at him or treat him like shit. He's walking around here treating me like I'm his enemy. Fuck him! I mean that shit, too. I'm done with the disrespect. Maybe if he brings his ass home and sees that his family is gone, he might realize how fucked up he's been."

"I'm not going. I want to stay here with Daddy."

"Heaven I advise you to get your back pack and go get in the car. I'm trying my best not to whoop your ass, but the way I feel right now, I will beat your ass raw."

Heaven stomped off and slammed the door behind her.

"I don't know what we're going to do with her and Ka'Jaiyah," I just shook my head because they were one and the same.

"I almost called her bad ass a bitch. I had to catch myself because she makes me so angry. Remy allows her to get away with murder. She's seen how he's been acting towards me, but he does no wrong in her eyes. I'm just fed up with all of this shit. I need a damn vacation away from all of this shit."

We both grabbed the bags and headed out of the house with the kids.

"That shit doesn't sound like a bad idea. I say we make it a girl's thing. Next week is Spring Break. Let's tear down South Beach, Boss Lady Inc. style."

I was in desperate need of a vacation myself. I love my husband and my kids, but I need some me time. I want to get fucked up, party, and of course, bullshit. My girls and I needed a vacation.

"I'm with it. Just let me know the details and I'm there with bells on. Thanks for coming over to check on us. I really appreciate it. I need to call Madear and let her know about this shit. She's going to have a fit knowing I walked out on Remy. Then again, I'm not going to even tell her. It's a shame I can't even go to my mother's house because her and my Daddy will tell him where I'm at. Fuck that, I'm going to a hotel."

"No problem. I'll call you and let you know all of the details. Everything is going to be just fine with you and Remy. Watch what I tell you. Love you, Boo."

Rosé and I hugged one another and parted ways. As I drove back towards the house, my phone was constantly going off. I looked at the screen and it was Python. I made sure to decline his calls. Thug would kill me if I had any contact with Python. Python rubs my husband the wrong way. He's cordial for the sake of me, but at the same time he flat out refuses for me to fuck with him on any level. The old Tahari would have defied Thug in a minute, but the new me knows better. Plus, we've been so good with regards to our relationship. There is no need for me to create unnecessary drama when we're on great terms. Lord knows Thug and I can go from lovey dovey to World War III in a matter of seconds. I don't want those types of problems with Thug.

When I pulled into the driveway, I was surprised to see Momma Peaches' car, especially this early in the day. Lately, she and Momma Gail have been doing nothing but partying and acting like teenagers again. Peaches and Quanie have been going at it because of it, and in a way, I don't blame him. She's walking around like she's not the mother of toddler twins.

Now don't get me wrong, I'm not bad mouthing my mother-in-law because she's the best. I'm just having a hard time understanding why she's behaving this way. I looked in my rearview and saw Malik pulling in behind me. I shook my head because I could only imagine what was going on. Before I could even get out of the car good, Malik had jumped out and rushed into the house. That made me put some pep in my step. I didn't want to miss a beat. I walked inside the living room and Thug was sitting in his recliner. Momma Peaches and Malik were sitting on the couch, looking like she had been crying.

"What do you mean you're not going to do shit?" Momma Peaches cried.

"Like I said, I'm not getting in that shit. That man had every right to drag your ass out the club. In case you forgot, you have small children. It would be different if the twins were grown, but they aren't. You need to be at home with your kids," Thug took a pull of the blunt and handed it to Malik.

"You and Gail need to sit ya asses down somewhere and act like the Golden Girls you are. All this drinking and hanging out don't make no sense. Plus, I'm tired of babysitting your damn kids. Last night was the last time, Ma. All they do is shit and cry. I was happy as hell Quanie came and got their ass. I was about to bring them right to that damn club," Malik added.

"Shut the fuck up, Malik. This shit is your fault anyway. Who told you to let Quanie take my fucking kids?"

"I wasn't about to deny that man access to his kids. Last time I checked, he was a good father to them and an even better husband to you. If I was him, I would have been laid hands on your ass. You need a foot up your ass for your behavior. You lucky you're my OG and I love you because I might do it myself."

"I wish the fuck you or Quanie would even try it. You and Thug got a lot of fucking nerve chastising me about my parenting. Last I remember, I raised both of y'all and your sister. Y'all never wanted for shit. Just because I want to hang out, it's a problem. At the same time, I never complain when I had to babysit them damn heathens you call kids. I love all my grandkids, but let's keep it real, they're bad as shit. I can't believe y'all sitting here acting like Quanie taking my kids is cool. I'm so done with y'all. Where the fuck is the loyalty at?" Peaches jumped up and grabbed her purse and rushed out of the door, damn near knocking me over. I wanted to go after her, but she really upset. I would just call and check on her later.

"What the hell going on?" I asked as I went and sat on Thug's lap.

"Ma mad at us because Quanie got the kids and won't answer the phone for her. All that partying with Gail has caught up to her ass. Now she wants to blame the world because Quanie done got fed up and took his kids," Thug said as him and Malik continued to pass the blunt back and forth.

"Ma knows better. I'm gone head over to her crib in a little while and talk to her. I don't like my baby being mad at me," Malik said with his spoiled ass. As much shit as he and Peaches talk to one another, they still have such a special bond.

"Get your soft ass out of here!" Thug said as snatched the blunt from him.

"That shit must be going around because Rosé just took the kids and left Remy. When I made it over there this morning, Rosé had stabbed him. He left out of the house and I don't know if he went to the hospital or what. I'm kind of worried about him because he was bleeding like crazy."

"Raise up, babe. Let me see if I can get in touch with this nigga. In the meantime, mind your business Ta-Baby. I know you mean well, but you be having all the ladies acting out with their niggas. Since when Rosé doing shit like that? I love you babe, but you're a bad influence on your whole crew."

I was appalled that Thug would even say some shit like that to me. I wanted to curse his ass out, but I knew that wouldn't be a good thing because I could tell that he was upset about Remy.

"All them Boss Lady Bitches is crazy. Barbie be stressing me out so much she got gray hairs growing on my dick."

"Really Malik?"

I swear he irritates my soul with the shit he says out of his mouth.

"Dead ass. I have to keep my shit shaved bald. I'm too fucking sexy for gray hairs to be anywhere on a sexy motherfucker like myself."

"Get the hell out of my house, Malik, and I'm telling Barbie what ya black ass said, too."

I headed upstairs and Thug was getting dressed. I wanted to ask questions but decided against it. I was just going to let him be. I knew that most likely he was on his way to check on Remy. Since I had a couple of hours to kill before the kids made it home from school, I decided to take me a much needed nap. Lord knows I needed all the rest I could get.

Before dozing off, I thought of Momma Peaches. In a way I could relate to her wanting to hang out and have fun. Motherhood has a way of stopping all the leisure activities for a woman. So I can understand her just wanting to get out and enjoy herself. The more I thought about it, the more I knew we ladies definitely needed us a get away. The problem was convincing our husbands to let us go without them.

Chapter 3- Torn Love

Peaches

Pissed was understatement to describe the way that I was feeling. Thug and Malik had really pissed me off acting like me hanging out was so wrong. It was bad enough I was fighting Quanie about it, but to be at odds with my boys was killing me. I wished Quaadir was here in Chicago. Out of all my sons, I could never do wrong in his eyes. I think that's because we not too long ago reunited. At any rate, he's always on my side. Which is more than I could say for Malik and Thug. Don't get me wrong, I love my boys. I just hate when they get all high and mighty on me like their shit don't stank.

Besides being mad at them, I was down right angry with Quanie. This nigga had taken my kids and flat out refused to come home with them. I was going crazy because I had no idea where they were. I just wanted my kids, and at this point, Quanie could take his ass on somewhere.

It had been a week and Quanie still hadn't come home. I had blocked everybody's number because I didn't want to hear shit. The only reason Quanie wasn't blocked was because of the kids. I was on my Petty Betty shit and I was going to make everybody feel it. Malik, Thug, and Ta'Jay had been at my house on several occasions, but I refused to answer my door. I was laughing my ass off because Malik sounded like he was going to cry begging me to open the door. Serves his spoiled ass right for going against the grain.

Despite being so angry, I was sick without my babies. Quanie just didn't understand. To be honest, I didn't understand either. I didn't know if I was having a midlife crisis, going through menopause, or having a nervous breakdown. Whatever was going on with me, it was causing me to go crazy and my mental state was in question. I loved my kids and I loved Quanie, but I was so afraid that I was going to hurt them. After all, I always find a way to bring some type of drama or grief into my kids' lives.

I've worked hard at being there for my kids no matter what and in my heart I know that they appreciate everything that I've done for them. I don't think they understand what I go through on a daily basis trying to keep this family together. All I wanted was some me time. Now I'm sitting up feeling like a bad parent because Quanie is punishing me for it. I had been in bed, too depressed to get up and do anything. I just wanted to sleep my life away. I wouldn't be so depressed about the situation if Quanie would just answer my phone calls.

I was going crazy, so I decided to go over to Gail's house just to get some air. She had been calling me like crazy. I knew she was going to curse me out. but shit, it's her damn fault anyway. I've been hanging out with her ass so that she can sneak off with Python. Mike is going to kill both of our asses if he finds out.

I walked inside of Gail's house and found her in the kitchen sitting at the table. I was glad she had the Patrón because I was in desperate need of a drink and a cigarette. Since I had the twins, I'd slowed down on the drinking and the smoking. Since I'd started back hanging out with Gail, I'd been back smoking and drinking, heavily. That was most likely a big issue with Quanie as well because I had promised that I would stop over indulging in Patrón and my Newports. Y'all know that shit was hard on me but for the sake of my children I did it.

Now I'm feeling like shit because I know that I love Quanie and he's the best thing that has ever happened to me. I had a feeling that I'd been being selfish to Quanie and his needs of me. I expected so much from him without giving him all of me. I'm far too old of a woman to be acting like a teenager without a care in the world. I need to make this shit right with Quanie. That is, if he'll allow me to.

Quanie is stubborn as fuck and knows how to hold a grudge. I really underestimated this young nigga. He did so much more than slang good ass cock. Lil' nigga wasn't playing no games with my ole ass. He was so much more than just the father of my kids. He was my husband and that changed the entire dynamic of the situation.

"It's about time you brought your ass out of that house. I thought I was gone have to call the fire department and have them kick the door in."

"I was okay, Gail. I just didn't want to be bothered with anybody. Quanie still hasn't brought my damn kids home or called. So I'm sorry if I have other shit to worry about," I poured me a shot of Patrón and knocked it back, followed by another.

"Calm down, bitch. I was joking. I think you should let Quanie keep them kids and stop worrying. He not gone let shit happen to them. I say you get dressed and let's go out tonight and get our step on."

I looked at this drunk pussy bitch like she had lost her mind. It was then I noticed something different, yet familiar, about my sister. Her ass was back getting high and I knew who was responsible for it.

"I'm gone ask you this once and one time only. On the lives of all my children, I'm gone beat your ass in this kitchen if you lie to me."

"Ask me what?"

"Are you back getting high, bitch?"

Gail stared at me long and hard before answering.

"I'm sorry, it was just once."

I jumped across the table and smacked the fuck out of her.

"You're a damn lie. After everything you've been through. You have a relationship with your kids and grandkids. Mike is the best thing to ever happen to you. Please don't let Python come into your life and fuck up everything you've worked so hard for. I'm going to tell you this once and one time only. If you don't straighten the fuck up and cut that nigga Python off, I'm through with your ass.

"Life is too good for us to be fucking over the people we love. I love you sis, but I'm done with the partying and all that hanging out shit. I have to get my family back on track. My kids and my husband deserve better than this."

I pushed her ass away from me causing her to stumble. I was so fucking disappointed in her right now. At the same time, I was mad at myself because she's a recovering addict. I had no business engaging in that type of behavior with her.

"I'm done with this shit, too. I promise you sis, I'm done with him and that drug shit. Please don't tell Markese and Aja. Mike already knows and got in my ass something serious. My only regret in all of this was letting Python come and fuck shit up. I can't blame him though because I should have known better than to be fucking with him anyway. That nigga is toxic. Always has been and always will be. I love Mike too much to put him through more than I already have."

I was glad to hear her say what she said. Looking at her let me know that she was indeed telling the truth about being done.

"I'm glad to hear that. Call me if you need me, sis. I love you."

"Okay I will and I love you, too. By the way bitch, make that the last time you put your hands on me. Heavy-handed hoe."

We both hugged one another and parted ways. Gail and I have come too far to lose it all. Especially her. Because of her drug use, she lost out on so many years with her children. Shit is real good for her and no matter how good Python tries to come off, he still shares the same blood as Snake and Venom. Down the road, there is bound to be some type of betrayal on his part. I can feel that shit. He smiles too motherfucking much for me and smiling faces tell lies.

I hope and pray Tahari stays far away from him like my son has demanded her to. Just seeing how vulnerable Gail was to their past makes me see how he can move in on Tahari. Outside of Keesha, he's her next of kin. No matter how strong Tahari is, she has a way of being vulnerable when it comes down to her relatives. Python better tread lightly though, because he's not prepared for Hurricane Thug. My son will definitely do damage behind his wife.

As I headed back home, my mind drifted to my twin sister, Sherita. I wanted nothing more but to be as close to her as I was with Gail. She flat out refuses to fuck with me. The shit that happened between us happened when we were younger, but she just won't let the shit go. Since finding out that Rosé was indeed my niece and her daughter, I've gone above and beyond to rebuild our relationship. She ignores and avoids me like the damn plague. We're missing out on precious time because this old bitch is still in her feelings after all these years. This bitch gets on my fucking nerves acting like she's so much better then Gail and I. I love Sherita, but I will love her from a distance. If there is one thing a motherfucker needs to know about Peaches, it's that she don't kiss nobody's ass. Hopefully, before one of us leaves this world, we will make things right. Until then, fuck her stuck up ass.

*****

As I pulled into my driveway, I was happy to see Quanie's truck. A smile crossed my face as I exited my car and rushed inside. My smile quickly turned into a frown as stumbled over his bags that were packed by the door. He was sitting on the couch and the twins were on his lap.

"Hey Momma's babies, I missed y'all so much," I rushed over towards the couch and I started hugging and kissing all over them. Quanie removed them from his lap and headed towards the door.

"Whatever they need, just call and I'll get it to you."

"Quanie, sit down and stop it with all the damn dramatics. Yes, I fucked up and I'm sorry. Please don't do this. Don't punish our kids because of my wrongdoing."

"I would never punish my kids. That's why I brought them back home to their mother. I am, however, punishing your ass. You want to act like you missing something in them streets, well now you're free to go out and find whatever you're looking for. Like I said, call me for whatever they need."

Quanie grabbed his bags and walked out of the door. It had been years since I cried over man. The tears were flowing freely, but I remained calm not to alert my kids of the sorrow that I felt inside of me. Just like that I had lost the only man who probably ever truly loved me. I wanted to go after him and beg him to forgive for me for my behavior, but I knew right now was too soon. Quanie was fed up and I brought the shit on myself.

I thought long and hard about what I was going to do. It had been so long since I sought guidance from someone. I'd been so busy giving my all to my family that I forgot about me. It had been so long since I'd seen or talked to my Aunt Ruth. She had been my biggest supporter, friend, and confidant when I gave birth to Thug and Quaadir. I was dead set against it, but she assured me that my baby would be well taken care of. I knew that she took my son in out of the kindness of her heart and the love she had for my mother.

On the other hand, I knew that my mother had done it out of spite to hurt me. I had no idea she was so heavy in the drug game until years after. Finding out she had Quaadir so heavy in the drug game threw me for a loop. At the same time, I was happy because it was in our blood to run drug empires. I wasn't proud of it but you can't control what you're born into.

After much thought, I got in touch with Quaadir and let him know that I was coming down to Atlanta to visit them. I knew that Thug, Malik, and Ta'Jay were going to be mad because I didn't tell them first. Hopefully, they would understand that I needed to get away for the sake of my sanity.

Right now there was no way I could stay here and live in this house without Quanie. We built this house from the ground up for our future. I see no sense in living in it without him. I packed lightly for the trip because I planned on shopping when I made it down there for everything we would need. I had no idea when I was coming back home. I laid across the couch and cuddled with my babies, praying for better days and hoping that Quanie would eventually forgive me.

Chapter 4- I Don't Mean It

Remy

I was mad at myself for choking Rosé. That was definitely out of character for me. Not to mention her stabbing my ass. That was out of character for her as well. We never fought to that extent. I hated that we'd been fighting like crazy in front of our kids. Heaven had a fit this morning when we were tussling. That shit hurt my heart because I love all my kids, but Heaven is my entire world. That little girl has given a nigga like me a purpose to live. That's why I have to make shit right with my wife. I never in my life want her to see what we have become and think that's how a relationship is supposed to be.

After receiving fifteen stitches in my arm, I headed back home only to find Rosé and my kids gone. The worst part was that she had left her ring behind accompanied by a fucking note. She knew how to piss me off because that's exactly what I was.

As a matter of fact, I was livid and had every intention on fucking her up for taking my kids. True I had been in a real fucked up mood lately, but after all the shit that I'd been through, a nigga deserved to have a bad day or two.

Rosé knows that I love her more than anything in this world. After all, I lost the life that was near and dear to me before I met her. It didn't matter that the shit was all a big lie. The way I feel now, I just wish none of the shit would've came to the light. Not saying that I regret my wife, because Rosé is the best thing outside of my kids to come out of all this bullshit. I just wish shit wouldn't have all came at me like a raging bull.

To go from being adored by your parents to them hating you and trying to kill you is some hard shit to swallow. Followed by learning that one of your best friends is really your brother because you share the same father. All my life I've been raised as Remy Ramirez, Jr. To know that he's not my father and Vinny Santerelli is had me fucked up. Not to mention my best friend really being my brother. That shit has me fucked up. Rosé thinks that I'm just supposed to get over everything. That's easy for her to say because her family has never betrayed or turned their backs on her.

Despite all of that, I've been acting pretty damn fucked up towards her. Rosé didn't deserve that at all. At the same time, I needed her to be more supportive of what I was going through. Rosé's trying to live life like shit normal and it's not. Nothing about what we've been through is normal.

I had been avoiding everybody like the fucking plague, especially Thug. That nigga, out of all people, knew what the fuck I was going through. He was never supposed to hold that shit to his chest like that. We were supposed to be better than that, so that's why I been on some fuck everybody type shit lately. I don't even know who the fuck I can trust.

Since Rosé wants to take my kids, I don't trust her ass, either. But she's in for a rude ass awakening if she thinks she gone take my kids from me.

*****

I'd been looking all over for Rosé and the kids. Her family hadn't heard from her and that caused me to worry like crazy. Regardless of being in retirement, I've acquired many enemies over the years. At this point, I just wanted to make sure she was straight. Even if she didn't to want come home.

I'd been out looking for her all day and I was exhausted from the damn pain medication they gave me at the hospital. I needed to lay my ass down for a couple of hours. I was mentally and physically drained from the day's events. I just wanted to lie down and regroup because I had every intention on finding my wife and kids.

When I pulled in my driveway, I had the right mind to reach for my gun. Thug and Malik were sitting on the hoods of Thug's Aston Martin. Last time I checked, I wasn't fucking with either of these cats. I thought I made that shit clear on several occasions, but I see motherfuckers didn't get the memo.

"It's about time you brought your ass home my nigga," Malik said as he jumped off of the car and Thug did as well. These niggas were standing here looking like the damn Double mint twins. I just shook my head because they were my fucking brothers and my biggest issue was the way I found out.

"Get the fuck off my property!"

"Nigga you need to get off all this bullshit. Okay, so we're brothers. You walking around here acting like a bitch. Like the shit is bad or something. I fell back for a minute because I knew the shit was fucked up, but at the same time nigga, this shit is a fucking blessing. I'm sick and tired of you walking around like this shit is the end of the world. I've always had respect for you and fucked with you the long way. However, I'm not feeling this soft shit you on!" Thug stepped closer to me and I stepper closer to him.

"Ain't no hoe in my blood so don't step to me with all this rah rah ass shit."

Before I knew Thug swung and caught me in the jaw. I immediately swung back and cracked his ass. We started going blow for blow. Older brother or not, I wasn't backing down.

"I got a stack on Remy! That's right my nigga, don't let him do you like that. World Star! I'm definitely uploading this motherfucker here! That's right Big Bro, handle that little nigga. I got a stack on Thug, too."

Malik was really clowning the both of us. We both continued to go blow for blow until we were tired out. Thug got the best of me, but I wasn't backing down from his ass. He already knows my gun blows just like his. All that fighting made me bust my damn stitches open and I was in pain. I sat on the doorstep and pulled my shirt over my head to wrap my arm. I spit the blood from my mouth that had pooled inside of it.

"Come on nigga, let me take ya ass back to the hospital. I think I need them to look at my nose. I swear to God if you broke my shit, I'm shooting ya bitch ass," Thug reached his hand out to help me up. He pulled me in for a hug and we both embraced.

"Aww ain't that shit sweet. I'm glad you young ladies made up."

"Shut the fuck up, Malik!" Thug said as he charged Malik but he ran towards his own car.

"Don't get mad at me because Lil' Bro was hanging with you. I can't wait to tell Quaadir this shit. As a matter of fact, let me FaceTime that nigga right now. Fuck y'all niggas. I'm headed home to get some pussy anyway. Have fun skipping down the street and holding hands," Malik peeled off in his car and I hopped in the car with Thug. It had been a minute since I had any interaction with him outside of us just fighting and getting shit off of our chests.

"I know that shit been fucked up with everything going on in your life. You must know and understand that it fucked me up when I found out that you were indeed my brother. You of all people know of all the fucking lies and secrets my mother kept from my siblings and me. Nigga, you think you got it bad finding out we're actually brothers. How in the fuck do you think I felt when it came to light that Quaadir was not only my brother, but my twin? Not to mention the fact that he fucked my wife. Now that's some shit that will make a nigga mad and want to kill his brother. Trust and believe me, had it not been for the love of my mother, he would be a dead motherfucker.

"Today I'm grateful to have him as my brother and the same goes for you. Now, let me clear anything up if you're confused. I know that family is the last thing you're trusting right now, but family is everything. I can assure you that you have a family. All you have to do is allow yourself to trust again. We're a family. Now don't get it twisted, it's always some bullshit when it comes to Peaches, and of course, our wives. Still and all we love each other and go to war with for each other. We good, Bro?" Thug handed me a blunt and I took a long pull off it. After that speech, how could I ever not want to be a part of this family?

"Yeah we good."

We pulled up to the hospital and sat smoking the entire blunt before heading in to get checked out.

"By the way, if you're looking for Rosé, she at the W Hotel on Michigan Ave. in the Executive Suite. I saw the text come through Ta-Baby's phone earlier. Don't tell them I told you. My wife would have a fit. But I hate that she has to meddle in matters that don't concern her. As you know, retirement is hard on her so she has to make up for it in shit that has no concern of hers. However, that's my baby and I love her. If Rosé becomes a part of that whole Boss Lady shit, be prepared because you'll have to lay hands on her ass because they don't listen."

"I've seen that crew in action. Rosé already nutting the fuck up on me. Let me get checked out and drag her ass up out of this hotel. Good looking, Bro."

*****

After sitting in the damn ER for three hours, I was finally stitched back up. I was glad Thug's nose wasn't broken because fighting that motherfucker was like fighting a damn bull. He doesn't even look that damn strong. I have to eat my Wheaties and get back in the gym tussling with his ass. Now that we got all of our frustrations out of the way with one another, I doubt that we'll ever have to come to blows again. It felt like a weight had been lifted off of my shoulders since we got that shit off of our chests. The more I thought about it, the more I realized I was overreacting about the entire situation. I should have been embracing the fact of having a family that I knew was loyal. Instead of dwelling on the family that wasn't. In the midst of my craziness, I got away from what was important and that was my wife and kids. There's no way in hell my family should be at a hotel when we have a multi-million dollar estate. That shit had me feeling all types of fucked up but not for long, because I was going to get my family. Rosé didn't have a choice because I was going to drag her ass out by that long ass hair she be rocking.

Chapter 5- Nothing Even Matters

Rosé

It hadn't even been a full day and I was missing Remy like crazy. I saw him calling me all day, but my pride wouldn't allow me to answer his call. Now as I lay here in bed next to my sleeping babies, I realize that Tahari was right. I did move far too fast. I felt so naked without my wedding ring. That was a token of our love and I never should've taken it off. I was just so mad and hurt about the way he'd been treating me lately. Walking around the house with all that pent up frustration and shutting me out was hurting me to my heart.

We'd been through so much together, so for us to be saying the nasty things that we'd been saying to each other really bothered me. It was hurting me to my heart that I had to actually slice his ass. The moment he wrapped his hands around my neck, I knew he needed a reality check. He wasn't listening to my words, but he damn sure heard my actions loud and clear when I let that blade do the talking. Although I'd been out of jail for years now, I still walked around with a blade on me. To a certain extent, I was still very much institutionalized.

Although it seemed like I was satisfied with what I'd done, I wasn't. Inside, I was sick about what I had to do. Regardless of anything Remy has done or said to me, I don't know where I would without him. He's been here for me since the moment we met. I couldn't help but feel like he lost everything by trying to be with me. I remember telling him that I wanted to leave because I couldn't handle him losing everything because of me. Remy flat out refused. I know that man loves me because he was willing to die for me. As I lay here I regret not having more understanding and patience with him. Out of all the events that had happened, the one that hurt and broke him the most, was when his father ordered his men to gun him down.

Finding out that Thug, Malik, and Quaadir were actually his brothers was the icing on the cake. Shit has been crazy ever since. I've been getting the brunt of all his anger and in a heated moment, I lost control. I just wanted things to get back to the way they were when we first met before all the betrayal. As much as I missed him and wanted to go home, I knew that I couldn't. I had to remain firm in letting him know that he couldn't treat me like shit just because he was mad. We're a team. We can't go around fighting each other, because no matter what at the end of the day all we have is each other. I might have a big family that loves me, but when we said our vows Remy became my family. He's mine and I'm his. This is just a bump in the road for us, but we've been through hurdles and obstacles and come out strong. So a bump ain't shit to some survivors like us. I lie in bed with my kids and stared at them sleeping peacefully until I dosed off.

*****

"Rosé! Get up, get my kids dressed, and let's go home."

At first I thought I was dreaming at the sound Remy's loud and powerful voice. Once I opened my eyes, I realized he was standing over me and it was far from a dream. I sat up in bed and stared at him through narrow eyes. The whole time I wondered how in the fuck he knew that I was even there. At the same time, he had a lot of nerve coming in here and demanding that I go home. I wanted to come home, but I didn't have to let him know that.

"What if I say I'm not ready to come home?" I folded my arms across my chest like the spoiled brat he's made me.

"What if I say that if you don't, I'm gone drag your ass out of here by your hair? Now like I said before get up, get my kids dressed, and let's go."

This time he was so loud that he woke up the kids. As soon as they realized he was in the room, they jumped up and were all over him.

"Daddy! Daddy!"

"Are you okay, Daddy?" Heaven asked as she rubbed his arm and hugged him. When she hugged him, she faced me. My heart sank as she gave me the nastiest look ever.

"Daddy is just fine. Help your Momma put your brothers' clothes on so we can go home."

Remy went and sat down in a chair that was in the corner of the room. I hesitated, but eventually I got up and got ready to head home. It was taking everything inside of me not to just burst out in tears because my feelings were hurt. It hurt for him to act like he didn't care about my feelings. I swear I wanted to just lash out, but that wasn't a good idea. Especially since the kids were all happy to see him. I decided to take one for the team, for the sake of my children.

When we made it home I got the kids situated and took a long, hot bath. I laid my head back and just thought about how Remy hadn't said one thing to me on the ride home. Somewhere inside of me, I was just praying that he would be the nice and gentle Remy I fell in love with. We didn't have to have some long, drawn-out conversation, confessing our love to one another. If there was nothing else I was sure of in life, it was our love for one another.

Right now I was sad as fuck because I didn't feel loved by him. Once I was finished bathing, I quickly dried off and headed out of the bathroom to get in bed. I was stopped dead in my tracks at the sight before me. I covered my mouth and tears ran down my face. Our bedroom was dimly lit and filled with candles and rose petals were all over the room. Remy hit the switch on our stereo system that was installed in the wall and R.Kelly's *I Will Never Leave* came on.

"I'm sorry for everything, babe. I love you more than life itself. I don't know what I would do without you. Forgive me for the way I've treated you. I'll do whatever it takes to make sure shit between us gets back right. I never want to fight like this again. Rosé we've come too far for this."

Remy had moved closer to me and lifted my chin so that I could look into his eyes. He wiped my tears with his thumbs. I wrapped my arms around him and hugged him tighter than ever before.

"Of course I forgive you. I'm sorry for cutting you."

Remy yanked my towel from around me and lifted me up. I wrapped my legs around his waist and we kissed passionately.

"I love you so much, Baby," I said as Remy roughly threw my naked body on our King-sized poster bed.

"I love you, too."

He placed his head in between my legs and began to devour my pussy. Remy was a beast in the bedroom. In all of our years of being married, he's never eaten my pussy the way he was doing. He had my legs wrapped around his neck with a death grip on them. I'd already cum several times, but he wasn't letting up. It was like he wanted to suck the soul of my pussy. I was gripping the covers tightly and punching the bed.

"Oh shit, Remy! I can't take no more! I feel like I'm about to piss on myself!" I yelled out in pleasure.

I was sure that I woke my kids up. I was trying my best to push his head from in between my legs. Although I was slightly able to push his head away, his long ass tongue was still able to assault my clit. He inserted two of his fingers inside of me and that broke the dam. I started squirting so hard that it was shooting damn near across the room. I was in shock because I'd never cum so hard in my life.

"That a girl. That's right, make that shit nasty for Daddy," Remy said as he crawled in between my legs. We stared into each other's eyes as he threw my limp legs over his shoulders. I closed my eyes as Remy placed his dick inside of me and gave my ass the business. I had no time to try and fuck back because he was in full beast mode. He had my body bent in so many different positions, one would think I was a contortionist. Nigga was just that fucking good with his dick game.

After a couple of hours of straight animalistic sex, we laid in our soaking wet bed. Our bodies were dripping wet from our sweat and from each other's sweat. I laid my head on his stomach as he ran his fingers through my hair. His soft touch sent chills through my body. His touch alone let me know that the Remy I fell in love with was back and in full effect.

"You know that no matter what I will never turn my back on you, Remy. When shit gets rough, I need for you to have trust in the fact that I'm here. I'm more than just your wife and the mother of your children. I'm your best friend, I'm your Bonnie, I'm your ride or die bitch, and most importantly, I'm your pain pill. It's my job to take the pain away. Let me be the sun and the rainbow in the midst of the storm that had placed this dark cloud over you. I love you Remy Ramirez and nothing will ever change that. Not even you being mean and pushing me away. Don't ever in life treat me like your enemy again because if we're fighting each other, we're opening the gates for the people on the outside to hurt us. We've had enough of that. Let's just live the happily ever after that we promised each other."

"Thank you for loving me when it was the hardest thing to do. I love you so much and I promise that I'll never ever mistreat you again. Especially if you're going to be slicing me up and shit. My arm hurts like hell and I need you to make it feel better."

I looked up at him and rolled my eyes because he thought that he was so slick. He smiled at me with those irresistible pearly whites that had their own way of making me give in to his ass. I placed soft kisses on his stomach as he gently pushed my head down towards his dick. After making love to his dick with my mouth, we made passionate love to each other until it was time to get up and start a new day.

Since we were all exhausted, we decided to keep the kids home from school and have a family day. It'd been so long since I allowed them to just eat junk food and pig out on whatever they wanted. We all made pallets in our movie theater and chilled back and watched movies all day long. It was just us and the kids, spending quality time like all families should. This was the best feeling in the world to me. Remy was in one of the best moods ever. I loved to see him smiling and spending time with the kids instead of sulking and getting fucked up in his office. This was the beginning of us getting back to the original Mr. and Mrs. Remy Ramirez, Jr.

*****

It had been a minute since I'd seen my mother. She'd been all in her feelings about me building a relationship with my aunts. She claimed that she didn't care because she didn't fuck with them like that, but in reality I knew that she did. I didn't understand why she acted the way that she did towards them. Peaches and Gail had been trying their best to get past the past, but she just wouldn't let go. At the same time, she thought that I was supposed to do the same thing to them. That just wasn't going to happen. Growing up the only family I had was my father's side of the family. Now that I've gotten to know my mother's side, I never want to be away from them. It's crazy how I'm married to my cousin's brother. Not only do I have more family members, but Remy has a family that loves him and wants to be in his life. Remy is blessed beyond measure. It was meant for him to go through all that shit with his parents, because there was something greater on the horizon for him.

Despite me building relationship with my aunts and cousins, I still missed my grandmother. Madear had picked up and moved down to Mississippi with Deacon Black. I still can't believe that man ended up leaving his wife for her. I really don't know why I'm all surprised, my grandmother was a damn heathen. She went and took all the holiness out of that man. He doesn't even like to be called Deacon anymore. Now you know they going straight to hell without passing go or collecting two hundred dollars.

I missed Boo and Honey, as well. They moved down to Atlanta and opened up their own strip club. Can you believe that? After all that shit Boo took Honey through in regards to her stripping, he follows her down to Atlanta to run a strip club that she inherited from one of her old bosses. They were down there doing the damn thing. Their club was one of the hottest in the A. Boo still ran shit with Peanut for Remy, but he spent most of his time down there.

Peanut and Neicee were still in the Chi. Thug had been trying to get him to join Thug Inc. but he hadn't decided yet. Peanut was good just running things for Remy. He felt like that's what he'd been doing for years and loved doing it. He just didn't feel good about being a part of it. Peanut is different like that. He just marches to a different beat than everyone else.

Neicee was now running Remy's strip club full-time and it's been doing really well. She's remodeled the club and hired all new dancers. My father has taken on all of Remy's businesses and business has been good. I'm thankful for my family, because they go so hard for Remy. I don't know where he would be without them.

Our journey had been long and hard, but we all made it. Our relationship's survived what the world thought it couldn't. I'll forever be grateful for the hard times because it made us appreciate the good times. Life is great for all of us. I just need to convince my mother to build a relationship with her sisters. I feel like we won't be fully complete until she does.

Chapter 6- Got Me Fucked Up

Malik

Peaches was being really petty at the moment by just picking up and going down to Atlanta without saying shit to me or Thug. I've been running around here looking for this nigga Quanie because I thought he did something to my Momma, but all along her ass was in Atlanta. To make matters worse, she took that man's kids without even telling him. It's safe to say that nigga was on his way to the A to drag her ass right back home. I know he ain't crazy, so he won't put his hands on her. Then again, that might just be what she and Gail need. I love them with all my heart, but they really need the men in their lives to break a good foot off up in their asses. Their thot ass behavior lately is cause for a good old-fashioned ass whooping. Peaches knows better. I'm kind of glad her ass is gone down there. Now she can't drop her damn BeBe's Kids off on me and my wife every chance she gets.

I barely want to watch my own kids, that's why I dropped them off on her ass. I'm still pissed she went and got pregnant. Knowing she got a damn slave ship full of grandchildren already. That's Peaches for you, though. She always springs some shit on you out of the blue. That's my baby, though. I miss that old bird. She's so mad at me I'm on the damn blocked list. Y'all know that hurt my heart.

Peaches is the first woman I knew how to love and she's pushing me away. All because she did wrong and she wants to play the victim. Y'all know I'm a momma's boy and proud of it. She gone make me jump on the plane my damn self and drag her ass back to the Chi my. Who in the hell gone cook for me on Sundays? I'm mad as hell just thinking about the shit.

*****

It had been a minute since I kicked it with my nigga's Sarge and Dro. Ever since the incident with Barbie fucking her baby Daddy, she's been on my dick. She thinks I'm on some revenge type shit, but I'm not that type of nigga anymore. Now, the old Malik would have been nailing hoes to the cross and giving out the good word with this dick. I'm on my grown man shit these days. Barbie and I have come to a place in our relationship were we don't have to go tit for tat with one another. We both agree to disagree. She might throw something across the room at me, and I might break my foot off in her ass then turn around and fuck the lining out her little pussy. That's just how we roll. That's our thing. It's not for anyone to like or understand because we have a love that no one understands but us, and we like it that way.

"What's up my niggas?" I said as I walked into Ta'Jay and Sarge's backyard. Sarge was on the grill and Dro was rolling a couple of blunts up.

"Waiting on your slow ass. What the fuck took you so long?" Sarge asked as I handed him the ice and liters of Remy that I'd grabbed.

"Nigga don't question my damn timing, my name Malik not Ta'Jay. By the way, where is my lil' baby anyway?" I observed Sarge's jaws clench in anger. I shook my head because I didn't have time for this shit with him and my sister. I thought their asses were cool but his actions showed different. I looked at Dro and he just shook his head and lit the blunt.

"She probably out with her nigga."

I looked at this motherfucker like he'd lost his mind.

"What the fuck is you trying to say?"

I was now standing to my feet because what he said pissed me off. That shit was nothing but a better way of calling my sister a hoe and that shit didn't sit right with me.

"I'm saying that Ta'Jay cheating on me with some nigga down at Chi-City Cutz, the barbershop in the complex where her boutique is,"

Sarge was talking so cool, calm, and collected. The shit was pissing me off because he was acting like it wasn't shit.

"So why the fuck is you flipping burgers and shit while she out popping that pussy for another nigga?"

"I did some fucked up shit to her in the past, so I guess she on her get back shit. I'm gone let her have her fun, though."

"Barbie pulled that same stunt and got a nigga decapitated behind it. I don't give a fuck about what the fuck I ever did to Barbie in the past. If I fucked every bitch in the city of Chicago, it's still not okay for her to be on revenge type of shit. Shit makes her look bad, that's just the way of the world. I can't tell you how to handle your wife, but as her big brother I'll put a bullet in any nigga that think fucking her is cool.

"Your ass almost got some hot shit, but you my nigga and I know you love her. Ta'Jay got life fucked up right now. Handle your shit, my nigga. I know you think some shit will happen behind getting in her shit. We're men before we're anything. Thug, Quaadir, and I are husbands so we know how this shit feels. Handle your wife as a husband because I'm definitely going to handle her ass as a big brother. I'll holla at you niggas later."

I was livid just knowing Ta'Jay was out on bullshit and she knew that she was dead ass wrong. Especially since I'm a silent owner in Chi-City Cutz because I run drugs through that bitch. Yeah, we got a motherfucking problem, businesswise and personally. I distinctly told this nigga Cam to stay the fuck away from my sister. I saw the way they were flirting with each other. She tried to act like it was nothing but I'm a nigga and I saw how this bitch ass nigga was fucking her with his eyes. I also saw how she was low key mind fucking him. It didn't take a rocket scientist to know what was going on.

As soon as Sarge said what he said I knew that he was talking about this bitch ass nigga Cam. He thought I was a motherfucking joke, but I was about to show his ass I most definitely wasn't. I can't stand a disrespectful ass nigga. Motherfuckers wonder why they get murked behind fucking a nigga's wife. He knows full and well that she's married. I have a problem with this nigga disrespecting my right hand man Sarge. Bitches gone be bitches. Niggas know the motherfucking code, though. Never fuck with another man's wife. That's law.

I headed straight to her boutique. This is why Peaches needs to be her ass here. I could tell shit was about to go left without her presence.

*****

"Oh shit Malik!" Ta'Jay yelled as she hurried up and jumped off of her desk in her office. This nigga Cam was eating my little sister pussy. I started having a heart attack like Fred Sanford, stumbling and every damn thing. I swear I felt dizzy and lightheaded. Once I gathered myself, I blanked the fuck out and started beating this nigga ass.

"Malik stop!" I heard Barbie's voice and looked up as she tried to get me off this nigga Cam's ass. I yanked away so hard her ass fell and I didn't care because she knew about the shit. Her and Ta'Jay are partners in crime. Once I was satisfied with beating his ass, I picked his ass up and put him on his shit.

"Now get ya bitch ass the fuck out of here. I told you to stay the fuck away from my sister. Now I come in here and you licking on her pussy and eating her groceries and shit."

"This shit ain't over nigga!" he said as he backed out the door.

"Is that a threat, my nigga?"

I pulled my gun from my waist and let off one. Made that nigga jump around like he was James Brown on the motherfucking good foot. He hauled ass out of there. I turned around and smacked the shit out of Ta'Jay. She looked at me with so much hurt and pain in her eyes.

My anger got the best of me. The last thing I wanted to do was hurt, but this shit she was doing was not cool and bad for business. She grabbed her purse and ran out of her office.

"Really Malik? Why would you hit her like that?" Barbie said as she stood to her feet.

"Shut the fuck up before I slap your ass for being in on that shit!" I said as I stepped in her face.

"I wish you would. I told your ass the last time you put your hands on me was the last time. I'm going straight to the County Jail," she said as she walked out of the office with her middle finger in the air

"Yeah aight. I'll see your ass at home and ya stanking ass better beat me there!"

She knew to get the fuck out of dodge with all that shit she was spitting. I was pissed the fuck off for catching this fuck nigga eating on my sister pussy. Not to mention I was mad at myself for losing control and hitting her. I knew she was gone call Thug and Peaches. Even if she was in the wrong, they were definitely going to be at my head. Ta'Jay does no wrong in any of our eyes. But she was wrong for doing this. I expect her to carry herself better than these thot ass bitches out here.

I looked at my nigga Sarge and he was hurt and that shit hurt me. I knew for a fact he'd changed and did it all for Ta'Jay. What the fuck was wrong with these Boss Lady Bitches? Their get a nigga back game is way too strong for me. Barbie had my ass crying and sucking my thumb in the damn corner when I overheard her on my voicemail fucking that nigga. I'm a living witness to not being able to take what I dish out with regards to cheating.

I already knew what my nigga was feeling. She has never looked at another nigga since they've been together, let alone let him fuck. The way he was eating her pussy let me know he'd done hit that shit several times. I needed to shake the image out of my head. Shit was disturbing as fuck. I needed to call my Momma and tell her about this shit here.

*****

I walked inside of my house and I was surprised to see Ta'Jay sitting at the table with Barbie. She looked up and had tears in her eyes. I felt bad but I was still mad about the shit. I grabbed me a Corona from the refrigerator and went to check on my kids.

Lil' Malik and Malikhi were playing his game and London was on the computer, as usual.

I headed straight to my man cave. I needed to calm the fuck down. Ta'Jay is my baby and we're close in our special way because we share a bond that's deeper than being brother and sister. Our childhood abuse made us stronger in the sense that it makes us depend on each other in adulthood. For some reason it's like we're each other's crutch when shit gets hectic. Ta'Jay should have come and told me that she was having problems. I can't help her with her womanly ways, but as a big brother I could have given her a male point of view.

Niggas in the barbershop talk about everything. If I ever hear those niggas in that bitch talking shit about my sister, I swear I'm airing that bitch out and burning it to the ground.

"I'm sorry, Malik."

I looked behind me and Ta'Jay was standing behind me. I turned around and drank the rest of the beer I had.

"I'm sorry for putting my hands on you. That shit wasn't cool at all."

"I fucked up, Malik. Sarge is going to kill me when he finds this shit out."

"He already knows, so you need to be trying to figure out how to make shit right with your husband."

She started crying like a motherfucker. One would think he was whooping her ass the way she was shaking and crying. I wanted to feel sorry for her, but I just couldn't because she brought this shit on herself. She's not a little girl anymore. Ta'Jay is an adult who made a poor decision and now she has to deal with it.

"What the fuck is going on?" Thug said as he walked in and sat next to us. I looked at Ta'Jay so she could tell him. Just thinking about the shit had me pissed off.

"I've been cheating on Sarge with Cam from the barbershop."

"Dead that shit immediately!" Thug roared. Nigga was so loud he made me jump.

"But I—"

"No buts, Ta'Jay. End that shit or that nigga life comes to an end!" Thug roared looking like the damn beast he is. See nothing I did was going to even compare to what he would do. He was, without a doubt, the father we never had. I talk shit and I play a lot, but at the end of the day, his word is law. Period and point blank. Ta'Jay ran out of my man cave crying. Thug and I looked at each other and shook our heads.

"Can you believe this shit, man?"

"I saw him eating her pussy with my own eyes and I still can't believe it," I said as I flamed up a cigarette. My nerves were bad as fuck being related to all these dysfunctional ass people.

"Don't even tell me anymore. This shit making me want to go and murk that nigga. Does Sarge know about this shit?"

"He told me. That's what made me go to the boutique to talk to her ass. That nigga calm as fuck. Over at the house cooking and acting like it's okay for her to be out here being a damn thot."

I was so mad that I wanted to go back to their house and kick his ass for being a weak ass nigga about the situation.

"Sarge better fuck that nigga up."

I nodded my head in agreeance with Thug. The nigga definitely had to do something.

"Have you talked to Ma?" I asked.

"Hell no. She got my number blocked. I just got off the phone with Quaadir. He want us all to come down there. I told him that I need to holler at my wife first. She always doing shit without running it by me first. Knowing her ass, she's probably planning trips to Europe and shit."

"Just let me know. I'm down for whatever."

"Let me get out of here. I promised Ka'Jaiyah I would pick her up from school and take her to get a dog."

"She ain't gone do shit but make this one kill itself, too."

Something was off about my niece and I don't care what anybody says. She worried the shit out of that damn dog. She changed its clothes all damn day, putting it on pampers and putting it in strollers and shit. She treated that dog like it was a human baby. Lil' nigga died to get away for her ass. Thug knows it's the truth, he just won't admit it.

"Don't do my baby like that. She's passionate about her animals."

We both laughed and dapped it up before he left. Since I'd cooled down, I walked through the house to find Barbie. I heard her and Ta'Jay talking. Of course my nosey ass wanted to know what was being said so I stood outside of the door.

"You have to tell Sarge, Ta'Jay."

"How can I tell my husband that our daughter might not be his?"

I appeared in the doorway and they immediately stopped talking. The look on my face let them know I'd heard what they said.

"Either you tell him or I am. I don't know what the fuck wrong with you but you better stop it with all this fucking thot ass behavior. You're my sister and I love you, but I will fuck you up. I'm not your husband who's sitting over there in the house waiting for your ass to come home, knowing that you out without another nigga. As a matter of fact, get the fuck out my house and take your ass home. Tell that man, Ta'Jay. He deserves to know."

"Stop being so hard on her, Malik. This is really hard for her."

"Shut the fuck up, Barbie! It wasn't hard when she had her legs in the air or her pussy in that nigga mouth. Sarge don't deserve this shit. It's one thing to be cheating, but a baby is involved. He crazy about Ta'Jariea and both of y'all know it. I'm not even surprised that you condoning this shit. I forgot you got sneaky pussy, too."

"Nigga please, you had community dick wayyy before I got sneaky pussy. While you talking shit nigga, you love this sneaky pussy. And while you worried about why her pussy in another nigga mouth, this one over here needs some mouth action. Nigga you slipping."

"Get the shit slapped out of you. While you running off at your mouth about what the fuck I need to be doing, I'm gone need some of that mouth from your ass. Quit talking shit, Barbie. I advise you to shut the fuck up before I drop something off in it. Get the fuck out Ta'Jay and go talk to Sarge. Barbie, bring your sneaky pussy ass on. My dick hard from all that talking you doing."

They both looked at me like I was crazy, but I was dead ass serious.

"You're one ignorant ass motherfucker. I swear to God don't you ever say shit else to me."

Ta'Jay pushed past me and walked out the door. I didn't care that she was mad about some shit that she created. I would be less of a brother to condone that shit. Sarge is so in love with their daughter. He prayed for a daughter for so long after they lost their first daughter. Don't get me wrong, he loves Lil' Sarge and Sema'Jay, but Ta'Jariea is his heart. So for Ta'Jay to be acting like this shit is okay is not cool at all. That man is over there feeling like shit for cheating on her so he's accepting her infidelity. Not fully knowing there's more to it. She might hate me now, but she'll love me later. They all hate me when I'm spitting real shit. I don't mind being hated because I speak the truth.

*****

"You gone do this dick, or nah?" I said as I laid back in our bed, asshole naked.

Barbie walked inside of the room looking sexy as fuck. It seemed like the older we got, the sexier she got. She's so self-conscious about her weight after our last baby that all she does is work out, waist train, and eat healthy. She's starving the shit out of me and our kids. I'm glad that she wants to keep her shit right and tight. There's nothing worse than a bitch that lets herself go. If your ass started out looking like Beyoncé, don't let a nigga wake up and ya looking like Precious. That shit is the ultimate deal breaker.

"I'll give you all the pussy you want if you give me money for a new wig," Barbie said as she stood in the mirror in nothing but a hot pink corset and thong. She made her ass jiggle on purpose, playing with a nigga.

"Hell no. That's why your ass bald-headed now," I jumped out of the bed and grabbed her ass around her waist.

"Let me go, Malik. You play too damn much."

"Don't get mad at me because you ain't got no edges. I told your ass a long time ago to stop wearing that shit in your head."

"Babe, you know that I hate my real hair."

Barbie turned around, wrapped her arms around my neck, and sucked on my bottom lip. She knew exactly what she was doing.

"You're my wife and I love you. So you don't have to lie to me. I know underneath all that shit, you're looking like Suge Knight. I'm glad you wear that shit though, because when I'm hitting it from the back you give a nigga something to pull on while I'm off in them guts. That's what I call teamwork. Now give Daddy a kiss," I puckered up my lips and she muffed me. I picked her ass up, threw her over my shoulder, and smacked her on her ass repeatedly, "You gone do this dick! You gone do this dick!"

"Ahhhhh! Yeah I'm gone do your dick!"

I threw her on the bed and we started wrestling. These days, no matter how much we might argue or fight, we intend to never go to bed mad. We just have a different type of way of showing our affection. She pushed me back on the bed and straddled me. I ripped her thong off and she slid down on my dick without hesitation. Barbie got that wet wet. My eyes started rolling in the back of my head as she began to rock back and forth. I had to grab her hips and try to take control so that I wouldn't bust quick. The sight of her bouncing up and down on my dick had a nigga about to be a minute man. Lord knows I've got the stamina of a bull, but she was just feeling too good at the moment.

"Slow down, Bae," I moaned out as I bit my bottom lip. She knocked my hands away and began to bounce hard as hell.

"You wanted me to do this dick, right?" she asked as she turned around and started riding me backwards.

"You doing that motherfucker, too."

I smacked her on both of her ass cheeks, making sure to leave my handprints. Not long after, I was cumming long and hard all up in her ass. Her ass better be lucky she's on birth control because those were twins right there.

"So are you going to buy me some hair or not?"

I knew that was coming. Damn shame my own wife was using her pussy to trick me out of some damn weave.

"Of course. You know you can have whatever you like."

"I'm glad you said that because the hair is four thousand dollars, but it's well worth it."

"Really, Barbie? You can go down there to the beauty supply and get some packs of Remy like all these other bitches do."

"That's the thing. I'm not average like these other bitches. I'm a Boss Lady. I roll with nothing but them pretty bitches and siddity bitches. Fuck I look like walking out the house with Giuseppe's on my feet and beauty supply hair in my head. Don't try me Malik, because you dress to impress. So don't try to send me out here looking a fool because you for damn sure don't walk out the door looking a fool."

I just shook my head because she was trying to figure out anything she could to make wanting four thousand dollar hair in her head okay. At any rate, of course she could get it. I love for her to look beautiful, so if the hair was forty thousand dollars I would have got it for her. I just like to talk shit. I wouldn't be me if I didn't.

As I lay in bed, I decided to flame up a blunt because I needed to relax my mind. I was so upset with Ta'Jay for being reckless. True she's a grown woman and very capable of making her own decisions. However, the one thing I know is that she can't handle the repercussions of her decisions. This nigga Cam ain't shit to her but something to do. I know for a fact she's not going to be able to handle it if Sarge leaves her. The more I laid here, the more a feeling came over me that I couldn't shake. I had a feeling some shit wasn't right. I jumped out of bed and started putting on my clothes.

"What's wrong?"

"I have a bad feeling, babe. I need to hit up Thug and head over to Ta'Jay house. Some shit don't feel right. Just stay by the phone."

I kissed Barbie on the forehead and I rushed out the house. Although Ta'Jay and I aren't twins, we just have this sixth sense about each other.

Chapter 7- Sins of the Wife

Ta'Jay

I sat in my driveway too afraid to go inside. This shit had been a long time coming, I just didn't know how to go about telling Sarge. A lot has happened in such a short time. I'm now the mother of a beautiful baby girl I named Ta'Jariea. Despite me being so in love with Sarge, I still felt as though I was missing something. I found that comfort and understanding in Cam. It started out as innocent flirting when I would take Sarge to the barbershop or go do pickups for Malik. One thing led to another when we started inboxing each other on Facebook. That led to us fucking via Facetime. It was crazy how he was able to get my body to do things without even physically touching me. It was the sound of his voice commanding me to cum and the way he jacked off as he watched me.

In that one time I did something with somebody outside of my husband and I loved it. As soon as I did it, I regretted it. But it made me want him in a more physical way. We'd been fucking around for months and I didn't stop until I was pregnant with my daughter. That was because I had no idea who the father was. There was a sixty percent chance it was my husband's and a strong ass forty percent chance it was Cam's. I thought that if I cut off all ties that would ease my worries, but my entire pregnancy I was scared shitless. The moment I gave birth and looked her, I was scared because she didn't look like Sarge. She was the splitting image of me. When Cam heard I gave birth, he started reaching out to me talking about he wanted to see his daughter. I didn't know what to do so I ignored his ass and avoided him.

This nigga was throwing out threats like my brothers wouldn't murder his ass. I didn't want to tell them about this shit. I thought that I could handle the shit on my own. That's how I ended up in the position I was in today. We were supposed to be discussing the baby but my pussy ended up in the nigga mouth. Now Thug and Malik know. I know it's about to be some shit because Cam thinks he tough and my brothers are beasts. Not to mention my husband. Sarge is going to murder him and me. I knew I couldn't sit in my car any longer. I got out of the car and headed inside to face the music.

As I walked up to my door I started reciting Psalm 23:4 in my head.

Yea though I walk through the valley of the shadow of death, I will fear no evil, for thou art with me; thy rod and thy staff they comfort me.

Laugh all you want to, death was in my near future and I needed a little more Jesus. I walked through the house looking for Sarge while I still had the courage to come clean. I knew once he found out about the possibility of our daughter not being his, our marriage was over. I can't blame anybody but myself, so I was prepared for whatever.

I found him out on the patio, smoking a blunt, and drinking out of a big ass Remy bottle. I sat beside him and I felt like shit. I looked at my hustling ass husband and then at the lavish ass estate we lived in. He's always given me the world. Cam had money, but nothing compared to my husband. I just became overwhelmed and started shedding tears. I reached and touched his leg but he knocked it off of him.

"Don't touch me!"

I bit my bottom lip and I rubbed my hands up and down my legs nervously.

"There's something I have to tell you."

"What? About that broke fuck nigga Cam. No need for you to confess shit, I already know. It was one thing for you to be out cheating. I would've fucked him over, but in the past I cheated. So I guess had that shit coming. But my daughter, Ta'Jay. That's my daughter. How could you do this to me? I've fucked bitches but I would never leave room for any bitch to bring a baby to our doorstep. No matter what I've done to you, I would never do no shit like. That's the ultimate disrespect.

"So, you fucked that nigga raw, huh? Turned around and looked me in my face everyday. Laid next to me and made love to me like it was nothing. I give you your props, though. That shit was real gangsta. I respect that, but I'm going to keep it gangsta with you as well. I been had her tested and that's my fucking daughter without a doubt. By the way, I want a divorce. You can keep all this shit."

Sarge grabbed some papers from under the lawn chair and threw them at me making sure they hit me in my face. I caught them and I looked at the DNA test and it read that at 99.9 percent, he was indeed her father. I folded it up and picked up the divorce papers. My tears were actually falling on the papers.

"Is this really what you want, Sarge? Can we at least try to get through this?"

"We can't try shit. The last bitch that hesitated when I wanted her to sign divorce papers is pushing up daises. Sign them papers. If you lied about our daughter's paternity, then I can't trust you. Just sign the papers. Let's not make this shit all long and drawn out. I'll take care of my kids. You can have everything I bought for you during the marriage, including the cars. You also still have access to our joint account. I'm here as the father of your children, but I simply can't be here to be your husband.

"This shit has been going on for months and I tried to give the chance to see if you would remember you were married. The last straw was when I physically saw you having sex with that nigga in the boutique that I put my blood, sweat, and tears in to make sure that you could pursue your dreams. Yeah, I saw everything, so don't deny shit. Please don't make this shit harder than it has to be. Sign the papers."

He threw a pen at me and I caught it before it fell. I sat in the lawn chair and cried the ugliest cry ever. The entire time he stood there without a care in the world. I looked in his eyes and I knew he was dead ass serious.

"You fucked up repeatedly during the course of our relationship and I accepted you back with open arms. I fuck up once and just like that it's over. Really, Sarge?"

He stood silent and continued to stare a hole through me. There was nothing I could say to persuade him to change his mind. I signed the divorce papers and handed them to him.

"I'll take the kids with me tonight and I'll bring them back sometime tomorrow."

He snatched the paper out of my hand and walked away. My head was spinning because I didn't expect for him to want a divorce. I woke up this morning with intentions of ending the shit with Cam once and for all. I had no idea I would go to bed divorced.

I hurried up and wiped the tears from my face as Lil' Sarge came and gave me a hug. He was such a big boy, standing tall at ten years old. He's grown up so fast on me it seems like yesterday I was in labor with him. Sema'Jay was standing off to the side being his usual quiet self. He was a momma's boy, so I knew at any minute he would be crying. At five years old, he was very smart and observant. Sarge looked away as he handed me our daughter so that I could kiss her. She'd just started walking and was getting into everything. He quickly walked out the house without looking at me. Seconds later, I could hear arguing. I cringed when I heard this nigga Cam outside acting a fool. I ran towards the front door and rushed outside. Cam had a big ass gun holding it down to the side.

"What the fuck are you doing, Cam?" I screamed jumping in front of Sarge and my kids.

"Take the kids and go in the house," Sarge roared.

"Take your sons in the house, but you can bring my daughter over here."

I looked at his ass and I tried to rush inside of the house. That's when I heard the first gun shot. I didn't feel the pain until I hit the ground, which made me drop my daughter. After that, the sound of gunfire was going off in rapid succession. I felt something on my back and I knew it was Sarge because he was grunting like he was in pain. I could hear my kids crying in the distance. The pain in my back was burning like hell and it was so painful.

"Oh fuck!" I heard Malik say.

"No! No! No!" I heard Thug say and it seemed like he was kicking something. I tried keeping my eyes open but I just couldn't. I was cold and sleepy.

"Hold on, sis! Don't close your eyes!"

"I'm sleepy, Thug."

"Ta'Jay! Ta'Jay!" The last thing I remembered was him calling my name before everything faded to black.

Chapter 8- Family Matters

Thug

When Malik called me I thought that he was exaggerating, but that shit changed when we pulled up in Sarge and Ta'Jay's driveway. I can still see it in my head when that nigga shot my sister in her back like a coward. Then he turned the gun on Sarge and fired. At the same time, we were letting off rounds in that nigga. He went out blazing all over some pussy that never belonged to him. Now my sister and Sarge are in the hospital fighting for their lives. The only reason we aren't sitting in jail is because they live on private land. That nigga was definitely sleeping with the fishes.

As I sit in this emergency room looking at my family and my crew, I can't help but think that I failed them. I'm supposed to know what the fuck is going on with my family at all times. I'm the head of this family. This shit was never supposed to happen. It had been hours and they were both still in surgery. My niece and nephews were shaken up, but they weren't hit. Thank God for that.

I just keep hearing my mother screaming and hollering through the phone. She was on her way out here on a private jet with Quaadir and Keesha. I had to close my eyes tight to keep from shedding tears. My sister and Sarge were really fucked up. Sarge looked dead. That nigga hit him all in his chest and stomach. I just started kicking the chair in front of me in anger. I was supposed to be there to protect them. There's no way my niece and nephews can grow up without their parents.

"Everything is going to be okay, baby."

Tahari rubbed her hand over my back trying to calm me down and in a way, it did. Her soft touch and angelic voice were the only things that could calm a nigga down at the moment.

"I fucked up, babe. I should've went and hollered at that nigga immediately when Malik told me about the shit. Did you know about this shit?" she hesitated to answer, so I knew she knew. I'm not surprised, though. All the Boss Ladies stick together and ride with each other until the very end.

"Yes, I knew. But it wasn't my business to tell her overprotective brothers. In case you forgot, she's my sister as well."

"Cut the bullshit. You knew that shit was wrong. Do you see what keeping secrets do? Because she felt like she needed some attention, she decided to step out on her husband with a fuck nigga. Now they're back there fighting for their lives. I know all y'all close, but this should be a lesson about keeping fucking secrets and being on that sneaky shit y'all be on. Watch out man."

I had to get up and take a walk to calm down. I felt myself taking my anger out on Tahari and the rest of the girls and they hadn't done any wrong. I stood outside the hospital and flamed up a fat ass blunt.

"Can I hit that?"

I looked up and it was a familiar face from my past. She looked even better now than she did then, but I wasn't fucking with her, period. Bitch lied and told me she was pregnant for money. Bitch got that money and I haven't seen her since.

"Knock yourself out, Pooh," I handed it to her and walked off.

I don't even entertain peasant ass bitches like that. No matter how good they look or how good they suck dick. This one right here was definitely a beast, but she was no Tahari. Nothing close to it. I've learned my lesson with that cheating shit. Last time it was a gun shot to my ass. Next it will be dirt on my coffin. I am not fucking around with Boss Lady.

"Damn, it's like that. When you start curving bitches?"

"When I put ring on his dick. Swerve bitch."

"Come on, they're out of surgery and the doctor wants to talk to us," Tahari came out of nowhere and we both left her ass looking crazy. I wanted to laugh but there was nothing to laugh at. Hearing that they were out of surgery had me on edge. When I walked inside of the family waiting room, the doctor was walking out. I looked at Malik and he was crying. I sat down and waited to get the bad news.

"What's going on?"

"Sarge gone be cool. All the bullets he took went in and out with out damaging anything. Ta'Jay wasn't so lucky. She might not ever walk again. They have her under sedation because they were unable to remove the bullet in her back. Her heart stopped on the table, but they got it back beating. They just want her body to heal so that's why they have her in a medically-induced coma for now. What the fuck, man? I was supposed to be there! This shit was never supposed to happen. I fucked up, Big Bro."

I had to stand up and grab my little brother in for a hug. We both felt guilty so I knew we needed each other. I felt a pair of hands wrap around us and looked up and it was Quaadir on one side and Remy on the other side. It felt good being with all my brothers at once. Now there was only one of us missing. Adonis had been MIA since he helped with the info on Tahari. Once all of this was over, I had every intention on making sure I reached out to him. Family is precious and we have to start living like everyday is our last.

"My baby has to be okay. Where were y'all at when all this shit was going down? Do you hear me, Thug? You're the oldest. You know you're supposed to protect your siblings!" Peaches was yelling at me from the seat she was sitting in.

"Ma, stop! It's my fault all this happened."

"Shut the fuck up, Malik! Thug is the head of this family. It's his job to protect us. Talk to me Ka'Jaire. What the fuck happened?"

"I fucked up, Ma! I'm sorry!"

"That shit ain't fair, Peaches. They've been blaming themselves from the moment they walked in the door," Tahari said jumping up in my defense.

"I love you Tahari, but Ka'Jaire is my son and I handle him my way. Don't get in between our shit!" Peaches was now standing up and in Tahari's face.

"Well I'm his wife and it's my duty to protect him when I feel like he's being wronged. Right now you're in the wrong for chastising him like he's a child when he goes above and beyond for this family."

"Stop all this shit. Ta'Jay and Sarge are in the back laid up from someone shooting them. It ain't nobody fault in this room!" Barbie said as she stood in between Peaches and Tahari.

The whole scene had me fucked up. I was hurt by Peaches' words because I could look at her and tell she was angry about something else and taking the shit out on me. I wanted to stay, but I knew if I did I'd blow the fuck up. The last thing I wanted to do was blow up and disrespect my mother. I wanted to go back and see my nigga Sarge and my sister, but I would wait until later. I walked out of there, refusing to look back and answer as they called out my name. I just wanted to be by myself and sort some shit out. As soon as I walked out of the emergency room doors, I walked right into Khia walking inside.

"Hey Bro. How are they?" she asked as we embraced one another.

"Sarge is good. Ta'Jay not so good, but she'll make it. I need to get out of here. By the way, that nigga Dro in there and well, you know the rest."

Khia looked almost afraid to walk in now but she needed to see that man. It's been well over year since we'd heard from or seen her. Dro had even hired a private detective but had no luck. I had enough on my plate. I was in condition to deal with Khia and Dro's shit. I was in need of peace of mind and went to the only place I knew where I could find it: in the walls of my home with my children. When I was with them, nothing else in the world mattered. They made the evils of the world look like candy and rainbows to a nigga. When I walked inside the house, Ka'Jairea was sitting on the couch watching TV.

"What you still doing up, baby girl?" I went and sat next to her on the couch and she hugged me.

"I was waiting up for you and Momma. Is Uncle Sarge and Auntie Ta'Jay okay?"

"Yeah, they're okay. Auntie Ta'Jay is still pretty sick, but she's going to be okay?"

"Can I ask you something, Daddy? Promise me that you won't get mad," she looked so sad and almost afraid to look at me. That was a first because she was the head strong one out of all the kids.

"Yesterday at school, I had a argument with this girl. I wanted to sit with her and the other girls at lunch but they didn't want me to. I asked her why she was being mean and she said that her mother told her to stay away from me because my parents were drug dealers and killers. Is that true, Daddy?"

I looked at my daughter. I realized she was not the same little girl that I fell in love with the moment I laid on her when she was three years old. She was now thirteen and looking just like Ta'Jay. I ran my hand over my face in frustration because I've worked so hard to shield my kids from the shit I do in the streets, only for some mean ass little girl to put something in her head. I could lie, but that would be wrong. The fact of the matter was her parents were everything the little girl said we were. But right now, I wasn't mentally prepared to have this talk with my daughter. This was more of Tahari's department.

"Don't listen to them little girls at school. They don't know nothing about your parents and the next time her or any other person disrespect you or your family, you go across they shit. They see you with everything they don't have and they're jealous of that. What your parent's do for a living shouldn't even be a topic of conversation at school. I want you to always remember that family is everything. Don't ever let someone disrespect your family. You got that."

"Yes, Daddy. I got it," she smiled and kissed me on the jaw.

"While we're talking. What's this I hear I about you liking Lil' Hassan?"

I had to see what was really good because Ka'Jaiyah had been telling me all types of shit about these two.

"I'm going to kill Ka'Jaiyah," she gritted.

"Don't kill my baby. Plus, you know that her ass can't hold hot water. Now come back over here and tell Daddy what's going on with you and Lil' Hassan."

I could tell she was hesitant to talk to me, but she didn't have to be.

"Nothing is going on, Daddy. I mean, I like him. I guess you can say he's my boyfriend. "

"Boyfriend, huh?

"Are you going to kill him, Daddy?"

I laughed because she was so dramatic when she said it. She looked like she was about to cry. I wanted to cry because my baby girl had her first crush.

"Of course I'm not going to kill him. However, he's not your boyfriend. You just have a little puppy love. You're too young to be talking about you having a boyfriend. What are you trying to do, give me a heart attack?"

"No, Daddy. I just like him. He's so cute."

I just shook my head at her because she was really sitting here blushing like it was nothing.

"Listen to me. Boys ain't shit but trouble. They come in like a thief in the night and steal your heart. Boys will make you sad and they will make you cry. I don't want nobody hurting my baby. If he does hurt you or make you cry, I might have to kill him. If I kill him then I have to turn around and kill his father Hassan. We do business together, so that wouldn't be a good look. I love you, baby girl. But I don't want to hear any more talk about Lil' Hassan again. Now go to bed before your Momma come in here cursing about you being up late."

She grabbed her throw blanket and headed up the stairs.

"Just so you know Daddy, I'm well aware of your lifestyle. I also want you to know that it doesn't matter what you do for a living. You and Momma have always made sure that we had everything we needed. I don't care what anyone says, you guys are the best parents in the world. I know that you told me that I can't have a boyfriend and for me to stop saying that Lil' Hassan is my boyfriend. Daddy, I just want you to know that one day I'm going to marry Lil' Hassan. I love you, Daddy."

"I love you too, baby girl."

I sat speechless, in awe of my daughter. She was no longer my little baby girl. I got a good look at her and one would think she was Tahari's biological daughter. She was so headstrong like her. That shit warmed my heart to hear her say Tahari and I are good parents. Just when I had the weight of the world on my shoulders, a simple conversation with my daughter lifted it off. Now I need to figure out what the hell am I going to do about her calling herself liking Lil' Hassan. I enjoy being a father, but nothing will ever prepare me for this shit here.

Chapter 9- Real Love

Tahari

I stood, watching my husband as he walked out of the family waiting room. That shit hurt me to the core the way Peaches had talked to him. My husband is not perfect, but he goes hard for his family. That's one of the things that attracted me to him. Family is everything to Thug and everybody around him knows that. For Peaches to say that shit to him pissed me off. I don't care about her being his mother. That shit was dead ass wrong on so many levels. I would be less than a wife not to address the situation.

"How could you do him like that, Peaches? Everybody else can stand around here and be quiet, but not me. Y'all know this shit is dead ass wrong. Thug does everything in his power to make sure everyone is okay. Thug didn't deserve that. I understand that you're his mother, but I'm his wife. I love him just like you do, Peaches. I'll even die for him just like I know you will.

"It's not my intention to disrespect you, Peaches. You know that I look at you like the mother I never had. However, please stop acting like my husband is your husband and it's his responsibility to be a father to your kids. He loves his brothers and sisters with everything in him. Sometimes Thug needs love and affection too, but I think everybody forgets that about him. Just talking to you about this makes me rethink the way I act towards him. I'm spoiled and bratty towards him on a daily basis, but no matter what he still goes hard for me and he does the same for everyone in this room. Thug is a thoroughbred and as hard as they come, but he needs someone to depend on just like everybody else. Please Peaches, watch how you handle my husband."

"He wouldn't even be your husband had we not felt sorry for your ass. As a matter of fact, a lot of the shit that we went through we've been going through it since your ass came along. Please don't ever in your life think it's cool to check me about my motherfucking son. I love you just like a daughter as well, but watch how the fuck you handle me when it comes to my son."

"I guess you been dying for a reason to throw that in my face. Kudos to you. Thank you for letting me know how the fuck you really feel. I admit I come from a fucked up bloodline. You, on the other hand, created your own chaos by fucking one brother that was a fucking pedophile and then fucking the other brother that was a sadistic son of a bitch. All of that shit happened before I met your son. Please don't blame me for your fuck ups. I'm glad we had this conversation. Now we both know how the other one really feels. You don't ever have to worry about my kids or me bothering with you again."

"Both of y'all shut the fuck up with all this shit. My sister is paralyzed! What part of that shit don't y'all get? This shit is petty. Both of y'all sitting her arguing back and forth over Thug. How in the fuck y'all think he gone feel knowing his mother and wife is disrespecting one another. I love you Ma, but you dead ass wrong. I'm sorry, Ma. I'm just being honest," Malik said before he grabbed Barbie's hand and they left out of the family waiting room.

Peaches wanted to say something but Quanie grabbed her roughly and yanked her out of the room. I was so over this whole scene so I grabbed my jacket and headed out to check on my husband. I already knew Malik's trick ass had called and told him by now. I just had to mentally prepare myself because I knew he was going to be upset with me. As I headed out the door, I ran dead smack into Khia. I rushed over and grabbed her tightly. I'd been extremely worried about her. She hadn't been in contact with us or anything.

"Hey, sis. I missed you so much."

"I missed you more. Let's hurry up and get out of here before Dro sees me."

"Khia! Khia!"

The sound of Dro's voice boomed and I tried to turn to look, but this bitch grabbed my hand and made me take off running with her.

"Really, bitch?" I said out of breath as we made it out to the parking lot with Dro hot on our asses. I swear to God I'd picked up a little weight so a bitch was in no shape to be out here running.

"I swear to God I'm gone shoot your ass if you keep running!"

"Don't stop, Ta-Baby!" Khia ass was running like Jackie Joyner Kersey. I gave up, I couldn't run anymore. That bitch hopped in her car and got the fuck out of dodge.

"Really, sis? That's how you do me? How could you let her get away like that? I just want to see my son."

"What was I supposed to do? That's my friend. Trust me, she'll be back. If she didn't want to see you, she never would have came back. Just give her some time. Especially since you're now with Brittany. If memory serves me right, you and that boot mouth bitch is the reason why she left in the first place. This shit ain't gone do nothing but cause more drama. I love you Dro and you know that, but you did this shit to yourself," I said out of breath, and headed to my car.

Today was just too much on me and I was mentally exhausted from the day's events. I just wanted to go home and cater to my husband and kids.

*****

I walked in the house and Thug was knocked out sleep on the couch. I checked on all the kids and they were asleep as well. Since they were all sound asleep, I decided to take that time to cater to Thug. I ran him some bath water and placed some rose petals inside of the tub. Since the water was a little too hot, I waited for his water to cool off before I woke him up. I used that time to roll him up a fat ass blunt and pour him a double shot of Remy.

"Wake up, Bae," I gently shook him and he sat up quickly.

"What's up?" he said as he wiped his eyes and looked at his phone.

"Nothing. I ran you some bath water. Come on upstairs so I can bathe you. I just want to make you feel better," I said as I tried to pull him up from the couch.

"Now you know damn well I don't take no baths. Real niggas take showers. Go and get the shower ready for me. I'll be up in a minute. Thanks, babe."

He kissed me on the forehead and started looking through his phone. I hurried up and walked away because I knew at any minute he was going to go ape shit about me arguing with Peaches. Just thinking about it had me feeling really bad. A part of me wanted to call her and apologize. But if I apologize, it would be like I was wrong. I stand firm in everything that I said to her with regards to Thug.

Pretty early in our relationship, I realized how much they depended on him and how much he catered to them and made sure they were okay. Now don't get me wrong, I love how he loves his family. I never had the type of love that they have for one another, so it's heartwarming to see their bond. However, Peaches has given Thug the responsibility of being the father that they never really had around. Malik and Ta'Jay look at him as a father figure because that's how he treats them and that's a good thing. He does that shit from his heart because he loves them. However, Peaches makes it like he's obligated to be their father figure. She might not see it that way, but that's how it looks to me.

"What the hell is Peaches talking about you disrespected her?"

Damn I thought it was going to be Malik, I thought to myself.

"I didn't disrespect her, Ka'Jaire. I spoke the truth and she got mad. I told her that she was wrong for the way she treated you. As your wife I have the right to speak in your defense, and if that's wrong, then so be it. Don't you dare tell me to apologize because I'm not."

I could see it all in his face that he wanted me to apologize but I had to let his know up front that shit wasn't happening at all.

"I'm not saying it's wrong, Ta-Baby and I'm not telling you to apologize. However, I'm a grown man and I can speak up for myself. I know that you love me and you go hard as fuck for me. I love you more because of the way that you love me. The sexiest thing outside of your beauty is how big your heart is on the inside. It's my job to take care of you, not the other way around."

I just shook my head at him because here he was standing in front of me being big, bad Thug. Acting like her behavior didn't faze him, but I know that I did. I wanted to snap on his ass. Instead, I just remained quiet and walked out of the bathroom and past him. I stripped down to my panties and bra and climbed up in my bed.

"You're just going to walk away and not say anything?" Thug sat next to me on the bed and flamed up the blunt.

"It's not that I don't want to say anything. It's just that you're making me feel like saying something was wrong. You're my husband and I have the right to defend your honor, even if it's your mother."

Thug grabbed my legs and placed my feet in his lap. He kissed on each one of my toes.

"I don't know what I would do without you, Tahari. I'm so appreciative and grateful for all that you do for me. Never think that shit go unnoticed. You were not wrong for defending me. I apologize if I made you feel that way. This shit is between you and Peaches. I'm not getting in the middle of that shit. Both of y'all know better than to be at odds with one another. We're a family and I expect y'all to fix it. I know it's hard for you to understand, but Peaches and I have a relationship that only we understand. Yeah her words hurt me, but I know that it wasn't her intention to do that. I'll handle it. I love you, man," he grabbed my face and kissed me.

"I love you, too."

He removed his clothes and climbed in bed. I laid my head on his chest and listened to his strong heartbeat. It was like a lullaby because it put me right to sleep. I was sleeping good too until Thug woke me up.

"Wakeup, Bae. Khia is here."

I sat straight up when I heard him say that. All I could think about was that bitch getting the fuck out of dodge on my ass yesterday.

"Let me handle my personal hygiene. Tell her I'll be down in a minute. I hope she ready to deal with Dro because all this running not right. She need to sit down and talk him."

"I'm glad she showed up too, but you know I try to stay out of people relationships. I'll go down and let her know."

"Wait a minute, nigga. I'm gone need you to put on a T-shirt and make sure it cover your dick print. Khia my bitch and all, but I'm not comfortable with her seeing your bare chest or your dick print in them basketball shorts. I'm not saying that you or her would take it there, but I want to take precautions for what's mine and at the same time refrain from murdering her ass."

I grabbed his dick and he made his chest jump like I like. I thought that he was going to say something smart but he grabbed a T-shirt and put it on.

"Are you happy now, Boss Lady?"

I nodded my head in approval and he headed out the door. My baby had become so mild-mannered and humble these days. Retirement has made him a better man.

When I walked into the living room, I was taken aback at the sight of Khia bouncing a baby girl on her leg. She looked up at me with the saddest eyes ever. I rushed over to her and she started to cry and hold the baby tighter.

"I never should have come back."

Tears were streaming down her face and she was shaking uncontrollably.

"Calm down, Khia and tell me what's wrong?"

She was crying so hard that I could barely get any understanding from her.

"I went over to the house and she answered the door. He got that bitch in my house, Ta-Baby. I wanted to be the bigger person and allow him to meet his daughter. Now I'm gone make sure he never sees her," Khia yelled, causing the baby to start crying. I grabbed the baby from her arms and rocked her.

"Now you know I'm Team Khia all day, but you left him. I know you didn't think that nigga was gone keep looking for you and you were purposely hiding from him. I'm not condoning a damn thing Dro has done because the shit is dead ass wrong on so many levels. However, that was your nigga and you never should've walked away. You left the door open for that bitch to slide right in your motherfucking spot. You're a motherfucking Boss Lady and we don't run from nothing. We fuck shit up. Now while you're sitting your ass on my couch crying, looking all ugly and shit, you need to be over there beating that bitch the fuck up."

Khia was pissing me off with this weak shit right now.

"I know that it's my fault he moved on, but what was I supposed to do when he was basically showing me that he didn't want to be with me. I was tired of fighting him and I wasn't about to let him hurt me anymore than he already had. I didn't start regretting it until I gave birth and looked into my daughter's beautiful face."

Before I could respond, someone begin ringing the doorbell repeatedly. Khia and I looked at each other and Thug came walking from the back with a smirk on his face.

"Really, Thug?"

He opened the door and Dro rushed in. Khia's ass took off again running up the stairs in my house with Dro hot on her ass. I looked at him and shook my head because he was a sneaky motherfucker for doing that. These niggas know they stick together. That's why me and my girls be on good bullshit with their asses.

"Don't say shit. My nigga deserves to know he has a daughter. Now sit there and mind your business."

I rolled my eyes and sat back to listen to Khia and Dro tearing shit up and I hoped they knew they were paying for whatever the fuck they broke in my shit.

Chapter 10- Is Your Heart Still Mine

Khia

I was so damn out of breath running from Dro. Tahari and Thug house was like a damn fortress so I was running all over the place but a bitch was tired. I looked behind me and noticed that Dro was on my ass. I tried to turn into one of the rooms but he caught me by my long ass weave and jerked my ass back so hard that he damn near broke my neck. I fell backwards on my ass hard as hell. He dragged me be my hair until he found a guest room.

"Let me go, Dro!"

"Shut the fuck up! You up and leave a year and half ago and come back only to have me chasing after your ass. Where the fuck have you been and where the fuck is my son?"

"Please Dro, just stop pulling my hair and I'll tell you!" He roughly pushed me away by my hair and I jumped up on his ass and started swinging like a mad woman.

"How dare you put your motherfucking hands on me like you give a fuck? Ya bitch ass laid up in my fucking house with that thot ass bitch Brittany and think the shit cool."

He lifted me up and pinned me down on the bed in way that the only thing I could move was my head from side to side.

"Calm your ass down. I fucked up okay and I didn't realize that until you and Khiandre were gone. I know that there is nothing I can say that will change all the hurt and pain that I caused you. Just give me a chance to do right by you and my son. Come home, Khia. I know you came by and saw Brittany but me and her are no longer together. We're just co-parenting for the sake of our daughter. Yes, I was fucking with her from time to time while you've been gone, but what the fuck did you expect me to do."

Dro let me go and sat down on the side of the bed next to me. He rubbed his hand over his face in frustration.

"I expected for you to not get another bitch pregnant and treat me like shit. Do you actually think I wanted to just up and leave you? Dro, you basically shitted on me for Brittany. After I made a mistake and shot Khiandre things were worse and you acted as if you hated me. I just couldn't take it so I took our son and left. During that time, I met someone and we've been together ever since. Three months after I was gone, I found out I was pregnant with your daughter. That little girl Tahari was holding is our daughter Khelani. Khiandre is here as well, I dropped him off over Barbie's house so he could play with Lil' Malik and Malikhi."

I reached out to touch Dro but he knocked my hand away and walked out of the room. I jumped up and followed him down the stairs. I made sure to keep some distance between us. He might get the urge to turn around and smack the shit out of me. Dro walked over to Tahari and she handed him Khelani . He just looked at her for a minute before kissing her all over her face.

"I don't know who the fuck that nigga is you been with and I don't give a fuck. All I know is you better tell that motherfucker it's over and bring ya ass home. I'm taking my fucking kids home with me. You have less than twenty four hours to bring your ass home."

Dro walked out of the door with our daughter and her diaper bag without so much as looking back. I sat down on the couch and put my head down in my hands.

"Go tell that nigga it's over lil' sis before shit get out of hand. You already know how Thug Inc. coming. Stop with all the bullshit and save that man life. He had no idea what he was getting himself into. I love you sis, and welcome back," Thug patted me on the shoulder and walked out of the door like it was nothing. I rolled my eyes at his ass too, because it's all his damn fault Dro caught up with my ass.

"I hate when they start with them egos and shit. However, you know they gone be at that nigga head. So it's up to you if you want that nigga blood on your hands. Who the fuck is he anyway?"

I was dreading that question but I knew I had to tell who it was.

"Adonis," I said just above a whisper.

"Come again."

"I've been in a relationship with Thug's brother Adonis. About a month after I left, I bumped into him at the mall. We exchanged numbers and we started talking on the phone. One thing led to another and we took things to the next level. Adonis was giving me everything that Dro wasn't. I think that's what made me fall for him so easy and so fast. We both knew that shit had the potential to get us both fucked up, but at the time we didn't care. We didn't want to cause any trouble so that's why we've been MIA.

"The sad part is that he's a really good guy. He's been good to me and my kids. This shit is going to be so hard because I was supposed to be coming here to tell Dro about my relationship with him. I never really wanted to do it because my heart was still with Dro. Now I have to go home and break this nigga heart."

"Oh my God, Khia. This shit has the potential to have bad ass consequences. Thug is going to spazz the fuck out when he finds out. Take your ass over there and end the shit immediately. Hurry up because Dro psycho ass is in rare form this morning."

Tahari and I embraced one another and I left. It only took me a little under a hour to get home. I was still living in the State of Illinois, just not Chicago. The whole ride over I was shaking in my Giuseppe's because this man had changed jobs and everything for me. I felt bad as fuck, but not bad to the point where I would change my mind about calling things off. In reality, it was the best thing to do because I'm not in love with Adonis. I have love for him and I appreciate everything he has done for me but my heart is with Dro. I shook my head at myself because I had to be the dumbest bitch on Earth to still love Dro. I'm learning the hard way that the heart wants who it wants, no matter who you're with.

*****

As I drove up to the house, I observed an all-black Lincoln Town car pulling out of the driveway. That was odd to me because we never had visitors. Although Adonis was a police officer and had a lot of powerful friends on the force, he still moved with caution because he was a Santerelli. From what he told me, he had to be careful at all times because there were still so many enemies lurking in the shadows. Being with Dro, I understood that firsthand.

Adonis was sitting on the couch when I walked inside of the house. I sat down next to him on the couch and reached out to touch his leg.

"There's something I need to tell you, Khia. I just hope when I'm finished telling you, we can still remain friends."

I laughed inwardly because this nigga was getting ready to dump my ass which was fine because it made me feel a lot better than just walking out on him. He'd been good to me and he didn't deserve for me to just leave him.

"Please don't spare my feelings, Adonis. Just tell me what's going on."

"I've been cheating on you with someone else and I really love her. I'm sorry to tell you like this, but I just can't keep living a lie and lying to you."

"How long has this been going on, Adonis?"

"Since before we met. We had a bad break up but we both realized that with each other is where we wanted to be. I'm really sorry, Khia. You know that I love you and the kids."

"It's fine, Adonis. I was actually coming here to tell you that I was going back to Dro. I'm sorry as well because you've been so good to us. We can both agree that this is over. No one knows about us but Tahari. I can assure you that our secret will not be revealed to the rest of the family. Let's just act like this has never happened. This actually works out perfect for you. I know how much you want to know your brothers. Now is the perfect time to start bonding with them. I'm going to grab a couple of items and I'll be out of your way. Thanks for being there when I needed you the most. Know that in me you have a friend for life.

"I'm glad to know that we can be friends. Call me if there is anything you or the kids need."

Adonis and I exchanged hugs and we officially parted ways. I packed as much as I could and headed back home to Dro. I didn't even know how to act being around Dro. It had been so long since we interacted with one another. I really had no idea what to expect from him. The one thing I did know was we had to have a conversation about him and the bitch Brittany, because I know while I was away they had something going on. Which is way more than them just co-parenting. That's bullshit and Dro is going to have to come better than that if he thinks things between us are going to just go back to normal.

Chapter 11- Where I Want to Be

Dro

A man will never see the error in his ways until he's left alone to fend for himself. I would be the first nigga to admit that it ain't no sunshine when she's gone. That's how I've been feeling since Khia walked out on me over a year and a half ago. I thought she was just in her feelings and she would come back in a week or so. She definitely showed my ass never to underestimate a hurt woman. I still can't believe that she up and left like that without so much as a word.

The thing that hurt me the most was the fact that she took Khiandre from me. I don't give fuck what I was doing in these streets. If she wanted to leave to find herself that was fine, but she was never supposed to take him away from me. What's worse is the fact that she had given birth to my daughter during her time away from me. She had been hiding good as fuck. I had one of the best private detectives looking for her and even he couldn't find her. It was like she had disappeared off the face of the Earth. Now that she was back, I wanted to know what nigga she'd been with.

I most definitely wanted to fuck the nigga over. Just thinking about this nigga being around my kids has me hot and wanting to beat Khia's ass. I know that I brought all of this shit on myself, but I'm a nigga and this is how the fuck we react when we aren't in control of the situation. There's nothing that I can do but sit back and pray she comes home to a nigga. In the meantime, I was enjoying this time getting to know my daughter.

Tears came to my eyes as she laid on my chest sleeping. I'd missed out on everything and that shit hurt. Khiandre was in bed, knocked out as well. He's been under me since I picked him up from Barbie's house.

I knew my little nigga had missed me just as much as I'd missed him. This shit was the life right here.

I had shared custody with my older kids' maternal grandmother. I only get to see them on holidays and weekends. I have my daughter by Brittany on a regular because all she wants to do is party and bullshit. Brittany and I were getting along until Khia came to the house while she was here. I don't know why the bitch was all in her feelings. She knew what the fuck it was when this shit got started. I told her ass from the jump Khia had my heart and whenever I found her, she was coming back home. This bitch was quick to say she was cool with the shit so I would continue fucking with her. Now she's in her feelings about Khia being back, but I don't give a fuck. My main concern is being in all my kids' lives. I just want to be a better father to them and an even better husband to Khia.

This shit with Sarge and Ta'Jay has put some shit on my heart. I need to make sure my home front is in order. I'd lost Khia to another nigga behind me chasing pussy out here in these streets. I don't have to be out here on that bullshit when I have everything in her. I could only hope that we can get back to our happy place. I promised to make her happy and never make her feel the way the nigga Nico did.

I have to make up for the promises that I broke. The sound of the alarm beeping made me remove my daughter from my chest and lay her next to her brother. I hopped up and stood at the top of the stairs, which overlooked the foyer of the house. I was happy as hell on the inside to see Khia was standing there with her suitcases. I walked down the stairs to grab the bags from her.

"Where are the kids?" she asked, not making eye contact with me.

"They're upstairs in the bed sleeping."

"I hope you weren't fucking that bitch in that bed. I don't want my fucking kids laying in that bitch pussy juice. As a matter of fact, that bitch has been in this house I don't even want to stay in this house!"

Khia turned around and tried to leave back out of the house but I pulled her in close to me. I hugged her so tight that she could barely move. I could tell from her touch she was trying not to give in, but that made me grab her face and kiss her.

"How could you do this to us?"

I was now rubbing my face where she had smacked the shit out of me. Before I could respond, she just starting hitting me. She was knocking the shit out of me, but I took the shit because I knew I deserved it.

"I'm sorry, Khia," I said as I pushed her up against the front door and held her hands above her head.

"No you're not. You just saying that shit to make me stay here," Khia said as she quickly wiped tears from her eyes.

"If you weren't staying, you never would have come back."

I ripped her blouse off of her, causing all of the buttons to fly off, exposing the black lace bra she was wearing. Her titties were sitting up just right. I couldn't help but to bend down and place succulent kisses on each one of them. I got down on my knees and unbuttoned her pants. I looked up at her just in case she wanted me to stop, but the way she was biting on her bottom lip in anticipation told me to keep going. I unzipped her pants and slowly removed them with her assistance. I turned her around so that she was facing the door. In one swift motion, I ripped her thong off of her. I ran my tongue up and down the crack of her ass. I went in for the kill and I started eating her ass like a buffet, fuck them groceries.

She reached back and grabbed my head pressing it farther into her ass. With her bent all the way over, I was able to dip my tongue in and out her pussy from time to time while I continued to eat her ass. I was trying to suck the soul out her ass and her pussy. I had to make her remember why she was sprung on a nigga at the age of fifteen, when I taught her how to suck dick. I might've fucked her over, but at the end of the day Khia knew I was the motherfucking truth. I raised up and dropped the basketball shorts I had on. I turned her around and lifted her up. She wrapped her legs around my waist and I walked her over to the couch, laying her body down gently.

"I missed the fuck out of you, Khia," I said as I penetrated her. I had to stop for a minute because her shit was gripping my dick like a glove.

"I missed you too, but you can't keep playing with my heart and thinking it's okay. I swear to God there will not be a next time. I'll leave with the kids and never come back."

She opened her legs wider and received my entire dick. I couldn't help it, I had to let out the moans. Khia's pussy was doing shit that it had never done for me. I got angry. Just thinking about her being with that nigga made my dick soft.

"What's wrong? Nigga, I was about to cum. How the fuck are you going to just stop in mid damn stroke? Your ass done fucked up my nut."

I didn't even say shit. I put my shorts back on and walked to my man cave. I needed a fucking blunt to deal with this shit. I needed to stimulate my mind and try to clear my head. Thinking about Khia and this nigga was fucking up my mental state. I always kept blunts rolled and in a cigar box on the bar. I didn't fuck with nothing but Remy so that's was all that was on top of the bar. I grabbed a bottle and poured me a shot. I know I'm being a bitch at the moment, but that shit got me hot.

I flamed up the blunt and inhaled deeply. I exhaled and Khia walked in the room completely naked. Her body was stacked in all the right places. She didn't even look like she had given birth to two kids. She didn't have a stretchmark in sight. Just admiring her curves reminded me of how thick she was for a teenager. Them niggas used to be at her and all she wanted was me. I've played many games with Khia, but that shit is dead and over with.

"Look, I now why you stopped and that shit ain't fair to me, Dro. I'm here although I shouldn't be. Just like the thought of a nigga fucking me is getting to you, it gets to me knowing that a bitch was able to come between us. Why, I don't know? I'm prettier than that bitch and my body is badder than hers. All the way around that hoe ain't fucking with me, period. So trust and believe me, it hurts me knowing that you were out giving that bitch what belonged to me. I sat back and watched you love her."

"Let me stop you right there. I don't love that bitch. Never have and I never will. I love my daughter that we share."

I knocked back a shot and watched as he shook her head. She grabbed the blunt from my hand and took a long pull from it.

"Did it ever occur to you how much it hurt me to know that you gave another woman outside of Keisha something that only I should be able to give to you? It was one thing for me to have to deal with Keisha and the fact that she'd always made life for me a living hell. When we were younger, I had to watch as you paraded her around the hood like she was a ghetto princess. I used to dream of the day when you would treat me like that.

"Then by luck, we found each other in the unluckiest of circumstances. Finally, you had chosen me and that shit had me feeling like fifteen year old Khia. You made me feel like I was the luckiest girl in the world. You came into my life at a time when my son and I needed you the most. You became everything we needed. Any doubts and fears I had about ever having a happy life subsided when you took us as your own. I had to be the stupidest bitch on Earth to think that I would ever get a chance at that happy life that I desired.

"You played me like I was that young stupid ass Khia that used to let you treat her like shit. I'm walking around here thinking that things are over with you and Keisha, but all along you were still fucking with the bitch. Playing with her emotions and shit. So she comes to our home and tries to kill me. She hated me so much that she killed our baby. It killed my soul to see my friends with their babies but mine was dead because his father couldn't keep his dick in his pants. I thought shit was going to get back to normal for us and then I find out that you have a baby with another bitch. Not only did you have a baby with the bitch, but you treated me like shit in the process.

"I'm saying all this to say that you have no reason to sit up and be in your feelings about a nigga fucking me. You need to accept it and move on just like I had to accept all the bullshit you put me through. We both know that had you never done these things to me, I never would've walked out you. I know you don't believe me, but I really hate that I kept Khelani and Khiandre from you.

"We're here now and that's all that matters. This is hard on me, too. It's like we have to start over from scratch and get back to the way we used to be. Back when nothing else mattered but us. You promised that you would take good care of my heart and all I want is for you to make good on that. I also want a brand new house with all new furnishings. I can smell that bitch in my bedroom. So until you get my house, the kids and I will be staying at a hotel."

Khia kissed me on the jaw and walked out. Everything she said was right so I couldn't argue with her. She wanted a new house, so first thing in the morning I was putting this one on the market and searching for a new one. I wanted my wife back so I had to do whatever I could to make it up to her. I could tell that she was going to make this hard on a nigga.

I knocked back another shot of Remy and I headed upstairs to get ready. If she was going to the hotel, I was going with her. I just want to lay in bed with my wife and kids. We needed to get back to the way we were. Before I fucked up and made her walk out of my life. I didn't know what I had until she was gone. Now that she's back, I'm going to do everything in my power to make good on my promises.

Chapter 12- Regrets of a Wife

Ta'Jay

One Month Later

The longer I sit in this hospital I feel like I'm about to go stir crazy. I just keep seeing myself laying on my doorstep and hearing the numerous gunshots that were going off around me. I woke up two weeks ago from a medically-induced coma. The surgery I had to undergo to remove the bullet that was lodged in my back was successful and I was not paralyzed like the doctor thought that I would be. It was nothing short of a miracle. I've been thanking God ever since I woke up. I'm so blessed to still have my mobility. But I feel so bad.

My actions have divided my family and it hurts my soul. Thug has yet to come up here and see me. That alone made me want to die because if I never had anyone in this life, I had my big brother. Thug is my safety net and I needed his security at the moment.

I needed him to assure me that everything would be okay just like he used to when I was younger. I'm a grown ass woman but when it comes to my brothers, I'm a little ass girl. It's always been that way. Thug, Malik, and Quaadir are pissed at me. I can tell in Thug's absence and Malik and Quaadir's voices when they talk to me.

Of course I had Tahari and the rest of my girls, but y'all know the bond I have with my brothers. This shit is damn worse than death. I need my backbone. Malik, Quaadir, and even Remy have been here around the clock, making sure I go to therapy and talking to the doctors. I loved them for catering to me despite the hurt and pain that I've caused. When I did what I did to Sarge, I didn't just hurt myself. I hurt my brothers too, because Sarge is family to them. I know the severity of the situation with regards to Thug Inc. and how they roll. So I'm fucked up about my decisions and I just want to make things right with everybody. They all look at me and say it's okay, but deep down inside I know they're judging me.

"I see you're dressed and all ready to go home. Here are your prescriptions and discharge papers. Remember, no strenuous activity of any kind for the next three months. Although your surgery was a success, you still have to take it easy and go to physical therapy twice a week to strengthen your mobility. Usually this is the nurse's job to get you all discharged, but I felt the need to be here personally. You're nothing short of a miracle and your case will go with me during the rest of my years. It was a joy treating you, Ms. Ta'Jay."

"Thank you so much. I promise to follow all of your instructions."

The doctor handed me all of my papers and left the room. Now I'm sitting here wondering how in the hell am I about to adapt to life without Sarge in it. I haven't heard from or seen him since the day we got shot. It's like he said fuck me and in reality, I couldn't blame him. However, if the shoe was on the other foot and it was him who was at fault for everything, I would be by his side with bells on. That's a nigga for you, though. They can get away with all types of shit, but when a woman does one wrong thing, it's the end of the world. I guess I shouldn't be surprised that he isn't here. After all, that nigga divorced my ass before we got hit up. So we were officially over.

"Come on let me get you home?" My mother said as she walked into the room looking like she was twenty-five years old. Peaches was beautiful for a forty-five year old woman with six kids. I could only hope to look like her at that age.

"Yeah, I'm all ready. Did you tell Thug that I was coming home?"

"I haven't talked to him, but I'm quite sure his wife told him," Peaches said as she rolled her eyes and grabbed my hand at the same time. She was trying her best to act as if she had an attitude with Thug and Tahari, but I know better. She was hurt that Thug and Tahari weren't speaking to her. At the same time, Peaches was wrong. She had no business talking to either of them the way that I heard she did. Peaches knows how Tahari is about Thug, so I don't understand why she's all in her feelings. I'm still pissed at her for blaming Thug for what happened to me. This shit is my fault and mine alone. If it wasn't for my brothers, Sarge, our kids, and me would probably be dead. So if anything, my brothers saved my life. I already knew that they took care of Cam and disposed of his ass. I didn't feel any remorse for him because I forewarned him about thinking it was sweet to play with his own life.

"Y'all really need to stop this silly bullshit."

"I know you just took some bullets, but watch your mouth Ta'Jay. I'm so fucking sick and tired of all this disrespect. Let me get you home so I can head back to Atlanta."

I looked at her like she had lost her mind.

"So you're just going to leave without fixing things."

"It's obvious I'm not needed here. Quanie don't want me no more. You, Thug, and Malik have made it perfectly clear you don't need me. The twins and I are out there with Aunt Ruth, and I actually love it out there with her."

I wasn't about to entertain Peaches or her pity party. She knows for a fact she's out there because she's too embarrassed to face the fact that Quanie left and it's her fault.

I'd created my own chaos with Sarge and it hurts me to the core that we are no longer together, but I refuse to run away. I'm going to hold my head up high and deal with it. I don't want to be looked at like a charity case. This my mess that I created and I intend on facing it head on. In the meantime, I couldn't deal with my mother and her issues. My plate was full as it was.

I think it's better if she does head out to Atlanta and work on herself. I've never seen her so broken in my life. The worst part about it is that she doesn't even realize how much her misery shows. She's so busy trying to be Super Peaches. I have to just let her be until she comes around.

"Before I drop you off, there's something I have to tell you?"

"What?"

She had me worried because of the look on her face.

"The kids are with Sarge. He came and got them from my house a couple of days ago.

"So you just let him take my kids, Ma?"

Tears welled up in my eyes because I couldn't believe this shit.

"I couldn't deny that man from seeing his kids. Plus, you know damn well Sarge ain't gone do shit to his kids."

I was sitting in the passenger seat looking at my mother like she was crazy. This is the same person who was walking around a complete fool when Quanie took the kids from her. She knew he wouldn't do shit to hurt them, yet she still caused all types of hell trying to find them. Now she's sitting here telling me he wouldn't hurt my kids. As if that mattered. That's not even the point. The fact is he took my kids and didn't tell me about it. As a matter of fact, I haven't heard from him since I've been awake.

"He's already divorced me, Ma. Now he wants to take my kids, too."

I was crying so badly I was trembling. That was until Peaches started hollering at me and hitting the steering wheel.

"Shut the fuck up Ta'Jay with all that weak bitch shit. You are a motherfucking Kenneth, not to mention a motherfucking Boss Lady. All of this crying and this depressed shit is not how we roll and you know that. So motherfucking what you cheated on your husband? It just so happened you put that pussy on a crazy motherfucker and he came gunning. You didn't know that shit was going to happen. At the end of the day, I know that you love Sarge. You were willing to lose everything just to be with that nigga. So your momma knows how deep your love is.

"At the same motherfucking time, stop blaming yourself for this shit that happened and try healing from it. Now if memory serves me right, Sarge was the same motherfucker married and you had no idea until the bitch made her presence known. Sarge is the same motherfucker that you and your son observed walking down Michigan Ave. holding some random bitch hand. Let's not forget this the same bitch was the one that was calling herself fucking with you about him so y'all had to get in that ass. Sarge ain't no saint. Don't let that nigga make you feel bad about cheating when he started the shit."

"It's too late, Ma. We signed the divorce papers."

She reached inside her purse and threw some papers at me. I looked and it was the same paperwork I signed that day at the house before the shooting.

"Tear that shit up, immediately. Don't you ever in your life agree to no bullshit like that. Ever. If that nigga wants a motherfucking divorce, you take his ass to court and drag that shit out. If he want to leave because you cheated, then you make that motherfucker pay you for all the shit he put you through over the years. You better wipe your fucking face right now. I've did my share of dirt in my lifetime, but I've never sat up and cried 'bout it because it wouldn't change my actions.

"You fucked up Ta'Jay, but it ain't the end of the world. It's actually your new beginning. Now the best advice I can give you as a mother is to Boss the fuck up and fight for your marriage. Sarge ain't crazy to fuck over you or them kids. He might be a part of Thug Inc., but we all know who hails supreme around this bitch. You know Thug ain't going at gunpoint when it comes to you. At the same time, you and I both know this shit more than personal for this family. It's business.

"Sarge brings in millions and The Kenneth Family is all about that money. If he doesn't want to reconcile, then you can't make him change his mind. However, I don't believe for a minute he wants to really divorce you. You know them Thug Inc. niggas let their egos get the best of them. I'm about to head back to Atlanta. I just need to get away from it all. Plus, Momma not gone lie to you, she's dick sick. I'm going crazy without Quanie, but I'll never let that motherfucker see me sweat. Quanie is teaching my ass a lesson, and trust me I'm learning that shit the hard way. Call me if you need me. I love you, baby."

"I love you too, Ma. I'm going to do everything you said, but I need you to do me a favor and go make things right with Thug and Tahari. You know they love you and you love them."

My momma was good at giving advice, but sometimes her ass needed a reality check.

"I already planned on doing that but I'm just not ready for all of that right now. Here are the keys. Don't fuck up shit in my house or I swear ya ass paying for it," she handed me the keys through the window and she blew me a kiss before she sped off.

I hoped like hell they made things right. It feels funny knowing that they were at odds. I walked inside my mother's house and I made myself comfortable in one of the guest bedrooms. My body was officially tired. All I did was sit up in the car and that had my back hurting like hell. The pain I was feeling reminded me that I needed to take it easy and try not to stress. The shit was hard as hell, though.

Once I got settled in bed, I pulled out my phone and I tried calling Sarge. I shook my head because this motherfucker had got his number changed on my ass. I was not about to play with his ass. If he wanted to pull a disappearing act then so be it, but he wasn't going to do it while he had my kids. As their mother, I deserved to at least know their whereabouts.

I couldn't wait to fully heal so that I could handle this shit accordingly. Sarge knew exactly what he was doing. He was trying his best to bring me down to my knees and make me pay for this shit. Little did he know, I was about to beat him at his own game. But first I needed to heal completely before I saw his ass. I might fuck around and kill him with my bare hands for taking my kids.

Chapter 13- Consequences and Repercussions

Sarge

I was sitting inside of the monthly Thug Inc. meeting and my mind was a million miles away. The last thing I wanted to do was have to sit in the room with Thug, Malik, and Quaadir. Shit was all bad between Ta'Jay and me so being in the room with her brothers didn't seem right at the moment. Granted we'd been through shit in the past, but never to this magnitude. I had the kids and I didn't want to give them back until I got ready to.

For the most part, they were keeping a nigga sane. I loved Ta'Jay more then anything in this world and her infidelity had gotten the best of me. I've always taken full responsibility for the pain I've caused her over the years. I know that she struggled over the years with being molested as a kid, but I stepped up in a major way with regards to how I handled her.

Ta'Jay was fragile and that's the way I had to treat her. When I saw her on that tape having sex wit that nigga in her office, I saw something different in her. I don't know what, but the look on her face showed she was enjoying that shit. I'm pissed off and I don't have a clue when I'll stop being pissed off.

"Have you talked to Ta'Jay yet?" Malik asked as he knocked back a shot. I swear we did more drinking and smoking at these meetings than talking.

"Nope."

"Well you need to go check on her and take the kids to see her. She's out of the hospital and staying over at Peaches' house. If you don't want to see her, I'll take the kids to see her myself."

"We good on that."

I didn't need this nigga getting in my business when it came down to my kids or their mother. I could care less if she was his sister or not. I just wanted to handle this situation my way.

"You been my nigga since the sandbox, but that's been my motherfucking sister since the womb. I understand that you're in your feelings about this shit and it's understandable, but don't forget that's still our sister. So I advise you watch what the fuck you say with regards to her," Malik pounded his fists on the table like that was supposed to make me jump or some shit.

"Or what?"

"Nigga you want to rock or something?" Malik stood up and knocked his chair over.

"It's whatever, my nigga. I know how you coming and you know how I'm coming," I said as I stood up. He got ready to walk around the table, but Thug stopped him.

"Both of yall shut the fuck up and sit down. This how this shit gone go and I wish a motherfucker would go against the grain. There is no need for you two motherfuckers to be in here about to fight about this shit. Malik, you of all people know what Ta'Jay did was dead ass wrong. So brother or not, we can't sit here and tell Sarge how to handle his wife. That's his decision. I love my sister and I will leave a nigga's brains on the motherfucking side of him for fucking with her. However, Sarge is a part of this family and we don't fight amongst each other. If I told you niggas once, I've told you niggas twice, we beef with them motherfuckers in the streets.

"As for you Sarge you're handling this shit your way, but you're going about the shit all wrong. Don't you know that you're not punishing her by taking the kids? If anything, you're giving her a much needed break while she recuperates. Not saying that she doesn't miss her kids, because I know she does. However, our wives wallow in the fact of having any moment's peace without the kids."

We all laughed because we knew that was the truth. I flamed up a much needed blunt and inhaled deeply.

"I love Ta'Jay, but this shit here got me fucked up. I've did my share of dirt, but she didn't have to get a nigga back like that. I'm not going to keep the kids from her, I just wanted my kids because they were keeping me sane. I'd been fucked up just thinking about how close we came to losing them. One of them bullets could have easily hit one of them. I know Ta'Jay had no idea that nigga was gone pull that bullshit, but she had no business fucking that nigga in the first place. I respect all of y'all but at the same time, I just want to handle this shit my way. I know that's y'all sister, but she's also my wife. I promise to drop the kids off to her, but I know for a fact I'm done with her."

"I can't tell you how to handle your wife, all I'm saying is watch how you handle my sister. You my motherfucking nigga. We've been through it all. Don't think shit one-sided because she our sister. We not sitting here making excuses for what the fuck happened. Ta'Jay fucked up and brought harm to her family and that's something she has to deal with. Don't you think she's suffered enough? You're not the only one who was shot. She was hurt, too. Imagine how she must feel sitting in that house alone unable to do shit because her spine fucked up. We all let our pride get in the way of doing what's right when it comes down to our wives. I don't know why you fronting my nigga, you still love her. You just mad. I suggest you get out your feelings and go talk to her before it be another nigga eating her pussy again."

"Shut the fuck up, Malik!"

"I'm just stating facts. Every time I'm telling the truth, you niggas tell me to shut the fuck up."

I just sat there in deep thought, thinking about what to do next. My sons had been asking to see their mother and had been worried about her, so I knew I had to just give in and take the kids to her.

*****

When I pulled up to my new spot, I knew it was about to be some bullshit. Ta'Jay, Tahari, Khia, Keesha, Dior, Gucci, Chanel, and Rosé were all blocking the doorway. Not to mention they were all standing with steel bats and their guns out. I knew they wanted to fuck me up so I called Thug Inc. These crazy bitches were not about to jump on me. I saw what they did to Quaadir and Malik. I'm not going at gunpoint. I'll fuck around and shoot one of their asses first. Since they like to fight, they can squad up with my crew. This shit been a long time coming. I was sitting and waiting patiently. That was, until Ta'Jay started busting out my windows with a steel bat.

"Get out the car, Sarge!"

"Hell no, you crazy ass bitch."

"I got your bitch, nigga."

I watched as she and started stuffing a rag into my gas tank. She took a lighter out of her pocket and started trying to light the end of the rag. I jumped out the car quick as hell and she hit my ass across the chest with the bat. Before I could swing, they were all on my ass with the quickness. They were getting some good ass licks off of me, too. I lost my damn balance and ended up on the ground. That's when them crazy bitches started stomping my ass out. I heard gunshots and them crazy bitches stop swinging on me and stomping my ass.

"Bring yo' ass here, Tahari!" I heard Thug say.

I got up off the ground and all I could see was my niggas yoking up their wives. I zoned in on Ta'Jay and I charged her ass. I yoked her up by her neck with the quickness, damn near lifting her off of her feet. My fucking driveway was filled with nothing but all of us fighting and tussling with one another.

"Let me go motherfucker! Give me my kids! I hate your ass!"

"You hate me bitch? I hate your ass, too! You mad at me because you cheated and that nigga shot us."

"No! I'm mad because you're acting like you never did shit wrong. I get it, Sarge. You don't want me and that's fine, but don't take my kids from me. Go get my motherfucking kids out that house now!" Ta'Jay was now pointing her gun at me. I walked closer so that the gun was pressing directly against my forehead.

"Pull the motherfucking trigger! You hate me that much then kill me dead. You've already killed my heart. Finish me, Ta'Jay!! You a big, bad ass Boss Lady, pull the trigger. I done seen it all and did it all."

"Put the fucking gun down, Ta'Jay. You're going too far!" Thug came over and snatched the gun from her hand.

"I just want my kids, Thug. Tell him to give me fucking kids," Ta'Jay was now crying and biting her bottom lip.

"Shut the fuck up with that crying. How in the fuck are you going to put a gun to someone head and then turn around crying? I'm so sick and tired of all of y'all walking around this motherfucker like y'all own shit. I know y'all Boss Lady Inc. and I respect that, but don't get it the fuck twisted. I'm the motherfucking Boss around this motherfucker. What? Y'all forgot who run shit?

"Cat got all y'all motherfucking tongue at the moment. Since ain't nobody talking, let me ask Boss Lady her motherfucking self since she's the head of Boss Lady Inc. Did you forget who the fuck the Boss is around this bitch?" Thug was now in Tahari's face and they were staring each other down, but she wasn't saying shit.

"Tahari Lashay Monroe-Kenneth, you don't hear me talking to you? I asked you a fucking question. Did you forget who the fuck run this city?"

"No, Thug. I didn't forget!" she yelled at him.

"Lower your motherfucking voice when you talking to a gangsta. Apparently you did, but I'm gone make sure I remind you. Since all y'all forgot who the fuck I am and how I get down. Boss Lady Inc. is no longer a faction of Thug Inc. Consider that shit canceled. All you bitches out of control and I mean that with the utmost respect.

"Go get your ass in the car Tahari, we'll finish this conversation at home. I don't want to hear no back talking or I'm gone hit your ass in the mouth. That's the problem, I ain't laid hands on ya ass in a while and you think Boss Lady Inc. is bigger than Thug Inc. You got me fucked up! As for the rest of y'all niggas, handle your shit!" Thug walked off and pushed Tahari towards the car.

"That's what the fuck I'm talking about, Bro! Bring yo ass on, Barbie."

"Don't touch me, Malik."

"Shut ya stanking ass up and bring your ass on. Don't start that rah rah shit with me because you already know it ain't gone do shit but make me lay hands on your ass. So I suggest you to keep a cool ass booty."

Barbie walked towards her car and peeled off and all the other girls followed suit. I had to sit my ass down on the porch because I felt like something was broken. I still hadn't fully healed from being hit up and I think Ta'Jay had fucked me up some more hitting me with that steel bat. I looked at her and she looked like she was about pass out. She knows for a fact she shouldn't even be doing this. From my understanding, her spine was still fucked up and she's supposed to be on bed rest.

"Come inside and lay down. You don't look good. I promise I'll go get the kids and bring them here and y'all can stay here with me until you heal up. Right now, I don't want to talk about what happened or what just happened here. You just need to take care of yourself. I'll make myself scarce and we don't even have to deal with each other while we're here. I'll just have the lawyer come over and we can discuss custody of the kids."

I tried to reach out and help her, but she knocked my hand away.

"I'm good. I don't want to be where I'm not welcome."

I quickly grabbed her ass by the hair because she was pissing me off like I had really done something to her.

"Stop trying to play the fucking victim, Ta'Jay. That shit is getting so fucking old to me. Yes, I cheated on you in the past. Yes, I was married and didn't tell you and yes, there was a time when I was emotionally disconnected from you because I didn't understand your apprehension when it came to having sex. No matter what I did to you, I took responsibility for my fuck ups. But as usual, you're being a spoiled ass brat about it. Own up to the fact that you fucked up our family. Do you not realize that shit? That bitch ass nigga could have not only killed us but killed our fucking kids as well."

I let her hair go and pushed her ass away from me. I had no words for her until she was ready to act like a grown woman and own up to her shit. I threw her the house keys and walked to one of my other cars. I called the Nanny and told her to drop the kids off. I needed to get away from her before I fucked around and paralyzed her ass myself. Just talking to her made me realize how much we were both hurting, but I was not about to apologize for her fuck up. Ta'Jay came off the porch and stood outside of the driver's side door.

"I do understand Sarge, but you don't want me to make it right. You just want a divorce and you want to take my kids. I was wrong and I'm sorry! I'm sorry! I'm sorry!"

"Move Ta'Jay, I have to go."

"I'm standing here crying my heart out and trying to apologize, but you still not letting me. I'm taking ownership of what I did. Just please give me a chance, Sarge."

I backed out of the driveway and peeled off, leaving her ass right there in the driveway crying. I knew I was breaking her down even more, but she needed to feel the repercussions from fucking with that nigga and hiding the fact that our daughter's paternity was in question.

Chapter 14- Twisted Hearts

Tahari

I sat in the passenger side of Thug's car not really knowing if I should have been mad or embarrassed. Thug didn't have to talk to me like I wasn't shit. Especially in front of my crew. I would never disrespect him in front of his crew so why would he do that shit to me. I understand that Thug is the Head of the family and the Boss out here in the streets. At the same time, I put in work as the Head of Boss Lady Inc. I deserve some respect as well. Who in the fuck is he to tell me and my crew that we shut down? I was so fucking heated that I was certain steam was coming from my ears. I looked over at Thug and this nigga had a mug out of this world on his face. His nose was flared and the veins in his head and neck were protruding. I rolled my eyes and stared out of the window.

"Roll them again," he said as he reached over and muffed my head.

"Keep your hands off of me, Ka'Jaire."

"Didn't I say don't say shit, Tahari?"

He put emphasis on my name, trying to be funny. This nigga was really trying to put his motherfucking pimp hand down. I just shut the fuck up, but you better believe I would be right back talking later. I didn't want to argue with him about none of this shit. I feel like we aren't in the wrong for getting Sarge's ass. He basically took her kids and wouldn't even say a word to her. They already know how we're coming when it comes down to each other. Sarge had to know the Boss Ladies couldn't just sit back and let that shit ride.

When we pulled up to our house, I hopped out of the car and rushed inside. Of course, Thug was hot on my ass, but I wasn't running from him. I just wanted to get away from him at the moment. There was no talking or compromising when he was mad like this. I just needed to give him space until he calmed down. I couldn't even go straight upstairs because all of our kids were in the living room watching TV and they knew better. Not to mention the house looked a hot ass mess.

"Ka'Jairea and KJ y'all both know better then to allow the kids to be in my living room. Now clean this shit up."

They were now thirteen and old enough to watch the kids without an adult being present. They knew the house rules, but of course they do whatever the fuck they want to do because Thug allows them to.

"Don't holler at them because you mad at me. I done told your ass about cursing at them like you crazy."

"See, this is exactly what I'm talking about. This is why they undermine my authority."

It's like when I tell them to do something they turn around and ask him. We're supposed to be a team and stick with one another when making decisions.

"I can't run Boss Lady Inc. or my household either, huh. Big, bad Thug got to be in control of everything. If I've told you once, I've told you twice, stop doing that shit. When I tell them something, they do it. I'm sick and tired of you doing that dumb ass shit."

All the kids started cleaning and making sure the living room was back in order. Thug was fuming mad and I could tell he was ready to blow up on my ass but I didn't give a fuck. I was just as mad as him.

"We're sorry, Ma. We're about to clean up now. Just please don't fight with Daddy."

"It's okay, Kane. I'm not about to say a word to your Daddy. Just straighten up for Momma and y'all can go in the theater and watch something."

I rolled my eyes and headed up the stairs to my bedroom. I went inside of Thug's weed stash and rolled my a fat blunt. The more I smoked, the more I started to replay the shit he had said back when we were at Sarge's house. I respected Thug and his position as Head of the family and King in these streets. My husband reigns supreme and I know that. From the moment I met him and we decided to make things official, he has always reminded me. Not that he had to, but that's Thug for you. I know who my husband is and what he's capable of, but he needs to remember who the fuck I am as well.

I walked over the wet bar we had installed in our room and I poured myself a glass of Red Moscato. I just needed to chill back and release some of this tension that was building up. I already knew that shit was about to get real between us. I was just waiting for the storm to come because it was definitely about to blow over. As soon as I laid across my custom made, all red and black Marilyn Monroe chaise, Thug walked into the room. I grabbed my phone and I started acting like I was really looking at something. He stood over me for what seemed like an eternity.

I just knew at any minute he was going to slap the shit out of me. Instead he snatched my phone out of my hand and threw it up against the wall. Before I could respond our bedroom door opened and KJ walked in. He had grown and sprouted up like a tree. My baby was now thirteen and as tall as his father. Not to mention as handsome as ever. He looks identical to Thug, but had strong features of his birth mother Kelis.

"You straight, Ma."

"Yeah, she straight. Next time you see that door closed, make sure you knock first." Thug walked over towards him and KJ kind of stood there looking over his father's shoulder at me. KJ was so overprotective of me. As I watched him and Thug damn near in each other's faces, it worried the hell out of me. It was then that I noticed just how much they were alike and I knew in the future they would both be a force to be reckoned with. KJ is, without a doubt, his father's son. At the same time, I knew that he was no match for his father, so I had to get my baby out of here before Thug smashed his ass. It warmed my heart to know that my son was looking out for me.

"I'm fine, baby. Go make sure your brothers and sisters are fine. Tell baby girl to order some pizza and hot wings for everybody. Thanks for checking on me. Now go on out and let me and your Daddy finish talking."

KJ walked out of the room, but I saw apprehension in the way he walked out.

"In a minute he gone think he can whoop his Pops. Did you see that little nigga swelling up at me?"

I could tell that KJ's demeanor upset Thug, but he was trying not to show it. I also knew that he was about to go even harder on me. I was prepared but he better be as well. I was not about to just sit here and let him chastise me like I was a child. That shit's dead.

"Back to you, Boss Lady. I was thinking about what I said about Boss Lady Inc. being shut down until further notice. I changed my mind and I've decided to make it indefinitely. This shit has went to your head and I'm done with the blatant disrespect. In the beginning, I thought the shit was cute. But now the shit is completely out of hand. Y'all have had your little fun with this shit, but it's officially over. You can call your crew and tell them it's a motherfucking wrap!"

"I'm not calling and telling them shit. Who are you to say that what the fuck I built is finished? In case you forgot, we're more than some bitches that meet up and sip wine and discuss their nothing ass husbands. We're some real ass bitches and we do real things. Last time I checked, Boss Lady Inc. had a body count out of this world. You think the streets only fear you? I understand you're the motherfucking Boss and you run shit. However, you run Thug Inc. That's your shit. I run boss Lady Inc. and we're in full effect.

"I respect you as my husband and your position in these streets, but I'm gone need you to respect me as well. The way you handled me today in front of everybody was downright disrespectful and embarrassing. If I had done that you, you would've beat my ass and you know it. Respect me and my position, Thug. You walk around all the time talking about the respect that you deserve. If you want respect, you have to earn it. You can say and do whatever the fuck you want to do to me, but I'm telling you right now Boss Lady Inc. is very much still in operation."

I sipped on my wine and stared at him dead in his eyes without as much as a blink. He just started laughing like some shit was funny and that made me mad. He didn't take one word I'd said seriously and that had me thinking he thought this shit was a joke. So, I threw the rest of the wine I had in my glass in his face.

I tried to walk away but he grabbed my by the back of my neck and slammed me face down on the chaise. I was squirming, kicking, and screaming trying get out of his grip, but he had me tight as hell. He had my arms twisted behind my back in a way that made me think he was going to break my shit if he applied anymore pressure.

"I will kill you in this motherfucker, Tahari. I've blew a nigga brains out simply for stepping on my motherfucking shoe and not apologizing. There are only three reasons you're still alive and breathing after all of the shit you've pulled over the years. One, I love the shit out of your ass. Two, you're the mother of my children. Three, and most importantly, you're my wife. Stop playing with me Tahari, and do what the fuck I said.

"You don't want to make me your enemy because I'll forget that you're my wife. I don't know why you continue to defy me and flat out say fuck me. That's that disrespectful shit that I don't like. I'm telling you the shit is over, but you want to defy me to prove a point. I'm telling you right now and this my last and final time saying it. Boss Lady Inc. is officially over. If you go against my wishes, consider yourself an enemy in these streets. If you continue to operate in the city without my permission, you will pay contributions just like everybody else. I want fifty thousand a month from you. If you want to play, you have to pay. It's the rule of the streets and I run these motherfuckers. You know how I get down, Tahari. We've been married some time now, so please don't take this shit lightly. The choice is yours and I advise you to choose wisely. We can either make passionate love or have an all out war around this bitch.

"I'm done playing and pacifying your ass when all you're going to do is turn around and disrespect not only me, but my crew as well. That shit is not cool that y'all be on. You bitches walking putting ya hands on gangsters. The only reason they haven't fucked y'all up is because we're all married. At one point the shit was funny, but it's not funny to me anymore. Boss Lady Inc. is a memory. I hope you had your fun while it lasted because the shit is over. Now, I'm gone let you up and if you swing on me I'm going to beat your ass."

Thug finally released my arms and let me up. As much I wanted to go across his shit, I didn't. At the moment I felt low, disrespected, and unappreciated. Despite the fact that from time to time me and the other girls stick up for each other when it comes to these fucked up husbands of ours, we've gone so hard for them in these streets. It's niggas out here in the streets that would kill to have a bitch that ain't scared to stand beside him laying his enemies down. Thug basically just said Boss Lady Inc. was a motherfucking joke and I couldn't get with that.

Outside of everything, I've been more than a wife and mother to this nigga's children. I've forgiven him for everything he has ever put me through and still stood firm beside him killing any and everything moving. These days him cheating on me doesn't even cross my mind because we're past that stage. However, I would much rather he had cheated opposed to telling me that what I've sacrificed for him is nothing more than a joke.

I hadn't cried over anything that Thug has done to me in years because we've been in a great space. I was hurt because I felt like everything I had ever done for him was in vain. It was obvious it meant nothing to him. So fuck him and Thug Inc. I calmly got up and went to check on my kids. They were all in the theater. I looked behind me and Thug was hot on my heels. he was trying to see what I was up to. It's not often he manhandles me and I let him. I walked outside and I went to the guest house to see Marta. She was outside planting flowers.

"Hey Marta, I need a really big favor from you."

"Anything for you Mrs. Kenneth. What do you need me to do?"

"As you know the kids are on spring break and I don't have any time to take them on vacation due to all the business that I need to handle here with the businesses. So, I was wondering if you can take them out to California for about two weeks. I would really appreciate it. They've been dying to go to Universal Studios."

"Of course, no problem. I'll pack their clothes now. Just get the itinerary together for me and I'll handle everything else. You look like you need a break. I'm so proud of you Mrs. Kenneth. Never in a million years did I think you had it in you to be a stay-at-home mom." We both laughed because Marta basically raised my kids and I'm so glad that I've been more hands-on with them.

"Thank you so much, Marta. You're the best." I turned around and headed back in the house to book their flights and hotel. I walked right past Thug who was confused as fuck because he had no idea what the fuck I was doing. I was just too calm and he knew I was on good bullshit.

"Guess what y'all? Marta is taking you guys to Universal Studios for spring break. I have some things I need to handle here so that's why I can't take you but I might fly down there and spend some days with y'all. Is that cool?

"Yeah, that's cool Ma. Don't worry about us. You and Daddy need a vacation anyway," Ka'Jairea said. It took everything in me not to say something smart. Instead, I smiled and headed in my office to book the flights and send out texts to all my girls to meet me the next day at our headquarters. There was some shit I needed to discuss with them with regards to the future of Boss Lady, Inc.

Once I had the hotels and flights booked, I went and spent some time with all of them before their flight in the morning. From time to time I would catch Thug looking at me with narrowed eyes. I had his ass perplexed. He didn't know what was going through my mind or what I was plotting. I was cool as a cucumber. He knew I was plotting but I didn't give a fuck. He better stay on his toes fucking with me. I'm not taking this shit lying down. For right now, I'll just smile, be the obedient and respectful wife that he wants me to be. I sat in the movie theater watching *Friday After Next* for the hundredth time with the kids. They watch this shit all day every day but I'll watch whenever they wanted if it meant I would get to spend these priceless moments with them.

"I don't know what the fuck you're up to but you better get it the fuck out of your head. All this shit is a front that you're putting up. Don't start nothing you aren't prepared to finish," he whispered in my ear and made sure to suck on my earlobe. If I wasn't so mad at him, it would have me ready to fuck the shit out of him. I didn't even bat my eyes or turn around to make eye contact with his ass.

"I'm already finished," I said in a low tone that only he could hear. I heard him blow out air in frustration and that made me laugh on the inside. I had him fucked up in the head. I didn't have to cut up or curse Thug out. Just me being nonchalant was driving his ass crazy, but I was not done just yet. This love and war he spoke on was just getting started.

Once all of the kids had gone to bed and the house was clean, I decided to lay it down. I was mentally and physically tired from the day's events. I just wanted to get in bed and lie down. I walked inside of my bedroom and was surprised to see Thug sitting up in bed with his back up against the headboard stroking his dick and staring at me lustfully. He was naked as the day he was born. There was something about the way his tatted hands glided up and down his dick. Call me crazy but that shit looked so damn sexy and gangsta.

Thug knew exactly what he was doing to me. I'm weak as fuck when it comes to his sex. I'm the true definition of being dick silly but he made me this way by giving me that thug passion. As much as I wanted to be mad at him, I couldn't deny the fact that my husband was even sexier than the first time I had sex with him in Peaches' room. He was now completely covered in tattoos. He damn near had no more room for anything else. He had just recently had his pussy monster tattoo redid and it was bright red with imprints of my lips surrounding it. It looked even better than it did before.

I was hurt by Thug's words and his actions towards me earlier. But, the feeling in my pussy wouldn't let that get in the way of my need to feel him inside me. I didn't speak a word as I undressed and walked up the steps to climb into our huge California king poster bed. I seductively stood over him and slowly glided down on his dick without hesitation. I didn't need him to do nothing to get me wet. His handsome face made my shit go drip drop on sight. I didn't want to speak a word to him. I just wanted to ride his ass to sleep because he when he woke up he was going to be mad as fuck.

"You know I love you right?" he said, as his eyes rolled to the back of his head.

"I love you more." I reached down and sucked on his bottom lip as I roughly bounced up and down on his dick. I wasn't trying to make love to him. I wanted to fuck his brains out. My husband had forgotten that I was a beast in the streets and the sheets. He was going to give me the fucking respect that I had earned over the years. I covered his mouth and rode his ass into a coma.

After fucking each other's brains out I was exhausted but unable to sleep. So, I got up and prepared myself for this war I was about to start. I never wanted to be at odds with my husband but this was the only way

I was going to get him to see that I took Boss Lady Inc. very serious. I was so fucking serious about the shit that I placed fifty thousand dollars on our bed as he slept along with a note that read: *I'm not defying you. I'm just doing what makes me happy. I love you but I'm ready for that war you spoke of.*

*****

I sat in the conference room of Boss Lady Inc. headquarters dressed in my hot pink and black biker suit. It was a beautiful April day in the Chi so I decided to take my brand new custom made motorcycle out. I sat in silence smoking on a fat ass Kush blunt watching as Barbie, Ta'Jay, Khia, Keesha, Rosé, Dior, Chanel, and Gucci walked into the conference room dressed in all black and pink as well. That was one of my rules: for us to always wear pink and black during meetings.

"How are you feeling, sis?" I asked Ta'Jay. She was walking real slow and she looked pale. Her ass needed to go back to that damn hospital. I was kind of mad at myself for edging her on to pop off on Sarge. I should have known better because she was in no condition to be swinging a steel bat or fucking Sarge's car up.

"I'm good, sis. My back hurting but I'll be okay. Sarge brought the kids to me last night but he left like it wasn't shit so I cut all the tongues of his Retro Jordans and the ass part out of his boxers. Then this morning he come in with a damn nanny and nurse to help me get better and help out with the kids. I kind of felt bed I fucked his shit up."

"You know Sarge is shoe fanatic. He's going to fuck you up for what you did to them shoes.'

"I know but fuck him. He wanted to make me suffer so I'm gone make him cry. That nigga love his Jordan collection more than he loves me and the kids. Besides that, it feels kind of good to be with the kids. Li'l Sarge and Sema'Jay have been sticking to me like glue. You know they're some momma's boys. Ta'Jariea loves her Daddy and her brothers. She don't fuck with me period. That's my little princess though."

"That's the same shit at my house." Just thinking about my kids made me miss them. I made sure to get all of them off to the airport before I got ready for this meeting that I had called. Thug's ass was still sleeping like a baby. This pussy put his ass to sleep just like I knew that it would. I shook the thought of Thug from my mind because he was the last thing I wanted to be thinking about while I was discussing Boss Lady Inc. business.

"I know y'all wondering why I called this meeting but after the events that transpired yesterday, I thought that it was well needed for all of us. I don't know what you and your husbands discuss behind closed doors with regards to Boss Lady Inc. and it's really not for me to know. I'm gone keep it one hundred with y'all because that's what I'm supposed to do. Thug has shut down Boss Lady Inc. indefinitely. He feels like I've taken my role as boss lady a little too far and he thinks this shit is one big joke.

"All of you know how dedicated I am to this movement. No, scratch that. All of you know how dedicated I am to my husband. Thug gets the highest honor. I hold that man down through thick and thin but he doesn't respect me and the sacrifices I've made for him. Fuck that. Everything I've done I did it for us. I deserve to be able to run Boss Lady Inc. my way. Of course with you guys' input.

"Yesterday he flat out embarrassed me not only in front of you guys, but in front of his crew as well. What we did to Sarge yesterday was apparently the last straw for him. He has put his foot down and said that Boss Lady Inc. is finished because he's Thug and of course, he's the boss. However, I'm Tahari and I'm the boss of this shit right here. Without you guys, I don't know where I would be. I've put my heart and soul into Boss Lady Inc. right along with you ladies. I feel like everything we do when it comes to our husbands has been to benefit them and to make our families flourish.

"I can't help but to think of where Thug Inc. would be without Boss Lady Inc. Like I'm sitting here thinking about when we did our first hit on the Santerelli family and took their asses out because they were fucking over our husbands. Or, that time I killed the head nigga in charge when I posed as a stripper. For my husband I would lay down and die a million times. So, excuse me if I'm in my feelings about him discrediting what it is we do and my intentions for Boss Lady Inc. I know that Thug is feared and the status that he holds in the streets. So, I understand if you guys want to follow his orders and be finished with Boss Lady Inc. This is something personally for me outside of the business aspect of it. So I have a point to prove and I will not walk away from Boss Lady Inc. because he wants me to.

"Boss Lady Inc. defines me as more than Thug's wife. I will not let him take me up out my glo. I've come too far with this to stop now. I've been giving in to Thug and I'm losing Tahari to make sure he's happy and content. I deserve the same in return and he's not giving me that. Now don't get me wrong, Thug loves me and Lord knows I love him. I'm just hurt that he feels the need to take something from me and threaten me if I don't abide by his rules. I'm his wife not his child. I'm getting all in my feelings so let me get straight to the point.

"I'm not stopping Boss Lady Inc. This is going to cause so much drama because I'm defying him. I do not want you guys to be in the middle of our shit because this shit will get ugly. Right here and now some decisions need to be made with regards to where we stand as a team. Please know that if you decide to stand down, that's fine and there will be no hard feelings. We are a family before anything so I respect your wishes." I leaned back in my seat and waited to hear what the girls felt. Their opinions and views mattered the most to me.

"I think that I could speak for everyone in this room when I say that without you some of our marriages probably never would have made it. I've always been the one to question you guys and judge your actions when it came down to the decisions you made with how to handle certain situations, especially you and Barbie. I used to be so hard on you guys about my brothers. I was young then and I didn't understand my role as a wife even though I had a husband.

"My family has always babied and shielded me from everything. I didn't realize all the things you had been trying to teach me until my husband wanted to leave me and in the process he was handling me like a whack bitch. Being around you ladies gave me the strength to fight back. I love my brother and I know that he's going to be mad but I'm a motherfucking boss lady," Ta'Jay said as she banged her fists on the table.

Before I could respond to what she said the warehouse door opened and in walked Thug Inc. with Thug standing front and center. He had one of the angriest looks on his face I had ever seen.

"How nice of you guys to join us. It's funny we were just talking about you." I stood to my feet as Thug walked around the table and stared down at me. He was trying his best to intimidate me but I was not giving in.

"So this is how you gone do it? I'm just making sure I know where we stand so anything transpires I won't feel bad about the shit."

"Get the fuck out of here Thug. I'm having a meeting in my headquarters." I pushed him back but he grabbed me by the back of my neck and dragged my ass to my office. The whole way there I was swinging and trying to bite a plug out of his ass. Everyone was trying to break us up but at the same time they didn't want to touch us because we were humbugging.

"It's like you want to test me to see how far you can take me." Thug was squeezing my jaws so tight I thought that he was going to break my shit. I was trying my best to respond but the way he was holding my jaws made it damn near impossible. He roughly pushed my head back making it bounce off of the wall behind me.

"I'm not trying to do shit to you Ka'Jaire. All I'm doing is making a decision that makes me happy for a change. I'm not trying to disrespect you Thug but you don't get to tell me what the fuck to do. You're my husband, not my father." He just sat stroking his chin in deep thought.

"Maybe if you would have had a father in your life I wouldn't have to treat your ass like you're my child. Ya' ass should know right from wrong."

"And maybe if you would have had a father in your life your mother would treat you like her son instead of her fucking husband."

"What the fuck you say?" Before I could respond Thug swung and hit me so hard that I lost my balance and fell. My mouth and my nose were leaking profusely. I was too dizzy to move and my vision was blurry. I wanted to cry but the shock of the blow had me just stuck but something inside of me went off in my head. Before I could fully think about what I was doing I had grabbed a letter opener from my desk and stabbed Thug repeatedly.

"Ahhhhhh!" He was screaming out in pain at the same time trying to get me to stop stabbing him. At that moment I didn't see Thug. I saw Nico. As I kept swinging the letter opener in my head I envisioned each and every time he had hit me.

"What the fuck did you do?" Malik yelled and it caused me to come back to reality and drop the letter opener. Thug was on the floor holding his chest and I could see the blood seeping through his hand.

"Bro, get me to the hospital," he said in a weak voice.

"Oh my God! What did you do to him?" Ta'Jay said as she ran past me and fell on the floor on top of Thug. My mind was racing and my heart was beating rapidly. Everybody was looking at me with judgment in their eyes. I wasn't thinking. I just ran out of the office.

"Tahari! Tahari! Wait." Keesha grabbed me and tried to pull me back, but I started swinging on her so she could let me go. I hit her one good time and she finally stopped tussling with me. I didn't understand what was wrong with me.

I hopped on my bike and got the fuck out of there. I don't know why I didn't stay and make sure Thug was okay. I guess I was just scared that I had possibly killed him. This was the second time I had physically done something to him that could kill him. I knew in my heart he wouldn't forgive me. My brain was drawing blanks and my body was numb.

I rushed to my house and packed some clothes and made sure to grab some money from the safe. Everything was a complete blur. I don't even remember how I made it to the airport. I cried as I sat on the airplane looking at my face in my compact. It was black, blue, and swollen. I looked like I had an abscess. That's how huge my jaw was. I placed my sunglasses over my face and sank down in my seat. I just wanted to sleep the entire flight.

Hours later I landed at Miami International and I powered my phone on. I had so many calls from everybody, and texts as well. The only one that stood out was the one from Thug.

Husband: So you want to kill me huh? That's what we on. You just run the fuck off and not even make sure I'm okay. I was wrong for hitting you so I guess I deserved to get stabbed but I would never leave you leaking like you did me. I guess I need to reevaluate who I made my wife. You're not the Tahari I married. Since you feel the need to abandon me and our kids, I advise you to stay gone."

My heart sank and I began to shake. I waited for my luggage and I headed over to South Beach and checked into the Fontainebleau Hotel. I made sure to get in contact with Marta to tell her what had happened. I talked to each one of my kids and let them know that I had to take a vacation and that I would see them soon. I laid in bed and I cried because this was not my intention. I just wanted to show Thug that I was independent and that I was dedicated to Boss Lady Inc. Things just escalated. The last thing I wanted to do was physically hurt him but I didn't want him to physically hurt me either. He hit me like I was a man. Granted he had hit me in the past but it was not like that. That hit was vicious and it reminded me of the ass whooping Nico used to give me.

I remember sitting at the kitchen table eating dinner that I had prepared for us. It wasn't hot enough for him so instead of him asking me to warm it up he dumped the plate into my lap and punched me in my face. The blow was so powerful he broke my nose and damaged my eye socket. To this day I have issues with my vision. From the moment I met Thug I felt safe and secure with him. In all of our nine years of being together he's never made me feel like I had to be scared to the point where I would leave the city.

I can honestly say I'm scared of the outcome behind me stabbing him. Honestly, it does look like I just ran and I didn't care if he was okay but that wasn't the case at all. I just panicked and I got the fuck out of dodge. Although I was afraid, I knew that I had to take my ass home and face Thug and deal with whatever consequences he has for me. In my heart I know that he's going to make me suffer and do whatever he can to mentally break me down. I know how he operates so I just have to stand firm and be the strong ass Tahari I've always been.

I was really mad at myself for running away like a coward ass bitch. For the first time in a long time I folded under pressure. I'm fucked up in the head about it because I'm that bitch that applies pressure. This shit is going to get worse before it gets better. If it gets better, that text has me thinking Thug is done with my ass. Shit was all good just a week ago now a bitch has to fight to prove her love.

Chapter 15- A Woman's Redemption

Peaches

The moment I got the call that my baby had been stabbed I caught a motherfucking red eye to Chicago. The plane ride over all I could think about was who could have possibly done that shit to him. I was so scared because of the way Malik sounded on the phone. I think he was crying but he told me that he wasn't. I was on pins and needles from the airport to Cook County Hospital. I knew shit was kind of bad if he had been taken there. They have the best trauma unit in the city. Just knowing that he had been taken there had me nervous as hell.

I didn't know what I would do if I didn't have Thug in my life. Just knowing that he was laid up in a hospital and I wasn't there made me realize just how stupid I had been. Lord knows I wouldn't have been any good had he left this world and we were on bad terms. I was beating myself up because I should have apologized to him and Tahari. They didn't deserve the way I treated them when Ta'Jay got hurt. I had been taking all my anger out on my family instead of being mad at myself.

Quanie leaving me was my fault and mine alone. I just couldn't bring myself to see that it was me who had ruined my own relationship. I blamed Quanie and he didn't deserve my behavior either. That man truly loved me and I pushed him away. For a minute I thought that we were back good. That was until I dropped the twins off at his house before heading over to the hospital.

Some bitch answered the door in a nightshirt. She was real pretty and much younger. I wanted to cut the fuck up and act a fool but I was trying to be a better person and mother to my children. I could tell that Quanie got a kick out of me seeing this. If he was trying to hurt my feelings, he had most definitely succeeded. I could have showed my emotions but instead I held them in and acted like a good baby momma who wasn't bitter because the father of her children no longer wanted her and had obviously moved on. She was his age. That alone let me know that I had been defeated.

Although Quanie made me feel like I was the most beautiful woman in the world, there were times when my insecurities got the best of me. Quanie would always reassure me that I was all he wanted. That's neither here nor there at this point. I fucked up and he's moved on. I just have to suck this shit up and be a woman about it. I guess I should be thankful he hasn't asked for a divorce yet. This shit hurts my soul but I've been hurt before. The only difference this time around was that I was the one who brought this shit on myself. I hurried up and shook Quanie, and our bullshit, from my mind as I walked through the emergency room at Cook County Hospital. Thug was my main concern at the moment.

"Hi, I'm Patrice Kenneth. My son Ka'Jaire Kenneth was brought in some time last night." I tapped my nails on the desk as the nurse looked him up in the computer.

"I'm sorry we don't have anyone here by that name. Wait a minute. Okay, we did have him here but he signed himself out of the hospital." I just shook my head and walked back out of the hospital. Malik called me acting like Thug was on his deathbed. This motherfucker had signed his damn self out of the hospital and ain't said shit.

I tried calling everybody but no one was answering the phone. I was getting pissed by the second because somebody needed to tell me something. I still had no idea how Thug had been stabbed but I was about to go to his house and find out. There might be beef between him, Tahari and me but at the end of the day I needed to see what the hell was going on. I know that I had said some shit to Tahari I shouldn't have said. However, I felt a certain type of way because she didn't have the common courtesy to call and tell me what the fuck was going on with my son. I knew she was mad at me but we were better than that.

******

I placed my key inside of the door at Thug and Tahari's house and walked all around looking for them. When I made it to their bedroom room I knocked but got no answer so I just walked in. Thug was lying in bed with like four big patches on his chest. My baby looked like he was in so much pain.

"Oh my God! Are you okay baby?" I rushed over and ran my hands over the patches. I didn't even know the tears were falling until I felt my face wet.

"I'm good Ma, stop crying."

"No you're not Ka'Jaire. Why in the fuck would you sign yourself out of that damn hospital? Why are you here by yourself? Where the fuck is Tahari or Marta?" Just seeing him in bed and home alone made me mad. He had just been seriously injured and was all by himself. I removed my jacket and started straightening up the room. I was about to get comfortable because I was not leaving my baby here alone.

"I don't know where Tahari at. Marta and the kids are in California. They should be back here within a couple of hours. I sent a private jet to bring them all back home." I looked at him as he spoke and something was off. The fact that he said he didn't know where Tahari was at made a light bulb go off in my head but I didn't want to jump to conclusions.

"What you mean you don't know where she at? You're laying here stabbed all up and shit and she's M.I.A. She stabbed you didn't she?"

"I hit her and she grabbed a letter opener and started stabbing me. I'm not even mad that she stabbed me Ma. I put my hands on her and that set her off. I'm mad because she just walked out and left me on the floor of her office leaking. I would never leave her in a state like that." My baby looked like he wanted to cry and that made me hurt. I wanted to be mad at Tahari for stabbing him but I knew that I couldn't. I was an abused woman so I know in the heat of the moment, we react. However, I am mad that she left him leaking. At the same time I know that Tahari loves Thug without a doubt.

"Thug, she was scared. Imagine how she felt once she realized that she had hurt you. Now I know that me and her aren't on the best of terms but I know her love for you is real. Have you heard from her or anything?"

"Nope, that bitch won't answer the phone. I've sent her several texts and I know she sees them. I told her ass since she decided to get ghost on me and our kids then her ass better stay gone." I watched as his eyes got glossy. He reached over on the nightstand and grabbed a Newport from the box. If his ass was smoking, he was stressed and I hated when he was stressed because we all got the brunt of his anger. Thug tripped me out trying to act all tough and she knew he loved Tahari more than he loved himself.

"You don't mean that and you know it. Let me call her and see if I can get her to come home. She's probably scared to face you. Seeing you laying there all bloody made her panic. You know she didn't mean to do it." I was trying my best to get him to calm down and stop talking crazy.

"She probably didn't mean to physically hurt me but she fucked me up in the head by just leaving like it was nothing. So like I said, her bitch ass could stay gone. End of discussion Ma." I looked at him like he was crazy talking about end of discussion. I didn't argue though. I just got up and headed towards the kitchen to cook him something to eat and make some phone calls. Malik, Quaadir, Ta'Jay and Remy needed to get their asses over here and talk some sense into his ass. Most importantly, Tahari needed to bring her ass home and get this shit straightened out.

I got in touch with everybody but Tahari's ass. She was sending me to voice mail but I made sure to leave her ass a nice message. If she knew like I knew, the sooner she got home the better. I was no longer in a mood to cook so I ordered as much Seafood Junction as I could since I had people coming over.

I sat at the bar drinking me some Patron and smoking on a cigarette in deep thought. I was thinking about all the bullshit that had transpired over the years and the pressure I had placed on my son.

"Pour me a shot, Ma." I looked up and Thug was standing over me.

"Now you know you have to pour your own troubles."

I grabbed him a bottle of Remy and a shot glass. I placed it in front of him and I just stared at him for the longest. I couldn't believe my baby was in his thirties. It seems like yesterday I was bringing him home from the hospital. The moment I gave birth to him and Quaadir, I saw greatness in their eyes. It was something about the way they looked at me for the first time. They had Vinnie's beautiful eyes and my caramel complexion. They were perfect in my eyes.

I laughed thinking about that damn Malik. I should have known he was going to be a damn fool. He came out laughing instead of crying. I swear when he was a baby he would be giving me the finger. People sit and think that Thug is my pick out of my kids but it's really Malik. That motherfucker got a hold my heart like no other. Just thinking about it makes me feel so bad about the responsibility I had put on Thug since he was younger. He never got a chance to enjoy childhood or being a teenager because he was too busy making sure I was okay and learning the family business.

"I'm sorry for ruining your life Ka'Jaire."

"What are you talking about Peaches? You didn't ruin my life. If anything, you made me the man I am today."

"That's the thing about it. Baby, I raised you to be a kingpin and I was wrong for that. A mother is supposed to raise her child to be a doctor, a lawyer, or hell-even the President of the United States. I taught you how to cook and package dope when you were nine years old. At eleven, I had you and Malik doing deliveries and picking up money from my workers. Day in and day out I drilled it in your head that you were the oldest and it was your responsibility to make sure that your brother and sister was okay at all times. Each and every time Snake did something to me, you were right there defending me.

"I remember one time he hit you with an extension cord and you choked the shit out of him. He was scared of you, he never let you know that but I knew that he was. I ruined you by making it so easy for you to catch your first body. I was supposed to get the fuck away from Snake the first time he hit me but the glitz, the glamour, and the money blinded me. In the beginning, my motive was to show y'all bitch ass Daddy that I didn't need him, his family, or his fucking money. After a while, I realized he didn't care about me or you boys but it was too late. By that time I was deep in with Cassie, Snake, and Venom there was no way out but you gave me a way out. To this day I blame myself for how fucked up you kids are. I should have been more protective of you guys instead of the other way around.

"I just keep thinking about how you used to sit outside of our building and buy all the kids who didn't have money anything they wanted. You were always so good with the ladies. They just loved them some Ka'Jaire. Hell, you always had a good heart and a good spirit. It's just that the way you were raised fucked you up as a grown man. I never should have exposed you to that lifestyle. I feel like that lifestyle blocks you from your softer side. I'm your momma so you don't always have to always have that thug ass demeanor with me. If you're hurt about this shit with Tahari, then let it out but don't let that anger block you from what your heart is telling you. You love that girl and you need to find out where the fuck she at and bring her home. Fuck this Thug Inc. and Boss Lady Inc. shit. It's fucking up all of y'all as families.

"This shit with Sarge and Ta'Jay should be an eye opener for all of us. That shit could have ended badly. I just don't want that for you and Tahari. Y'all have come too far and fought too many battles to be together. Please son, I'm begging you. Don't give up on the best thing that has ever happened to you. That's your wife, not some random ass bitch you fucked and had a couple of seeds with. I can look at you and tell you fucked up without her. I'm almost certain that wherever she is at, she's feeling fucked up too. I always knew Tahari loved you. She showed me to not even fuck with her husband. Boss Lady had fire in her eyes when she got on me about the way I was treating you. That made me realize the error in my ways and how I've overstepped my boundaries.

"I'm your momma but your wife trumps that. Tahari do not play about her Thug. If I wasn't your momma I think she would have killed my ass right there in that family room. You know she didn't mean to do this to you. I'm begging you to not ruin your life making hasty decisions. I don't want you to grow old and alone like I'm going to be. You and Tahari need to grow old together. It's in the universe. You and her were made for each other."

I flamed up a cigarette and just stared at him as he looked down at his phone. At the same time Malik and Ta'Jay came strolling in the back door. Ta'Jay rushed in and headed straight to Thug, hugging all over him. Malik walked over to me and kissed me on the forehead.

"I missed you Ma."

"I missed you too baby. I'm glad somebody missed me," I said, rolling my eyes at Ta'Jay but I was just kidding with her.

"You know I miss you too, Ma. It's just that I been worried about my brother. You know how I am about my brothers. Plus, I'm worried about my sister too. Did you talk to her Thug?"

"I'm worried about her too baby." We all just looked at Thug waiting for him to say something with regards to Tahari but he didn't.

"Bro, you really need to find out where sis at. You know she probably somewhere crying and shit. You need to let her know the shit over and for her to come home. It's too much going on out here for her to just be M.I.A," Malik said as he fired up a blunt and knocked back a shot of Patron.

"I'm glad y'all here but I don't want to talk about Tahari right now. However, I do want y'all to hear some real shit. Before any of the success we've had, it's always been us four. We did whatever the fuck we had to do to survive. All of our life you made sure we had everything that we needed. We never had a hungry or cold day. I don't give a fuck how you got that bread, you got it and in the process you taught us to get down how the fuck we live. By any means necessary and that's always been my motto. I never in my life want you to ever feel like you failed as a parent.

The lifestyle you showed us made me the beast I am today. Let's get something clear right now. You're the epitome of a good mother. No, let me rephrase that, you're a great mother so stop walking around and thinking that you're not because you have flaws. All of your flaws make you special in our eyes because it makes you who you are as our mother. I don't think I would even be who I am if I had some square ass woman for a mother. You've always been down to ride until the very end for us. You do the things you do because you love us. Don't ever beat yourself up for he things we endured growing up because it made us. The Kenneth Family ain't shit without the backbone and the foundation. You built us Ford tough and don't you ever forget it."

"Thanks Ka'Jaire. I needed to hear that." Tears welled up in my eyes and I reached over and hugged him. Malik and Ta'Jay joined in on the hug as well. He kissed me on the jaw and hurriedly walked away.

"Where you going, Bro? Ole soft ass nigga," Malik yelled and Ta'Jay popped him upside the head to make him shut up.

"Shut up Malik and leave my baby alone."

"Y'all know that nigga about to cry right?" Malik said, as he knocked back another shot.

"Is he okay Ma? I'm about to go check on him. I don't like how he acting." She tried to walk off but I grabbed her back.

"Your brother is just fine. That ain't nothing but growing pains. This thing with Tahari has him all in his feelings. So, let's just give him his space to get it together. Speaking of Tahari, I wonder where in the hell she could be?"

"Ain't no telling with her but I want to find her. I can't take my brother holding his pillow tight at night crying and listening to Keith Sweat."

I just shook my head and went to check on Thug. Malik's ass could never take shit serious but I knew that was his way of coping. I'm amazed at how much he's grown. When Malik was younger he stopped talking for like a year and that was because Snake was molesting him. Once they killed his ass it was like he started a new life. If only I could get him to stop talking now.

After having some much needed conversations with them I prepared myself to go and pick my kids up from Quanie. I hoped and prayed that bitch was gone. The Patron was kicking in. Not to mention, I had hit Malik's blunt a couple of times so I was on good bullshit. However, I knew I had to control myself and my liquor. Quanie was just looking for a reason to call me a bad mother or a horrible wife. I'm neither of those things so it was imperative I act accordingly. Even though I want to be on good bullshit.

*****

"I'm sorry I'm so late picking them up. I was dealing with this Thug situation. Plus, I was able to sit down with him, Malik, and Ta'Jay. We were in need of some one on one family therapy." I was standing on his porch and he was talking to me through the door.

"That's what up. I'm glad you were able to spend some time with them. Wait right here. I'll bring them out to you." He slammed the door in my face and it made me jump. I couldn't believe he wouldn't even let me inside. I counted to ten trying to calm down but I just couldn't. I politely twisted the door knob and walked in. He and this bitch were getting my kids dressed. I didn't know this girl from a can of paint so why in the fuck was she even touching my kids.

"I don't know who you are but could you excuse us for a minute." She looked at me and then at him. "This shit ain't even up for debate Li'l Momma. Get the fuck out so I can talk to my husband!" I walked over and I snatched Quanye away from her. She put her hands up in defeat and walked to the back of the house.

"Really Peaches?"

"What the fuck you mean really?"

"You know what, shut the fuck up talking to me and get the fuck out. You're too damn old to be on this bullshit." Just him calling me old was too much for me to take. Now all of sudden I was old because he had a younger bitch. I just turned my back to him and started grabbing my kid's things that I saw, placing it in their book bags. I hurried up and wiped the tears from my face that had fallen. The last thing I wanted was for him to see, or his new bitch, to see me crying.

"Don't cry Mommy," Quanie said as he reached up and wiped my face. That only made the tears flow like a river.

"Come on now man, you crying for nothing." Quanie grabbed me and pulled me into his embrace.

"What you mean I'm crying for nothing?"

"Quantez, I'm about to go. I'll leave so I can give you guys some privacy. It's obvious that you guys need to sit and have a much needed conversation."

"You don't have to leave sweetie. It's obvious we don't have shit to talk about." I started grabbing my kids and we headed towards the door. I needed to get the fuck out of there with the quickness because I felt myself about to shoot these bitches. I hated when I cried, especially when it was over a man. That shit is so weak to me but even the strongest of women get weak over a man and wear their emotions on their sleeves. It's just that I don't want to be one of those women.

"Quantez, would you please tell your wife that I'm your sister. This is getting out of hand."

"I don't have to tell her shit. She's just assuming some shit without asking. Last time I checked, we weren't even together so it wouldn't be any of her concern anyway. This isn't nothing but another one of her childish ass antics and I'm tired of the shit." Quanie kicked over the flat screen and that made the kids start crying.

"See what the fuck you did Quantez!" I hollered as I tried to calm the kids down.

"I'm Quanisha, his older sister. You've never met me because I live in Dubai. I'll calm them down. Please go back there and talk to him. He's been walking around here like a sad ass puppy dog and I can't take it."

"I'm sorry about the way I acted towards you."

"It's cool. I probably would have acted the same way with my husband." I walked away and found Quanie sitting on the patio smoking a blunt. I just stood behind him a minute because I didn't know what to say to him. I just shook my head at myself. This little nigga had my head gone but I would be lying if I said I didn't love him.

"I'm sorry for jumping to conclusions but how did you expect me to react? I come over here and there's some random ass chick in your house and I don't know who she is.

"I expected for you to act your age and not your shoe size. This is the reason why we're separated now. If I wanted a young random ass bitch I could easily get me one and have several of them bitches on speed dial to do this dick and swallow it too, but I'm not on that with these hoes. I wifed you because you have everything I want and need in my life. You're the mother of my children and we have to set an example for them Peaches. "

"Damn Quanie! I said I was sorry." Quanie jumped up and got in my face like he was going to hit me.

"See that's the thing. Your ass is forever sorry for your behavior. You say that shit and then you turn around and do the same motherfucking thing. I'm sick and tired of you trying to play with me like I'm some motherfucking joke. I might be younger than you are but that don't mean shit to a gangsta ass nigga like me. I'm not that nigga Vinnie and I for damn sho' ain't that bitch ass nigga Snake. I'm more than some handsome ass nigga with a big dick that dropped some seeds off in you. Respect me as a man Peaches or get the fuck on with your bullshit. Don't think you're the only one that can make this dick do tricks. My job is to sling cock and your job is to ride it. Play your position and we'll be just fine."

I didn't know if I should be mad at his choice of words or go sit in the corner because he definitely just bossed the fuck up on my ass. That shit had turned me completely on.

"I'm serious when I tell you that I'm sorry Quantez. I'm sorry about everything. I'm sorry for all of the partying and just flat out disrespecting you as a man. You didn't deserve that because you've been nothing but good to me since the moment we decided to make things official. I guess I started with all the partying because somewhere inside of me I thought that you were going to leave me for someone that was younger. I don't know, I just felt like I had to start acting a little younger just so I can keep up with you."

"Stop right there. Have I ever made you feel like you had to be a younger woman? Your age is what made me attracted to you. I keep telling your ass I love you Peaches. Fuck these young bitches. They don't have shit on you. Bring your ass here man." I put my head down and slowly walked over to him. He pulled me in close and hugged me tight.

"I love you, bae and you know that. You don't have to act out to get my attention. You got all of me for the rest of our lives. It's always been about you and the kids but I had to distance myself to let you know to stop fucking playing with me. I need you to be a wife and a mother to our kids. I'm your man. Just fall back and let me do what the fuck I have to do. Now is this going to be the last time we have this conversation?"

"Yes, Quanie, this is the last time."

"Now give Daddy a kiss with your old ass."

"Don't play with me Quanie," I said as I playfully hit him. We both laughed and it felt so good. I couldn't remember the last time we actually smiled. I will never take his love for me for granted. I've never had a man that truly loved me without an ulterior motive in my life. Quanie loves me for me and brings so much to my table that I don't even have to add anything to it. I love how he loves me and lets my ass know when I'm fucking up. Yep, that lil nigga got my old ass in line and in check. Now that I have fixed my relationship with my husband, it's time I get shit in order with Thug and Tahari. I'm not gone rest until I find out where the fuck my daughter-in-law is.

Chapter 16- Tragedy

Keesha

I was doing my best at holding it in where Tahari was. If Quaadir found out I was lying to him he would have a fit. Thug is his brother and Tahari is my sister. My loyalty is to her before anybody. She's all I have in this world with regards to blood family outside of my kids. I could care less about Python. I tolerated him to a certain extent but I didn't trust him as far as I could throw him. He came out of the blue too fucking nice for me. I learned to never get comfortable because everybody has a motive. He could stay his ass away from me and my kids.

At first I welcomed him into our life and things were cool. Up until we told him that we were retiring and we could no longer do hits for him. Quaadir was dead set against it from the jump but gave in because he knew how I wanted to be closer to my family. Once we told Python and he started bad-mouthing Thug Inc., I knew I would never fuck with him again in life. I blocked his ass from calling me. If you don't like my husband, then you don't like me. We are as one. No matter what the case may be I'm riding for my husband.

Although Thug Inc. had went into retirement back in Chicago, Quaadir was very much still in business here in Atlanta. Or shall I say God was still in business. That's what he goes by and that's how the streets address him. Being in Chicago all that time made me forget just how powerful my husband was back home. I was so mad at him when he told me he was back running things for Aunt Ruth.

At sixty-five she was still in the dope game strong with no end in sight. It's amazing how she still hanging with the best of these niggas. Quaadir is her baby and she loves him like her own. People that know us out here would never believe just how deep his family is back home besides the ones who know that Thug is his brother. Quaadir is the boss of all bosses out here and just as lethal as they come. He's one way when he's with his brothers and Thug Inc. but he's a different person when he's out here. Either way, I love him for him and who he is. I just wish that he would give this shit up all the way. But, of course he's not listening to me.

I'm irritated with him because he's back keeping late hours and barely being at home. I've gotten to a point where I don't even care anymore. For the sake of my sanity, I have to put my focus on my kids and making sure they're straight. Quaadir is not going to give me gray hair worrying and stressing over him. I've been with this man since I was fifteen and I've been going through the same shit since then. Now don't get me wrong when I say that because he's much better than he used to be. It's just that we aren't getting any younger. It's time to leave all the bullshit behind us and grow old together. I'm sick and tired of being worried sick about him being out in the streets at all times of night. Quaadir is getting too damn old for that shit.

*****

"Hey Aunt Ruth. What are you up to?" I walked inside of her beautiful Alpharetta home and she was sitting up in her recliner watching Law and Order: Special Victim's Unit. I laughed as she hollered at the TV like the people could really hear her. That shit used to make me so mad when I first moved in with them. She would be up late as hell hollering at the TV. Now it's funny as hell to me.

"Just sitting here watching my shows. Where my babies at?"

"The girls are at cheerleading practice and the boys are home with Nanny."

"I done told you and Quaadir about leaving those kids with a nanny. Black folks don't have no nannies. We keep our own damn kids. Bring them over here to me. Grandma take care of them real good."

"Now Aunt Ruth you know you ain't got no time to be keeping no kids. You be out in the streets just as much as Quaadir do." Aunt Ruth always complaining about us leaving the kids with a nanny but she knows damn well she ain't got no time to keep them. She loves them dearly but babysitting is not on her resume. Plus, I'd rather them be with a nanny. The last time the girls spent the weekend with her she taught them how to cook and measure coke. I was pissed because I don't want that for them. Quaadir thought the shit was so cute.

"Well, I'll be home more. Them doctors saying I have stage IV lung cancer." I jumped up and grabbed the cigarette from her hand that she had flamed up. I was in shock but I had to muster up the courage to keep a straight face. I wanted to crumble because this woman had been a mother and my best friend for many years. Without her I don't know where I would be.

"How long have you known?"

"About two months. I was trying to decide on what I wanted to do. I decided not to get chemotherapy or radiation. I'm too far gone so there's no reason for me try it. I have about six months left. So I'm gone sit here in the comfort of my home and live out my last days. Now, I see you over there getting ready to start that crying but don't cry for me. I lived a long, prosperous and luxurious lifestyle. I lived everyday like it was my last day on Earth. Aunt Ruth gone be just fine. I just want you to promise me one thing." I hurriedly wiped my face and listened to her intently.

"Take care of my baby. I know he's a hard man to love. He needs you to always be with him. You're the voice of reason that he needs when life gets hectic. Please don't ever give up on him. You know that Quaadir is my world. It don't matter that I didn't give birth to him and he's built a bond with Peaches and the rest of the kids. I raised him and taught him everything. That's my baby and it's killing me to know that

I'll have to leave him in this world alone. As long as he has you and the kids, I know that he will be okay.

"And another thing, this is strictly between you and me. I do not want Quaadir stressing about my sickness. I also don't want Peaches, Gail, or Sherita coming up here worrying the hell out of me. I just want a peace of mind. My last will and testament is in my top drawer in room. Please abide by my wishes. I don't want no funeral or no memorial service. Just cremate me and keep my ashes in your house. I want to always be where Quaadir lays his head. I'm his guardian angel in life and I want to be in death. I think I'll be able to rest easy being close to him. I know it sounds crazy but those are my wishes. Now, I'm counting on you Keesha to do that for me. Promise me that you won't tell the rest of the family."

I walked over and bent down over the recliner and hugged her for what seemed like an eternity.

"I promise I won't tell anybody." After I cried on her shoulder, I left her house and headed back home. Tears blinded me all the way home. I hate cancer. That shit sucks. When I pulled into the driveway, Quaadir was home. I had to gather myself because he would know something was wrong with me.

When I walked inside the house, he was talking on the phone. It sounded like business so I just walked over and kissed him on the cheek and headed upstairs to check on the kids. I knew that the nanny had dropped them off to him because she sent me a text letting me know. Niveaa and Nadiaa were on their phones as usual. They were straight divas and that shit got on my nerves. Their Daddy makes sure they get their hair, nails, and toes done every other week. I walked inside of my twins' room but they weren't in there. All of a sudden I heard a gunshot go off. The sound came from our bedroom so I took off running in that direction.

"Ahhhhhhhh!" I screamed out as Li'l Quaadir stood over Quameer with a gun in his hand. I rushed over and that's when I saw that Quameer had a huge hole in his chest.

"I'm sorry Momma we were playing. I thought it was a toy. I didn't mean to hurt him Momma." He wrapped his arms around my neck as I rocked back and forth on the floor holding my son's lifeless body. I knew that he was dead. I could feel it. My daughters ran over to us and they were crying hysterically but I was zoned out. I heard everything going on around me but it was like I was frozen in time. That was until I heard Quaadir crying.

"No! No! No!" I looked up and Quaadir was standing over us. He dropped down to his knees. Tears were flowing down his face. I stared at him with so much hate in my eyes. I tell him every time he comes in to put his gun away. He always puts it on the nightstand like we don't have mischievous three-year-olds running around. He reached out to touch him but I started hitting him.

"Don't touch him! Don't touch him! This is your fault! I told you to put that gun up! My baby! My baby! Please wake up! Momma is so sorry I left you today. Just please wake up."

"I'm sorry bae. I laid it on the bed and I had to quickly run downstairs. They were both asleep when I went downstairs. I'm sorry. I'm so sorry." We all sat on the floor crying and holding Quameer's body until the police came and EMTs came and took him away. They couldn't pronounce him dead so we still ended up going to the hospital.

For hours I sat in the emergency room waiting for the doctors to come out and tell me what I already knew. Quameer had passed from a gunshot wound to the chest. Quaadir had been taken into custody because the gun was his and he admitted to leaving it unattended. It was registered and we were both licensed firearm carriers. I didn't know if he was going to be charged with anything. Hell, there was a possibility that I could be charged. At this point I didn't even care what happened to me. There was no way I was going to be able to live without my baby. They might as well bury me next to him because I'm dead.

"Are you mad at me mommy?" I was sitting in the middle of my bedroom floor trying my best to remove my son's blood from the carpet but it seemed as if the spot was getting bigger and bigger. I looked up when I heard Li'l Quaadir talking. He was so sad without Quameer and I was trying my best not to cry or be angry around him. I reached my arm out so that he could come to me.

"No baby. Mommy is not mad at you. What happened was a big mistake. You didn't mean to hurt your brother. I love you very much and we're going to be okay." I hid my face in his shoulder as I cried. I was lying to my baby. I had no idea if things would be okay ever again. I looked up and saw Tahari standing in the doorway crying.

"Come here Quaadir baby. I want you to go downstairs and watch TV with your Daddy. If you be a good boy, auntie is going to take you and your sisters to get some ice cream. Now give me a hug." I was so glad my sister came on the first thing smoking when I told her what had happened. She walked over to me and wiped my tears with her hands. I just went back to scrubbing the blood.

"Why won't it come out?" I said as I started to scrub the blood stain with everything inside of me. Tahari yanked the scrub brush from me and held onto me as tight as ever as I began to wail and cry loudly. I had cried so much that I could barely see out of my eyes.

"That's right. Let it out sis."

"I just want my baby back. I don't care about the money, the houses, the cars, or the street status. I just want my baby."

"I know you do Keesha but he's not coming back. He's in Heaven with God now. He's up there with his cousins Angelica and Ka'Jariana. We're going to get through this together as a family. I'm your big sister and I promise you that we will." I knew that both of my sisters had went through this but I couldn't rely on a promise that I would get through this. At this moment there was nothing that made me feel like I would get through this shit. I stood up and I climbed up in my bed. I just wanted to sleep and never wake up.

Chapter 17- A Father's Anguish

Quaadir

Shit had been a complete blur from the moment I heard that gunshot go off. Seeing my son lying on the floor lifeless will always be in my mind. Each and every time I closed my eyes I could see him. That shit was fucking with my mental. I had been charged with reckless child endangerment and I was given a fifty-thousand-dollar bond. I expected Keesha to be there to bond me out, instead I couldn't get out until Aunt Ruth came.

I knew that Keesha was mad at me and she had every right to be. It was my fault Quameer was dead. I left the gun unattended and my boys got a hold to it. At the same time, we needed each other to get through this but Keesha refuses to talk to me. She won't even look at me. This shit is killing me slowly. I've not only lost my son but I've lost my wife too. I'm built Ford tough but I'm not built for this shit here. You see this type of shit on the news all the time but you never think it will happen to you.

*****

"Come on Bro. The service is starting." I was sitting on the church steps too afraid to go inside and join my family. I couldn't even bring myself to go inside and see my little nigga laid up like that.

"I can't do it." Thug sat down next to me and we both just sat in silence for a minute.

"It killed my soul to have to see a daughter I never got a chance to know lying in a casket. To this day I wonder what color was her eyes. We have no pictures, no blankets, no toys, or anything that reminds us of her. You on the other hand have had the blessing of having Quameer in your life for three years. At least you have the memories. Your little man loved you and you got a chance to shower him with nothing but love. This is the last time you will get to see him. Come on in here and say goodbye to your son. If you don't, you'll regret it for the rest of your life. Don't make Keesh sit up there alone."

"I fucked up big bro!" I hadn't really cried but right now I was crying like a newborn on my brother's shoulder. Thug pulled me up to my feet and he held me close.

"It was a mistake Bro. You can't keep blaming yourself. Get yourself together. We have to send Meer Meer off the right way." Thug walked back in to the church and I followed close behind him. I slowly made my way up to the custom made Spider-man casket. The inside had his name engraved. There were also Spider-man figurines placed inside. I wanted him to wear a nice suit but Li'l Quaadir said we should let him wear his favorite Spider-man costume and cape. I smiled as I pictured him in my head running around the house in full Spider-man mode. I bent down and kissed him on the forehead.

"I love you son and I'm so sorry." My emotions got the best of me and I couldn't control the tears.

"Come on baby," Peaches said, rubbing my back. She was finally able to grab me away from the casket and I sat down next to Keesha and my kids. I tried to grab her hand but she yanked it away.

"That's enough Keesha. You and Quaadir need each other right now. It's time you stop all of this stubbornness," Aunt Ruth said in a low tone.

"If he had put his gun up then we wouldn't be here right now." I was officially done at that moment and I couldn't even sit there any longer. That only made me jump up and leave out of the service. My whole family had flown in from Chicago and I knew they would represent me to the fullest. I would just have to be there in spirit. That wasn't my son lying in that casket. That was just his vessel. I knew that his soul was in Heaven with God and he was now our guardian angel.

I headed straight to the crib and to the bar. I had been drinking like crazy. It was the only thing that was numbing me from all the pain and hurt that I was going through. I went inside of my office and I opened up my lock box where I kept my hidden stash of PCP. I honestly didn't even know why I still had it in my possession. I hadn't smoked the shit since that time I went off and beat the shit out of Keesh.

I laughed on the inside as I thought about when I cut that nigga's head off. I took my custom made Glock out of the book and set it in front of me. I laid back and stared at the PCP, not really sure if I wanted to smoke that shit but knowing it would numb me. I just wanted to stop seeing my son dead on the bedroom floor lifeless. I grabbed the lighter and I flamed it up. As soon as the drugs hit my lungs I started floating into another fucking world. That's exactly where the fuck I needed to be in order to deal with this shit.

Chapter 18- In My Feelings

Keesha

I had just watched my son be lowered into his final resting place. The hardest part was leaving my baby out there alone. I felt like a bad mother as I rode back home in the family car. Regardless of the tragedy that had just hit my family, I knew I had to get it together for my kids that were still here on Earth. They had been just as out of it as I was. I needed to find Quaadir because I was pissed he left the service. I don't care what I said or how I was acting with him. How could he just leave like that and not see our son laid to rest? I'm so fucking angry with Quaadir right now. I can't even stand to look at him. Never in all of my years of being with him have I ever hated him as much as I do right now. Hate is such a strong word but I swear to God I hate him. It's his fault my son is dead and I just can't forgive him for being so fucking reckless right now.

*****

"We need to talk Keesha." I looked up from the glass of Remy I was drinking. Quaadir was standing over me with a bottle in his hand. The repast was in full swing and everybody was getting fucked up and enjoying one another despite our reason for being there.

"I don't feel like talking right now."

"It wasn't a motherfucking question. Either you get up and take this walk with me or I'm gone drag your ass out of here!"

"I wish the fuck I would." I looked at him in his eyes and I knew that he was high off of that shit. That alone made me want to cry because shit was going to get worse before the shit gets better. When he smoked that shit he was a different type of animal and it scared me. At that moment I knew I had fucked up by shutting him out but I just wasn't ready to talk to him. I turned around and got ready to turn my cup up but he grabbed me by my hair and started dragging me by my hair.

"Nigga you done lost your motherfucking mind dragging her like that!" I managed to look up and see Python standing there with his gun pointed at Quaadir.

"And you must have lost yours pulling that shit on my blood. You better put that shit up my nigga," Thug said, with his gun pointed in the back of his head.

"Big bro got you in the back and I most definitely got you up front," Malik said with his gun pointed at Python's forehead. Python also had a crew of people with him. King, Dutch, Nasir, Quanie, Dro, Sarge and Remy had their guns pointed at his men. What confused me was that I don't remember seeing Python at the service. Quaadir still had a firm ass grip on my hair.

"You better pull that trigger motherfucker! Because you better believe it's wartime."

"Nigga you done lost your motherfucking mind pulling a gun on my son in his motherfucking house. Get the fuck out of here!" Before I knew it Peaches rushed Python and started swinging on his ass and that made Tahari, Barbie, Rosé, Ta'Jay, Dior , Gucci, Chanel, and Khia start swinging on him and all his men. Mind you, Quaadir still had my hair tight. It was like he was stuck in a zone and wasn't letting me go. He started dragging me again towards the back of the house. Out of nowhere Peaches stepped in and slapped the shit out of him and he eventually let my hair go.

"Let her the fuck go. I've told you to keep your hands off of her. What the fuck is wrong with you? I need y'all to get it the fuck together. I understand that your son is dead and you're beating yourself up. but fighting her won't help you cope."

"I hate your ass!" I screamed out.

"You're dead ass wrong Keesha. You're not the only one who lost a motherfucking son. How dare you treat him like an enemy when he lost his child too? I've watched you be downright spiteful and mean to him from the moment this shit happened. You know Quaadir would lay down and die for them kids but you sitting here talking about you hate him. Really? After everything he has done for you. Now I don't condone him for his behavior because from day one I've always got on his ass for hitting you and you for staying. However, you shouldn't be blaming him."

"Fuck her Momma!" Quaadir said, as he threw the bottle up against the wall and it shattered everywhere."

"Calm the fuck down Quaadir!" Thug said and that made them start fighting one another. Everybody was trying to break them up. It all just became too much for me and I got the fuck out of there. Out of all days for us to be clowning, we did it on the day of my baby's funeral. This shit is sad on all of our parts.

*****

"You just gone sit out here all night by yourself," Tahari said as she came and sat down beside me. I was sitting on the edge of my pool with my feet in the water.

"I just needed some time to myself. It's too much going on in the house. Can you believe the way Quaadir acting?"

"Not any of them Thug Inc. niggas surprise me with their behavior. We all know they are passionate about what they believe in. I am, however, surprised at how you're acting." She handed me a glass and poured me a shot of Remy and then one for herself.

"What's that supposed to mean?"

"It means exactly the way it sounded. You're punishing Quaadir and it's not fair. You guys need to be supporting one another not fighting each other. Quameer is gone and I know it's hard but you guys still have three other children in there who need you. Y'all need to get your shit together and fix your relationship." I shook my head and just laughed at her loudly.

"What the fuck is so funny?"

"Your ass is funny." I poured me another shot and just stared at her because she was a cold piece of work my big sister.

"Enlighten me Keesha because I seem to have missed the joke. I must have on a big red nose and big ass clown shoes on the way your ass is laughing."

"I'm laughing because I find it funny how you always sit back and get on the rest of us about our relationships and how we need to fix things. Meanwhile, you sitting over here with a bruised ass face and your husband is in there all stitched up from you stabbing him and fleeing the scene. By the way, have you guys said anything to each other? From what I see, you've been avoiding him like the plague. So please don't sit here and judge me about how I need to treat Quaadir or handle him. That's my husband and I don't need nobody telling me how I should handle things. I handle shit my way. Oh yeah, I forgot you know him real well. Maybe I should take your advice. After all, he wishes I was you anyway."

"Come on now Keesha. That's not fair. You know damn well that thing with me and Quaadir has been over for years. Please watch what the fuck you say before you get anymore fucking drama started. I hate that you feel that way. Outside of anything that transpired between Quaadir and me, the fact is he loves his wife and I without a doubt love my husband. I'll be the first to admit that I need to work on my relationship with my husband with regards to how we behave towards one another in the heat of passion but what the fuck you got to know is what Thug and I have is real and it's always been that way. Don't worry about how I handle Thug or how he handles me. We go together like a hand in a glove but you already knew that. You're my sister and I love you with everything inside of me but please don't ever come for me with regards to my nigga. Your focus should be on Quaadir and why the fuck he keeps comparing you to me."

Before I could respond, she walked away but I didn't care. I wasn't about to go after her because that wasn't going to do anything but make us continue arguing with one another. There's enough bullshit going on already so it was never my intention. I don't want to fight with my sister. If anything I need her but Tahari always has a comeback for something no matter how much the shit hurts. I would be lying if I said my feelings weren't hurt behind her making that last statement but I do take ownership of the things I said to her with regards to Quaadir.

I know Tahari like a book and the way she responded had nothing to do with the statement I made about Quaadir. Tahari's problem is it's okay for her to tell everybody off for their behavior but when you say some shit to her she goes into boss lady mode. I love her but fuck her and that bullshit shit she was on. I poured me another drink and as soon as I knocked it back all I could hear was commotion in the house again. I thought death was supposed to bring a family together but it seems like it's tearing this family apart.

Chapter 19- Family Drama

Tahari

I felt bad after I spoke those words to my sister because I know she is really bothered by the fact that Quaadir and I had sex. It's crazy because we've become so close as a family it seems like the shit never happened. At first I used to get vibes and I would catch him looking at my ass but that shit stopped a long time ago after we had that first talk. I know for a fact that Quaadir doesn't even look at me like that. I can name one reason and that's Thug. Trust me, Quaadir values life. It took a long time for Thug to get to a point where he was comfortable with us being alone together. Despite all of that, I know that it's no solace to my sister if she feels in her heart that her husband still has a thing for me.

Although I had no idea about her or who he was for that matter, I still feel bad for sleeping with him. Being in the room with your husband and his brother knowing you fucked both of them is so awkward. I sit there so fucking ashamed. Over the years I've gotten past the shit and I just want my sister to be comfortable around me. I don't want her thinking she's not good enough for Quaadir because of me. I really don't even think that's the case. I think right now she's just in her feelings.

I got up and walked away because I felt the conversation escalating into something else. Plus, I wanted to talk to Quaadir and make sure that he wasn't making my sister feel some type of way. It might not have been the best time but I couldn't wait knowing my sister felt that way.

When I walked inside of the house everybody was back drinking and kicking it like it just wasn't about to be a fucking shootout in the living room. I looked around but I didn't see Quaadir. Peaches kept staring at me. I could tell that she wanted us to talk and without a doubt I knew that we needed to make things right but for some reason I was on my Petty Betty shit. So there was no way I was apologizing to her or Thug first. I was fucked up about hurting him when it happened and I had every intention of giving in and asking for his forgiveness. That was until I made it out here and he was acting as if I didn't even exist. It was like we didn't even know each other. He was walking past me and talking to everyone in the room but me. He even went so far as to put the kids on a red eye back to Chicago with Marta after the funeral without me knowing. We were able to sit together at the funeral but after the service I was under the impression that they were on their way to Keesha's house but when he arrived without them, I knew what he had done. I wasn't about to stoop to his level because I don't have time for it. Right now, this isn't about me and him. It's about trying to help Quaadir and Keesha cope with losing their son. At this point, everything else is irrelevant. Thug was trying his best to hurt me with his actions and I was trying my best to ignore his psychotic ass. He was itching to do something to me. I could feel it.

"Where Quaadir at?" I asked Ta'Jay. She was sitting in the kitchen at the table with Peaches, Gail, and Sherita. It's still so hard to believe that they are kin. Then again, it shouldn't be because all they do is talk shit and mind their kids' business but I ain't trying to argue.

"He in the back I think." I headed towards the back of the house and found him in the twins' room going through a baby photo book. I felt so bad for him and my sister. I walked inside and I sat on the floor beside him.

"Man, sis. I swear if I could I would change places with my little nigga. I'm so fucking stupid for leaving that gun out like that. Keesha got on me every day about coming in and just laying it down. How the fuck am I supposed to cope if my wife hates me and blames me for our son's death?"

"I just talked to her about that and told her to stop blaming you. I think it's just her way of coping with things. Keesha really needs you Quaadir. You know how she can get. That's actually why I came back here to talk to you. She told me you wish that she is me. Please tell me you didn't tell my sister that."

"Come on now Boss Lady. That shit is dead to me. I love my wife and I'm sorry you or any other woman could never be Keesh. That woman out there is everything to me. Anytime we get into it or have a disagreement, it's her who throws your name in it. I've become a broken record trying to explain to her that I no longer look at you like that. I love my fucking brother and I would never be on no shit like that with you anymore. Keesha loves you and she hates herself for feeling insecure about what went down between us. Don't take it personal though because it's not just you. Any woman that she knows I fucked with she feels insecure about. I haven't cheated on her since that shit with the correctional officer and I'll never cheat on her again. I just want her to trust in me that I'm a good nigga. Yeah, I know I put her through some shit but I'm done with that life. I just want her to let me make this shit right." Quaadir had tears streaming down his face and it hurt me to see him like that. I reached over and pulled him in for a hug so that I could comfort him.

"Ahem!" I looked up and Thug was standing in the doorway with the meanest look on his face. I knew he was about to be on good bullshit and I was in no mood for it. I took a good look at him and he was good and tipsy.

"What's good Bro?" Quaadir said, as we both stood up.

"Shit. I'm just wondering why the fuck my wife back here with you all hugged up. So, you need to tell me what the fuck is really good?"

"Stop this shit Ka'Jaire. I was just back here making sure he was okay."

"Did I ask you any motherfucking thing? Huh?" he yelled and it made me jump.

"No I –"

"Shut the fuck up then. Back to you my nigga. You still want to fuck my wife don't you? I see the way you stare at her and watch her ass when she walks by." Now the rest of the family and others that I didn't know had all rushed back to where we were and heard everything. I was so embarrassed for both for our families.

"Man Bro, stop tripping. Let me holler at you." Quaadir started walking towards Thug and he swung and him in his shit. Quaadir's nose started leaking instantly.

"Why did you do that Thug?" I cried as I rushed over to make sure Quaadir was okay at the same time Keesha and Peaches rushed over and started putting shit up to his nose to stop it from bleeding.

"What the hell are y'all fighting for now?" Keesha said, as she looked from Quaadir to Thug.

"Because my wife pussy so motherfucking good that he can't keep his fucking hands to himself." Keesha looked at me with so much hurt in her eyes. She just turned her head and focused back on Quaadir.

"Why are you acting like this Ka'Jaire? You know all I was doing was consoling him. There is nothing going on between us and everybody in here who knows us knows that. Yes, I had sex with Quaadir but I didn't know that he was my husband's twin brother. It only happened once and that's it. You're dead ass wrong for this shit, Thug."

"Bitch, you want to talk about what's wrong. Let's talk about me laying on the floor of your office bleeding to death. You getting ghost and leaving me leaking like it wasn't shit."

"I'm not gone be too many more of your bitches and I left your ass leaking because you put your fucking hands on me. Your stupid ass mad at me and you taking it out on your brother and the shit ain't cool." Thug rushed me and slammed me into the wall. He was choking me so hard that I felt like I was going to pass out. I was looking right into his eyes and they were black and cold as ice.

"Let her the fuck go!" Peaches said from behind him and hit him at the same time. The next thing I saw was all my Boss Ladies getting Thug's ass. He was drunk ass fuck and no match for them. Eventually he let me go and I collapsed on the floor. I started to vomit and cry uncontrollably. This shit was just too much. Why was he physically trying to hurt me? I didn't know who he was but this was not the man I married.

"Okay that's enough. Get the fuck back. I advise y'all to get the fuck gone because when I let him go, he gone fuck y'all up." Malik was now holding Thug back. If I was in the mood to laugh, I would have because you should have seen them bitches getting out of dodge except for Peaches, Keesha, and Quaadir.

"This shit is ridiculous. I'm so fucking embarrassed," I heard Peaches' voice crack. I had never heard her sound like that. I managed to look at her and tears were streaming down her face. We were all a disgrace. At this moment it didn't matter who was right or who was wrong.

"I don't mean no harm but could y'all please leave my house," Keesha said as she walked out of the bedroom. I felt horrible and I wished this shit had never happened. I tried getting up but I was too dizzy. Malik let Thug go and he looked like he was about to walk out of the door but he quickly walked back over to me and yoked my ass up quick. He threw me over his shoulder. The last place I wanted to be was with him but I was too weak and dizzy to tussle with his drunk ass.

*****

I woke up in complete darkness with the most excruciating headache ever. I had no idea where I was. It took me a minute to realize that I was in my hotel room. How I had gotten there was beyond me. The sound of light snoring made me jump up and cut the light on. Looking at Thug sleeping without a care in the world jarred all my damn memories of his silly ass behavior. Then he had the nerve to be naked. I looked down and I had my same clothes on that I wore to the funeral earlier. Just the thought of my nephew being dead made me sad all over again. I missed my kids like crazy and all I needed to see was their faces to make me feel better. I could tell that they were missing me as well when I saw them at the service. I also thought about my sister and Quaadir. I felt so bad about everything that had happened. I had to make it my business to go and check on them before I headed back to Chicago.

I felt so dirty because I was in bed with my clothes on. Thug knows I hate that shit. I looked over at him and rolled my eyes at his eyes. Sleeping like he hadn't shown his natural black ass. I gathered me some items from my suitcase to take a bath and headed into the bathroom. I removed my clothes and I looked in the mirror. The whites of my eyes were damn near bloodshot from him choking the shit out of me. I became angry as fuck looking at this shit. I had scratches all over my shit and his handprint was very visible. I hated how I looked and I hated how I felt. It was then I realized the shit between us had gotten way out of hand. I had the right mind to go across his shit while he was asleep but that would only make him want to get up and kick my ass some more. I knew I couldn't beat his ass but we needed to have a much needed conversation. I need to know if he's about to become the abusive ass man he told me would never become. He promised me that he would never fight me. Each and every time Thug hits me I get a flashback of Nico whooping on my ass. That's not good. I might fuck around and kill his ass the next time he puts his motherfucking hands on me. It's one thing for him to be overprotective and domineering, but abusive is something I can't even accept.

I walked out of the bathroom and stood over him as he slept. I couldn't help it so I reached down and smacked the shit out him.

"Wake the fuck up right now Thug!" He jumped up fast as hell looking all around the room like he didn't know what had hit him. Then he looked up at me and realized who the fuck had slapped his ass.

"What the fuck is wrong with you?"

"That's the same thing I want to know nigga. Get your ass up because we 'bout to get something straight right here and now." I stood over him in my black panty and bra set with my hands on my hips. I cut on the light and stared at him to let him know I wasn't playing with his ass. For a minute I thought that he was going to get up but instead he rolled over and turned his back to me.

"You better cut that light off and lay your ass down."

"Fine motherfucker, have it your way. I'll cut the light off and you better believe I won't be laying down next to your ass. As a matter fact, fuck you nigga. I'm calling my lawyer first thing in the morning. I want a divorce from your black ass." I walked away and started grabbing my luggage. I was so fucking for real with Thug. He had me fucked up if he thought things were going to go his way this time around. Sometimes desperate times call for desperate measures.

"You better sit your ass down Tahari!

"No! Fuck this shit. I'm going home. I ain't got time for this bullshit. Do you see my face Ka'Jaire? Look at me!" I had to scream at him to get him to look at me in my face because he was trying his best not to look at me. I just shook my head and I walked into the bathroom and slammed the door. I stripped out of my bra and panties and stepped inside the shower. I leaned my head forward on the wall as all of the water ran all over me. I wasn't even hurt about the situation. I was more mad about him acting nonchalant about the shit.

I squeezed my eyes together as tight as I could because I could feel his presence in the bathroom. He was so close to me that I could smell the natural scent of his body. Yes, my husband had his own special sweet smelling scent. I knew he was close because I could smell him.

Thug didn't even need cologne, he smelled that damn good. At that moment I didn't want to smell him, touch him, or feel him. I shook my head as I felt his arms wrap around my waist. Thug wasn't playing fair at all. I knew he was about to fuck the lining out of me. Not that I didn't welcome it but it would not fix the problem that we were going through. Thug needed to understand me and who I was as a person. You would think after all of these years he would know me by now. In reality, he does know it's just that he likes to be in control so it's blocking him from seeing how I'm affected by his behavior.

Thug roughly turned me around and pushed my legs apart. He got down on his knees looking at me the entire time. I quickly turned my head because I no longer wanted to look at him in his face. I leaned my head back as soon as I felt Thug's tongue on my pussy lips. His fingers slipped inside me with ease. I bit down on my bottom lip trying to stifle the moans that were threatening to escape my mouth. My breathing sped up and heart began to race as Thug sucked and licked every inch of my pussy. He threw my leg over his shoulder and went in full force.

"Ahhhhhhh! I'm about to cum."

"Let that shit go then. I want you to cum all in my mouth." Thug sped up his tongue action along with his fingers as he drilled them in and out of me. I started to cum all over his face and in his mouth at full force. My pussy juices mixed with the shower water that was still pouring all over us made the scene that much more sensual. My legs felt like noodles as Thug stood up and placed his lips on mine. I finally had the courage to stare at him in his eyes. He stood up and picked me up as well. I wrapped my legs around his waist and slid his dick inside of me without hesitation. Thug started to bounce me up and down on his dick with so much force. That shit hurt but it felt good at the same time. Thug was fucking me like an animal in heat but I knew it was all his pent up anger, stress, and frustration. So I let him release all his tension on my pussy. We fucked for what seemed like hours. We took it from the shower, to the balcony, to the floor and then to the bed. It was one of the best sex sessions we had ever had during the course of our marriage. Thug had taken my body to heights of pleasure beyond my wildest dreams. It was as if he was making love to me for the first time or the last time. Thug was fucking me like he was trying to prove a point. Either way he was fucking my brains out and I was enjoying each and every minute of it.

The next morning I stood over Thug for the second time and watched him as he slept peacefully. I kissed him on the forehead and I grabbed my suitcases to leave. Yes, I was still leaving his ass and going back home to Chicago. It's going to take more than just some good ass dick from Thug to make me forget about what had transpired between us. I loved Thug with all my heart but I had to show him that he can't hit me and think that things will go back to normal after he makes loves to me. I looked at him one last time before I exited the suite. I had a plane to catch back to the Chi and I was not going to miss it. I had an appointment with a divorce attorney. What? You motherfuckers thought I was bullshitting? Thug's ass is going to learn today what I'm about and that I'm not all talk when it comes to him because I'm definitely about that action. He's going to do right by me as his wife or lose me as his wife. Point blank and period.

******

My flight from Atlanta had been delayed due to severe weather so I didn't make it home until the next morning. I was surprised when I walked in my house and Peaches was in my kitchen cooking. She must have caught a red eye flight after Keesha put our asses out of her house. At the same time, I wondered why she was in my house and we weren't even on speaking terms. Where they do that at?

"Hi Mommy!" all my kids said in unison and they all jumped up and swarmed around me. It warmed my heart to see my kids and the smiles that were on their faces.

"What happened to your eyes?" KJ asked. I forgot all about my father being here. Yes, I said father. KJ be on me how a father is over their daughter. He's been that way since I met him.

"I'm fine. It's just my allergies." KJ and Ka'Jairea looked at me like they knew I was lying and that made me feel so low. What type of mother and father are we to even let our kids know that we physically hit each other.

"Where is my Daddy? Something is wrong with Prada, Ma. I need him to take her to the doctor so that she can feel better." I looked at Ka'Jaiyah and I shook my head because I knew something was going to happen to that dog. I begged Thug not to buy her another pet but he just wouldn't listen to me.

"What do you mean something is wrong with her?" I reached over and grabbed Prada out of her arms. She started yelping as soon as I tried to stand her up and take a good look at her. I looked at her legs and that's when I noticed that they looked broken. How in the hell did she break this dog legs?

"Come on Yah-Yah. I'll take you and Prada to the vet," Marta said as she came over and took Prada from me.

"Wait Marta, she needs to put on her clothes. I can't take my child out in the streets looking any kind of way." We all started laughing because my baby was dead ass serious. She is a fashionista.

"Adios Mios," Marta said as she threw her hands up in the air and followed her up the stairs to get Prada dressed. Marta loved all my kids and they loved her as well but I knew for a fact that she hated to deal with Yah-Yah. Hell, we all hated to. Thug was the only one she behaved for. Each and every time I look at her she's a reminder of when Thug "died". To this day I still get teary-eyed when I think of how I made it a year without him. Marta and Quaadir made it easy. All this time I forgot how much he helped me out with the kids during that time. Neither one us knew of the consequences that would possibly follow us for the rest of our lives.

"I hope you know that she gone kill that dog too," Ka'Jairea said and walked off without a care in the world. I shook my head because I knew it was true.

"What's good Kaine and Kash? Mommy missed y'all. Did y'all miss me? No hugs or nothing."

"What's good Ma?" they said in unison. I smiled because they always said the same thing at the same time. It was so creepy. They're so mild-mannered and well-behaved now. Who would have thought these were the same little boys who used to kill all the damn fish and write all over my walls. They were the epitome of terrible twos. Marta was the one who could tame them and make them act right.

I looked over at Kaia and Kahari and they were the last of my babies. They grew up too fast for me. They were now going on six and were very smart. They love me but they go to Ka'Jairea for everything and that's mainly because she's basically helped with her brothers and sisters for as long as I could remember. I don't know where I would be without her sometimes. I just hate that our relationship has changed since she's gotten older. She's into boys and into social media. Her Daddy hates it but there's nothing we can do about it. She's a teenager. Thug is going to have a fit when he finds out about her liking Li'l Hassan. I think that it's so cute she has her first crush.

I observed Kylie and she fit right in with us as a family. I just hate that she has been diagnosed with having a mild case of Autism. After we got full custody of her, we found out that she had some issues but she's been doing well with her therapy and tutors. I hope that her mother is looking down on us and happy about the decision she made. I looked around at all of my kids and silently thanked God for each and every one of them. They give me a purpose and a reason to live.

My phone began going off and I knew it was Thug. I ignored that shit and headed up the stairs to my bedroom. I didn't have time to talk to him at the moment.

"Can we talk Ta-Baby?" I looked up and Momma Peaches was standing in the doorway of my bedroom. I had actually tuned out the fact that she was here in my house.

"Sure come in." I sat down on my bed and waited to hear whatever it was she had to say. I knew sooner or later she would be coming and saying something to me with regards to me stabbing her son. I'm surprised we hadn't come to blows because after the disagreement in the hospital, I just knew it was on whenever we saw each other again.

"I know that I'm the last person you want to talk to but I just want to clear the air and move on from the shit that went on between us. These last couple of months has been the hardest on me and it's been an eye-opening experience as well. I never apologize for anything but it's only right I apologize to you for overstepping my boundaries with regards to Thug.

"At the same time, you know how I am about my baby. That boy is literally my life and I just can't see myself living without him. From the bottom of my heart, during the course of your marriage if I ever disrespected your place as his wife, I apologize. I also want to apologize for the statement I made with regards to my family going through shit ever since you came in the picture. Like you said this shit been fucked up way before you ever came into the picture. The things I said to Thug back at that hospital was wrong. Ta'Jay is a grown ass woman and it's not his or Malik's responsibility to make sure she doesn't go out and fuck psychotic ass niggas.

"I also had a long talk with Thug and I apologized to him for everything. I just want the best for my family. I also want the best for you guys. I see how you love my son and I've always loved that about you. The first time I laid eyes on you I knew you were going to be my daughter-in-law. You had this look in your eyes that let me know how much you loved my son. I just had no idea your ass was batshit crazy over his nutty ass."

We both laughed and I walked over and hugged her tight as ever.

"I'm sorry for the things I said as well. Although I was mad it was never my intention to disrespect you as his mother. Let me rephrase that. I meant as our mother. You're the only person outside of my grandma Lucy that was a real parent to me. I'm forever grateful for you inviting me into your close-knit family and making me a part of it.

Thug loves you so much and he feels like if he lets you down then he has failed you. So it hurt me for him just hearing you say what you said but I'm glad we've cleared the air. It felt so awkward being in a room with you and not saying anything to each other."

"Exactly. Now that that's out of the way. Have you talked to your sister? Her or Quaadir not answering the phone for anybody. I'm so worried about them. My grandbaby dying and all that bullshit that happened after the funeral had me fucked up. This family needs to come together. I don't like what's going on at all."

"I tried to call her but she's not answering either. I really hope no one thinks that there was anything inappropriate going on between Quaadir and me. I swear to God Momma Peaches Quaadir and I don't look at each other like that period. Thug just happened to walk past the room and see us hugging. The hug was nothing but a comforting hug. I'm disappointed that Thug would behave like that."

"You already know how he feels about that situation. Thug and Quaadir are the best of friends and brothers. However, it doesn't change the fact that his wife and brother fucked before. Just like Keesha loves you and y'all have become close. It still doesn't change the fact that her husband and her sister had sex before. There is nothing wrong with Keesha feeling inadequate when it comes to you. After all, you're Boss Lady right? I don't condone the shit Thug did that's why I went across his shit. As a matter of fact, where is that motherfucker anyway? He's the main reason I'm over here. Malik called and told me that Quaadir nose is broke and I'm pissed the fuck off about that shit." I just shook my head hearing that Thug had broken Quaadir's nose.

"I left his ass in Atlanta. When I saw my eyes and my neck I was so outdone. I packed my shit and now I'm here ready to file for divorce." Peaches just starting dying laughing like something was funny. That was the same thing Keesha did before I read her ass for filth. Peaches was going to get her cursed out again laughing at me.

"You and your husband are truly made for each other. The both of you are so fucking dramatic when you get into it that it don't make no sense. I understand that you're trying to prove a point but that's a drastic decision to make. You know damn well if you file some damn divorce papers and he signs them you're going to be all in your feelings. You and Thug need to learn how to communicate with your words instead of with your hands. Over the years you guys have prospered into one of the most wonderful couples out of everybody.

"Y'all problem is both of you want to be the boss of the relationship. Listen to me baby, and listen to me well. You have these bitches out here admiring the way you bossed up and overcame that shit with Nico. They also love how you carry yourself as a woman and how you will kill anything moving. There's nothing wrong with that. What's wrong is you always bossing up to Thug. Now don't get me wrong, you don't have to lay down and take his shit. You're supposed to stand up for yourself and speak about it when something is wrong. The fact remains the same that Thug is the man in the relationship and you have to let him be that.

I'm telling you this because I learned this shit the hard way with Quanie. It took for him to leave me completely alone in order for me to see the error in my ways. Nothing is wrong with going across his shit if he puts his hands on you. Never let that shit slide. We are both victims of domestic violence so there is absolutely no way we would even be cool with any man hitting on us. I don't condone you stabbing him up either. Y'all both have to be careful. That shit could have went left on both of y'all parts. He could hit you the wrong way or you could have killed him had you hit a main artery or something.

"I know it's hard to talk to Thug but you guys have to sit down and have an adult conversation. Y'all have eight damn kids, ain't no motherfucking breaking up. I'm gone need the both of you to get it together immediately. Thug will kill your ass before he let you divorce him. Come on and help me get this menu together. It's time for this family to sit down and have a dinner. We need to get back to us. The Kenneth Family never folds under pressure."

Peaches had said a mouthful and I never had chance to even respond because she kissed me on the jaw and hurriedly walked out of the room. I totally agreed with her. I didn't really want a divorce from my husband. I was just doing it to get his damn attention. I'll just wait until he comes home and hopefully we can sit down and have an adult conversation. I really don't know what's going to happen to us if he continues to act the way he's been acting.

I can't believe Peaches wants to have one of her famous family dinners. Those things never turn out right. After all of these years you would think she was done with this shit. This should be interesting with all the drama this family got going on.

Chapter 20- New Secrets

Barbie

I had been trying my best to keep it together but I was slowly losing my mind. Darro's wife, Michelle, had been a real pain in my ass and I was tired of her flat booty ass. Since Malik killed Darro, my daughter has lived with me. The thing about that was that she had been with me illegally. During the course of Darro and Michelle's marriage she had legally adopted my daughter. I didn't know the shit until like a month later when she showed up on my doorstep trying to take Zaria.

At first I thought the bitch was joking but I quickly knew that she wasn't when she produced legal documents. I was crushed but I had no other choice than to hand my daughter over to her. We went to court and I tried to fight it. I had to take a DNA test and everything to prove that I was, in fact, her birth mother. Thank God I never turned over my parental rights to my daughter when I left her with Darro. That's why she is now in my custody and living with us. Malik has adopted her as his own and I'm so happy. She loves her some Malik. I'm not surprised though because all of the kids love his silly ass.

The joy of being able to raise my daughter and live happily ever after with her was short-lived. Michelle has been hell bent on making Malik and me pay for whatever she thinks happened to Darro.

They still haven't found Darro's body and as you all know, they never will. I still get sick to my stomach when I think of how Malik had cut his damn body into all those pieces. Darro is still considered a missing person but this bitch refuses to leave me the fuck alone. I had been keeping the shit from Malik a secret because I knew that he would most likely go ape shit. I didn't need him catching any more bodies.

That part of our lives was over and done with. I just wanted us to sit back and enjoy the life we've worked so hard to have.

This bitch Michelle was working on my last good nerve with all these threats and accusations. I decided to meet up with her just to see what was really good with this green ass bitch. All this tough talking over the phone had me hyped. I wanted to tag this bitch one good ass time but I knew that I couldn't. I had to play it smart with this hoe because I had no idea where her head was really. It was a good thing Malik was still in Atlanta or else he would have been asking all types of fucking questions.

*****

I sat inside of Starbucks impatiently waiting for Michelle to arrive. She was already thirty minutes late and I knew she was doing the shit on purpose. I was done waiting for the bitch. She had me fifty ways to fucked up if she thought that I was going to sit and wait for her to come to a meeting that she had set up.

As soon as I made it out to the parking lot her car was pulling inside. She honked her horn and pulled into a parking spot.

"You're late."

"I ran into traffic. Let's go back inside and discuss some things." She stepped out of the car and strutted past me like she was walking on the catwalk. I looked around the parking lot to see who the fuck she was strutting for. My True Religion pants cost more than everything she had on and we all know True Religion ain't that damn expensive. I caught up with her and we grabbed a table.

"Did you want anything?"

"Cut the bullshit Michelle. What the fuck do you want from me and my husband?" This bitch was acting all nonchalant and I wanted to slap the shit out of her. Calling herself playing this fucking mind game with me.

"Straight to the point huh?" I observed her as she leaned forward and that's when I noticed what looked like a piece of black wire on the inside of her collar. It took everything inside of me not to reach across the table and snatch her ass bald. This bitch was wearing a wire.

"You know what Michelle, I just remembered I need to pick the kids up from afterschool. Let's reschedule this for another time." I grabbed my purse and walked out of there fast as I could. I jumped in my car and got the fuck out of there with the quickness. I was so damn nervous and paranoid that I was shaking. I could barely drive so I pulled over to the side of the road. I had to think of what I needed to do next. If this bitch was wearing a wire, there was no telling what she had told the damn police. Malik was going to go ballistic when he found this shit out. He was still in Atlanta and I didn't want to ruin whatever business meeting that he and Thug had out there. I was all out of options and Ta-Baby was my only hope.

******

"Tell me again Barbie. How do you know that the bitch was wearing a wire?" Tahari had been asking me question after question. I felt like I was in a fucking interrogation room. Dior, Gucci, Chanel, and Rosé were also in my living room. Ta'Jay had to be put back on bed rest because she messed up her back helping us whoop Thug's ass. I still can't believe we fought him.

"I'm telling you the bitch bent down and I saw the wire taped underneath her collar. She called herself leaning forward to go inside of her purse but really she made her shirt move. That's when I saw her collar pop up. It was right there. I swear Tahari, that bitch was rocking a wire.

"Did you tell her or say anything incriminating?" Gucci asked.

"No never. I thought the bitch was about to extort me out of some money just because she was a greedy bitch. In reality, I know it was a setup to get me to incriminate me or Malik."

"The nigga ain't even been declared dead and that bitch out here on a witch hunt over a missing person," Rosé said.

"Either way, that bitch got to go immediately," Chanel said.

"We can't do shit Chanel. You must have forgot Thug shut Boss Lady Inc. down," Dior said matter-of-factly. We all turned and looked at Tahari. I could tell she was in deep thought about what we should do. Her ass was on the fence about whether or not she should defy Thug. I understood her position. It's hard as hell being at odds with your husband and he's the boss of the motherfucking city. Over the years I've sat and watched wondering how in the hell she has survived Thug's wrath. People can say what they want about my husband but I'll take his ignorant bipolar ass any day over Thug. He ain't even my husband and I'm scared to defy him. So if Tahari decides to not go after the bitch Michelle, I totally understand.

"Suit up. Y'all know the colors. We need to make this shit count. I'm retiring Boss Lady Inc. and we will only come out to play when we have no other choice. I know that we can all agree that motherhood and our wifely duties trump everything. I'm not getting soft on you guys. I've just come to a place in my life where I realize that I have too much going on in my home life. I've missed so many milestones with my kids trying to prove a point to my husband when in reality, I didn't have to. I had already showed Thug that I was down for him from the jump just by being the wife he needed me to be.

"In other words, I love my husband more than I love the adrenaline rush of being the head of Boss Lady Inc. Now don't get me wrong, I'm still the baddest bitch known as Boss Lady. I just choose to take motherhood and being a wife more serious." We all understood her because we had all sacrificed so much over the years to support our husbands. I hated to admit it but it was definitely time to retire Boss Lady Inc. for good. We had a good ass run and without a doubt, we'll go down in history as some of the baddest bitches that ever did it."

We all got up and walked over to where Tahari was and had a group hug. It was well needed. We had all grown up tremendously over the years and that was because we had each other. We've fought together and cried together. I couldn't ask for a better set of females to not only call my friends, but to call my family. Our love for them Thug Inc. niggas will have us all forever connected to one another.

"Let's do this shit before Thug and the rest of them fools make it back to the Chi."

"Yes. Let's get to it. I don't have time to be fighting his ass no more. His ass is strong as an ox."

"Bitch you should have saw me running my ass up out of there after I got me a couple of licks in. I just knew he was about to turn around and start shooting our asses," I said and we all laughed. Them bitches laughing but I didn't see shit funny. Thug was going to get our asses for this shit. He and Tahari needed to make up so we could be off the hook. When they are all in love that nigga will say yes to anything.

*****

"This bitch sleep hard as hell," Gucci said as she blew smoke from her mouth. Every time we were about to kill somebody this bitch needed to smoke a cigarette. It gets more and more annoying to me. Especially since I stopped smoking them things. We were inside of Michelle's bedroom. She stayed in the same house that she and Darro stayed in when he was alive. The bitch looked like her room was a shrine of him. That shit was creeping me out and I needed to hurry up and get the fuck out of dodge. Malik had been calling me back to back and I just let it go to voicemail. I knew when we finally did talk he was going to act a damn fool about me not answering. Not because he was jealous but because he would be worried about me and the kids. Despite me standing in this woman's room getting ready to kill her ass, I smiled at the very thought of my husband. Despite Malik's silly ways, my baby has grown up tremendously. I never would have thought he would have been able to overcome his childhood demons. I'm just glad I was there to see him through it.

"Her ass snore like a grown ass man mixed with a fucking bear," Chanel said as she continued to tie her feet to the bedpost while I was tying her arms up.

"I can't believe this bitch is sleeping through all of this shit," Rosé said as she and Tahari slid a big ass barrel in the room.

"Me either but I'm about to wake her ass up," I said as I walked over and slapped the shit out of her twice.

"Whaatttt!" That bitch jumped up but she was delirious as hell. She looked around and saw nothing but us surrounding her bed in all black with hoodies on. I leaned forward so she could get a good look at me, I wanted that bitch to see me before she checks out. She tried to get up but quickly realized that she was tied down and couldn't move.

"Surprised huh?"

"Please let me go! Why are you doing this?"

"Don't y'all hate bitches like this? They kill me acting oblivious to what the fuck is going on. Open that container Rosé," Tahari said as she walked over and pulled out the biggest rat I had ever seen. Motherfucker was big as a damn raccoon. Shit, she caused all of us to jump the fuck out of the way. She dangled the rat over Michelle's body and she begin to squirm like crazy.

"No! No! Please don't put that on me!" She was begging and pleading but it wasn't helping because Tahari dropped the rat on her chest. Shit made me cringe like a motherfucker.

"You are a rat aren't you? Rats like to hang with other rats. Now there's more where that come from so bitch you better get to talking. I don't have all motherfucking day to play with you, " Tahari said as she slapped her ass across the face.

"What have you told the police about me and my husband?" I walked over to the container and I was scared as fuck looking at all of those damn rats but I knew I had to grab one. I needed this bitch to get to talking and fast. I grabbed one of the rats by its tail and dangled it over her face.

"Okay! Okay! I'll tell you everything just please don't put another one of those things on me.

"Get to talking bitch!"

"Darrow and I are federal agents. We had been sent here from Atlanta to build a case against Thug Inc. All attempts in the past by other federal jurisdictions had failed to come up with anything solid to get them convicted. Their case was put on our desk and immediately it became personal for Darro. He noticed you in some of the surveillance photos that had been taken of you guys coming out of your home. There were also pictures of Thug. He was the target of the investigation. That's who the government wanted and they won't rest until they get him. The government had no idea that you were Darro's baby mother.

"I never knew anything about Zaria's mother until that day when he came clean at our headquarters. He immediately came up with this elaborate ass scheme to take you guys down. That's where he fucked up at. He never revealed to our superiors the connection between you two. If he did they would have taken him off of the case immediately. Darro couldn't have that because he wanted to make you pay for leaving him and your daughter. Had he did what was right, he would still be alive today and we would be enjoying our life.

"Your mother and sister had no idea that Darro was simply using them to get closer to you. Chrissy really thought he just wanted them to get to know Zaria but she had become a pawn against you as well. Each time she went over to your house he had tiny recording devices hid in her clothing. That's how I knew Malik killed Darro. I have the whole thing on tape. Zaria's clothing had to be in the basement at some point during that time. I heard him beating you, Barbie.

"That motherfucker crazy. He tortured the shit out of Darro. I was stuck between a rock and hard place because we were never given permission to hide those devices in her clothing. So I decided to just keep them for safe keeping in the hopes that I could extort money from you and get the fuck out of dodge. I had to come clean to my superiors about the connection between you and Darro when he disappeared. One thing the government is not, is stupid. They know Thug Inc. is responsible for that man's disappearance. I wish his ass was here to fix this mess because he's ruined my fucking career because he was still infatuated with you and you weren't thinking about his ass. I lost my job because of his ass.

"Now I'm stuck here in Chicago with no family or nothing. All I had was Zaria and when I lost her, I knew I needed to come up with another plan. That's when I decided to hit you up in the hopes that I could come up off some cash from you."

I was standing over this bitch still dangling this rat over her trying to take in everything she had said about this motherfucker Darro and his motives. He claimed to love our daughter so much but all along he was using her as a pawn to get back at me and to take Malik down.

I feel so stupid for feeling bad about what Malik had done to him. I looked over at Tahari and the rest of the girls and I knew that they were fuming after hearing what this bitch said. I just dropped the rat directly on her face because she had made me that mad. She laid there and blamed it all on Darro knowing full and well she had a hand in the shit too.

"Ahhhhhhhhhhh! Please! I told you what you wanted to know! Why are you doing this?"

"Bitch you're a rat just like ya nigga was. Why in the fuck should we spare your life? You basically just told me that you have evidence that not only incriminates my husband, but me as well."

"Just you mentioning Thug's name is a death sentence bitch. I don't play behind that one. My husband moves with ease and precision. You cracker motherfuckers will never be able to lose my husband in the system. As a matter of fact, I'm done talking to this rat ass bitch. Hand me the whole container. I'm about to dump all these rats on her rat ass. Then again, since this is my last hoorah, a simple bullet in the bitch will suffice."

"I promise you I won't say anything. Please Barbie. Promise me you won't do this. I have some information I think might help you. I'll tell you if you untie me." I looked over to Tahari and she nodded for us to untie her.

"You got less than a minute starting now fifty-nine, fifty-eight, fifty-seven. . ." I started to count backwards letting her know she better get the fuck to talking.

"The government is no longer trying to build a case against Thug Inc. That has been put on hold since they've been receiving vital information on Boss Lady Inc. courtesy of Python."

"Who did you just say?" Tahari said and it looked like all the color had drained from her face. We were all in shock hearing her say Python's name.

"My best friend still works for the government and Python is a criminal informant against you ladies. It seems that you didn't choose him over your husband so he wants to take everything from you and your sisters, including your freedom." Tahari was breathing heavily and biting her bottom lip,

"Dump that container on her ass Barbie!" I lifted up the container along with the help of Rosé. At the same time Dior, Chanel, and Gucci begin to pour gasoline all over the room and on Michelle's body.

"You promised you wouldn't kill me! Michelle cried out.

"Barbie promised you that shit. I didn't." Tahari let off two rounds in her skull, lit a match, and threw it on her body. We rushed out of there before the whole damn place was engulfed in flames.

As we rode back in Tahari's Denali truck, I could tell her mind was somewhere else. It was yet again another heartbreak and betrayal from a family member who claimed to love her and not be like the other ones who claimed to love her. I felt so bad for her.

"What are we going to do now Ta-Baby?"

"I have no idea Barbie. I just need to go home and think about how I'm going to tell Thug how I allowed yet another snake into our operation by not listening." The rest of the ride was silent. We were all speechless because we had come to grow fond of Python too. We had all agreed to allow him to train us to be assassins for him.

I could tell the dynamic between us had changed the moment our husbands stepped in and said we were all retired. Python had been in his feelings. The look in his eyes when he pulled that gun out on Quaadir let me know that if given the opportunity, he would without a doubt pull the trigger. As I observed the look on Thug's face, I knew he wanted Python to move a muscle so that he could end his ass. It's about to be some shit and I'm almost certain Thug Inc. is about to come out of retirement, if only for one night.

Chapter 21- Back to Us

Thug

When I woke up the next morning to find Tahari gone, I was pissed. At the same time I couldn't be mad at her. I didn't even know what came over me. I just became enraged when I saw her and Quaadir in such close proximity to one another. It was just them two alone so my mind began to wonder as I saw them engaged in a hug. My mind raced and I spazzed the fuck out. After all these years I still get angry at the fact that my brother and my wife fucked before. When I looked at Quaadir at that moment, I didn't see my brother. I saw the nigga God who wanted to kill me and take my bitch. Yeah, a nigga was tripping hard as fuck because neither of them had given me an inkling that they were on that with one another.

My mother had been calling me nonstop and I knew it was because I fucked around and broke Quaadir's nose. That Remy mixed with that damn Kush had me in a zone. Not to mention the fact that this nigga Python had pulled a rookie motherfucking mistake the moment he upped on my brother. We can fight amongst each other but all bets were off when it came to an outsider getting in nation business that doesn't fucking concern them. I had eyes on this nigga anyway from the jump. Y'all know how the fuck I roll when it comes to these niggas in these streets. From the moment Python magically appeared bearing gifts I didn't trust him but I put my feelings on the back burner for the sake of my wife.

Tahari longed for a relationship with anybody who had the same blood as her and that was her problem. She saw the good in people even when they meant her no good, and that includes me. The shit I got on this nigga Python is going to kill my wife's soul and I'm mad about that shit. Tahari believed everything about him and that he really wanted to be in her, Ta'Jay, and Keesha's lives. For a minute I thought he was one hundred until I found texts in her phone from him popping smart shit to my wife with regards to her listening to what the fuck her man say instead of his ass. This nigga really didn't know who the fuck I was. My motherfucking name been Daddy for a long time. I'm the only Daddy she knows. Yep, I'm a cocky ass nigga and after all these years of being with Tahari, I'm still that nigga she calls Daddy when I'm knee-deep in the pussy or she giving me that million-dollar mouth. That's just the way we roll. Despite the current state of our relationship, how hard we go for one another will never change. I'm sitting here still bandaged up from her stabbing my ass up but it don't mean shit to me. Nobody fucks with my wife's heart and live to snitch about it.

I never would have known what the fuck Python was up to had I not reached out to my brother Adonis. Although he had left the force, he still had people in high places that he goes to and finds shit out. I was thanking my lucky stars to have a brother that was at least legit. I long ago stopped fucking with them dirty ass cops on the inside because they were out to get a nigga's freedom in the long run. Over the years I'd grown tired of the snake ass niggas coming for my head. The streets ain't playing fair no more. I had a long ass run and made millions on top of millions. I walked away from it with my freedom and my life.

That's more than majority of kingpins can say because they're either dead or in jail. I chose retirement because I had done it all and seen it all. My crew and I had a long run on the streets of Chicago. Now it's time to groom our sons to get ready to take over what's rightfully theirs. It's their birthright to stunt on these niggas, fuck their bitches, and stack that bread. I wouldn't have it any other way for my sons.

My intentions were to get back at this nigga Python before I left Atlanta but I had more pressing issues that needed to be dealt with. For so many years I had put business before my children and my wife. That shit can wait until later. I needed to get home to my wife. That is if I still had one. I was weak in the knees just thinking of her talking about a divorce. I would never let that shit happen because it's til death do us part. That didn't mean it didn't fuck me up that she said some shit like that out of her mouth. I knew I had fucked up big time because she would never say any shit like that to me.

I hopped my ass on my private jet and headed back to Chi. Hopefully I can fix this shit with my wife so that I can get back to this business of finding the motherfucker Python. I knew he wasn't that far because he was too cocky and too busy trying to prove a point that he could outdo Thug Inc. I guess my goons and I could come out of retirement and remind the streets that we ain't sleep, we just relaxing.

*****

When I finally made it home it was well after midnight and the entire house was quiet. I turned the security system back on and I headed up the stairs. I checked on all of the kids and they were asleep in their beds. A dim light was shining from our bedroom so I knew Tahari was most likely up. I walked inside of the room and she was slipping her pajama shirt over her head.

"Oh shit, you scared me. I didn't even hear you come in." She grabbed her bonnet from her vanity and put it on her head. I hated that damn thing but she insisted on wearing it to bed and all over the house if I didn't snatch it off her head in the morning when she would get up.

"That's because you forgot to turn on the alarm system again. I told you to stop doing that shit. Just because we live in this gated community around all these rich white folks doesn't mean shit." Tahari always forgot to cut the damn security system on before going to bed. I was dog ass tired so I just removed my clothes and climbed in bed.

"I know Thug. Apparently you tell me to do a lot of shit," she said in a sarcastic tone. She climbed in bed, turned her back to me, and cut of the lights off. Minutes later I heard her sniffling and I knew she was crying. I rolled over and tried to grab her but she yanked away from me.

"Come on now bae. Stop crying. Tell me what's wrong so I can fix it."

"Everything is wrong Thug. Things were not supposed to be this way. You know what, never mind because no matter what I say nothing will change and I don't want to fight with you no more. I just want to be happy and stay happy. I just want to get in my happy place and be able to stay there. It seems like no matter how happy I am, there's always something in the shadows waiting." She was crying harder than ever and that made me forcefully pull her closer to me. I already knew that she was most likely crying from all the bullshit that had been going on between us. I was angry as fuck at myself looking at the bruises on her neck. That shit wasn't cool at all.

"I don't want us to fight no more either. I'm sorry for everything." I kissed her on the back of her neck as I spoke gently in her ear.

"That's just it. You're always sorry and you turn around and do the same shit. You promised me that you would never hurt me like Nico did. You might not have hurt me to the extent that he did but you have hurt me nonetheless."

"I know that I hurt you bae and I'm sorry for all that shit. I'm fucked up behind putting my hands on you. You making me feel like I've been a fucked up husband to you. I've done nothing but try to give you the best of everything. A nigga has went through hell and back to be the husband that you need me to be. I've killed motherfuckers behind fucking with you. You don't have to ask because you already know the shit I've sacrificed to be with you. I'm feeling like you holding some shit in that you need to get off of your chest. What's good bae?" I was now standing over Tahari and staring her down because I was having a hard time understanding where she was going with this. It sounded like she was upset about way more than me putting my hands on her.

"I know all the drama I caused by us getting together. I know what you sacrificed out here in these streets for me and that's the problem. I feel like because you saved me that fateful night after Nico beat me with that extension cord, I'm your property. You treat me like your child sometimes instead of your wife. Now don't get me wrong Ka'Jaire, because I would never take away from how you love me or how you cater to me. I've never wanted for anything. If I wanted it, no matter what it was, you went out and got it for me.

I'll never assassinate your character as a husband with regards to taking care of your responsibilities. You love me in a way that I know another man in this world could never love me. You love me with your whole heart and I love you with mine. People look at us and want the type of love that we have. They see you that nigga they call "Thug", the handsome, sexy, rich, big dick, pussy monster ass nigga and they lust over you. These bitches see how you love me and they want my life. Not knowing the full story of what I've been through over the years being your wife. Oh my God! Just sitting here thinking about all of the bullshit I've endured over the years is pissing me off."

Tahari jumped up and started swinging on me and I let her get her row out. She was punching the shit out of me in the same places where she had stabbed me at. That shit was painful but I took it because she needs to get all this pent up anger and frustration out of her. She was amped and all out of breath.

"That's right, get that shit off your chest!" I sat on the edge of the bed and flamed up a blunt because I knew I needed to be high fucking with Tahari when she gets like this. Ain't no telling what the fuck she gone hit me with or when one of them hard ass slaps was coming. I needed to be under the influence because that shit hurt like hell.

"I remember when I was pregnant with our first baby and I was so excited. Only for you to turn around and tell me you thought it was best I get an abortion. In comes Kelis with KJ and baby girl. Then it was okay for me to keep my baby but then I lost him due to stress and pneumonia only for you to turn around and leave me when I got out of the hospital. I could have died when I saw you fucking that hoe in Peaches' bathroom hours after you had broken up with me.

"For months I wondered what I had did to make you treat me so bad. Then we got back together and I got pregnant with Kaine and Kash and you started fucking with that bitch Sabrina. That was one bitch's ass I enjoyed murking. There I was, pregnant with your twin sons and you were out fucking the help. I knew you were cheating on me with her and you continued to lie about it. That's why I broke that bitch jaw and had her sucking out of a straw. I didn't do that bitch dirty because she was fucking you. I toe tagged that hoe for thinking it was cool to fuck my husband and play them teenage ass games with me. Then there was what's her name. The one I shot in her chest and ended up killing her in the end because she thought shit was sweet. I can't even remember it but I bet you and your ass remember. See that's the problem. I've gotten too soft and all in my feelings over shit." I watched as Tahari walked over to her nightstand and pulled out her custom made Tiffany and Co. diamond encrusted nine millimeter.

"What the fuck? Aye man put that shit up!" Now her ass was going too far. I regret the day I taught her ass how to shoot. Tahari pulled the ottoman that was in our bedroom right in front of me and sat in-between my legs with her gun. I just took a long pull off my blunt because she was in rare form. Not to mention on good bullshit with a nigga.

"What you keep scooting back for? I'm not about to shoot you Thug. I'm just holding the gun in my hand that's all," she said, with a devilish grin on her face.

"Quit playing with me. You waving that shit all around and you got that look in your eye like you had when you shot me in the ass. I swear to God if you shoot me this time I'm pressing charges." I was dead ass serious. My ass be hurting like hell from time to time. She has sent my ass to the hospital twice. The third time I might not make it out that bitch.

"The hardest thing I ever had to deal with was you dying on me. I cried every day for you Thug. Then I find out that you were very much alive and fucking your physical therapist who turned out to be a fucking undercover agent. She was another one of your bitches that thought she was slick.

"Ta-Baby you enjoy killing everybody. I understand that you're reminding me of all the pain I caused you, but at the same time you forgave me for all of those things. If you forgive me then that's some shit that you shouldn't bring up. I would hate to think that you were walking around harboring all this resentment towards me. Just recently you were telling me how happy you were with me and how I've been a good husband to you. I'm listening to you right now and you're sounding different."

"I do forgive you, Thug. If I didn't I wouldn't still be here trying to get you to see where it is I'm coming from. In a nutshell, over the years I've been through it all and still stood beside you as your wife. I've told you over the years that I never want to be just your wife. It's imperative that I have an opinion, a voice, and an identity. Boss Lady Inc. is all me. That gives me something to be proud of outside of being your wife. When you just flat out said that we were done, that shit was wrong on so many levels. It would have been different if you had sat me down and we came to a mutual understanding. Instead, you scolded me and treated me like a child and that made me act out.

I understand you're the Head Nigga in Charge and you get the highest honor. However, I'm Boss Lady and I earned that shit. That title wasn't given to me. I put in major work over the years to reach Boss status. If I've never done anything I've earned my respect from the bitches and niggas in the streets. Most importantly, you need to give me the respect that I earned. I just want you to treat me like I'm somebody at all times. I'm really sorry for stabbing you and leaving you like that. I was just scared and I didn't know what to do.

"You know that I love you, I just hate when you get mad at me. You have no limits or boundaries, Ka'Jaire. Going forward, I just want both of us to think before we act. This time around, I don't want you to apologize because I know you're sorry. I just want you to listen."

I grabbed her face and kissed her long and hard. There was so much I wanted to say to her, but I decided to respect her wishes and just take in everything that she'd said. I never want my wife to think that I take her for granted because I don't. Just like most niggas, we get content and forget what's important in a relationship. Yes, I'm comfortable with Tahari and where we are in our marriage. I might be just a little too comfortable because I thought I knew her inside and out. She brought feelings out that I didn't know she had. I never want her to feel like she's less than a woman because she's my wife. There's a method to my madness. She just doesn't understand that when I tell her something, it's for her own good. But of course, she doesn't see it that way.

I was glad that we were at least on speaking terms because I needed to figure out how I was going to tell her about this Python situation. I know that it's going to hurt her, but I would rather she know now than later.

The next morning, I woke up and Tahari wasn't next to me. I swear to God if she'd left, hopped on a plane, and disappeared on my ass again, I was gone fuck her up. She has to stop doing that shit. I pulled the covers back and hopped out of bed. I looked inside all of the kids' rooms and they were empty. I went down the stairs and found Tahari in the kitchen with an apron on, cooking breakfast. I shook my head because if she was cooking that meant she was up to something, or she was about to confess some shit.

"What happened? What did you do and how much will it cost me?" I said as I sat at the table.

"Good Morning to you, too. Why is that the first thing you say when you see me cooking breakfast?"

She came over and placed a plate of fresh fruit in front of me. She dipped one of the strawberries in some whipped cream and fed it to me. Yeah, she was definitely up to something.

"Because I know you and you're up to something. You hate cooking, Ta-Baby."

"I know I do. I just wanted to fix you breakfast for a change."

She placed a plate of blueberry pancakes, turkey bacon, cheese eggs, grits and biscuits in front of me. Tahari can cook her ass off. Her Grandma Lucy taught her well. I wish her ass would cook more often. She sat across from me just staring at me. I knew she was trying to figure out the right time to break whatever news that she was holding in.

"You were right, Thug."

"What are you talking about?" I stopped eating and pushed my plate away. I reached across the table and grabbed her hand. She looked sad all of a sudden.

"You were right about Python. He wasn't genuine with his intentions for me or my sisters."

"You better not cry. Fuck that motherfucker! I already know and that's the real reason I wanted you to end Boss Lady Inc. You guys are on the Fed's radar. I didn't want to come right out and say it because I still needed to get the rest of the information."

"Oh my God, Thug. Why didn't you just tell me? We went through all these unnecessary changes. I stabbed you, for Christ's sake."

Tahari jumped up from her seat and wrapped her arms around me.

"Anything we go through is more of a lesson. It teaches us to love each other and respect one another. I'm fine, my wounds are healing just fine. I want you to tell the rest of your crew about you guys being on the radar. I can't deal with y'all sitting in prison. Make sure you tell them I'm not Sarge, Malik, or Quaadir. I'm getting them bitches back for jumping on me. Peaches gone get it too, because she kicked it off."

I laughed because I still couldn't believe that those bitches had the courage to actually hit Thug.

"They scared to see you, babe. Leave my girls alone."

Tahari walked in front of me and started kissing my wounds on my chest. My dick sat straight up. Tahari put her hand inside my Polo boxers and begin to stroke my manhood. She licked her lips and pulled my dick out.

"I know damn well y'all ain't about to do that nasty shit around all this damn food."

Tahari jumped up and hurriedly put my dick away. I knew I never should have given Malik a fucking key to my crib.

"How in the hell did you get in my house?" Tahari yelled, looking all embarrassed.

Malik dangled his keys in the air and sat down at the table. He grabbed the plate I had and started eating what I hadn't finished.

"Don't try to get off the subject, sis. I see I have to wash the cups before I drink out of them over here, too."

"Stop acting like Barbie don't do dick!"

"I wash the cups behind her ass, too."

I fell out laughing because this nigga is a straight fool. I love my Lil Bro.

"I can't stand you, Malik. Get the hell out of my house!"

Tahari reached for a biscuit, threw it at him, and ran out of the kitchen before he could throw it back at her.

"What the fuck you want, nigga? It better be good, too. Your ass just fucked up a nigga nut."

"You and her are the most dysfunctional couple I've ever met. She was just stabbed you, you was crying about it, she left your ass, she came back, you choked her, and now she in here about to salute you."

"Ain't nobody no more dysfunctional than you and Barbie. I blame you though, because you made that girl crazy whooping on her ass back in the day."

"There you go bringing up old shit. Let me get down to why I'm here. Have you talked to Ma or Markese?"

"Nope. Why you ask that?"

"Aunt Gail missing. Uncle Mike woke up and she was gone. Get dressed so we can get out here and try to figure out where she at. Markese going crazy and Ma is, too."

I hurried up and got dressed because this shit had Python written all over it. I just hope Gail ain't up and walked on Uncle Mike. That shit would be so fucked up. Not to mention if that's the case Markese and Aja will never forgive her. I planned on spending the rest of the day with my wife and kids. So much for a day or rest and relaxation.

Chapter 22- Regretful Love

Gail

This morning I woke up bright and early just like I did every day. Since Mike was still asleep I decided to go to IHOP and grab us some breakfast to go. I walked out and was not paying any attention to my surroundings. As soon as I placed my keys inside my car door, a bag was placed over my head and I was thrown into the trunk of a car. I'd been kidnapped for ransom years back, so I knew not to panic and remain calm. The entire time I was in the damn trunk of the car I was trying to think who in the fuck wanted to kidnap my ass.

During my days of being on drugs I got over on any and everybody I could. Then I thought that it could possibly be someone trying to get back at my son or my nephews. I stopped thinking so that I could focus on what the hell was going on around me. It seemed like I'd been in the car for hours, but I knew it hadn't been that long. This damn trunk was hot as hell. I felt like I was going to die from heat exhaustion. Not to mention the damn gas fumes. I wanted to cry, but I closed my eyes as tight as I could and thought about Mike, my kids, my grandkids, and the rest of my family instead. Lord I've come too far for this to be my ending. How in the hell would they survive without me?"

*****

"Wake up, G-Baby."

The sound of Python's deep voice jarred me from my sleep. The feel of his hand caressing my face made me jump from my not so peaceful slumber. I sat up and looked around. I was on the couch in the living room of his condo. He was sitting across from me smoking on a cigar, looking like the snake that he was.

"Why would you kidnap me like that? I know my kids are worried sick about me."

"I kidnapped you because you won't return my calls and do what the fuck I've asked you to do."

"Well you might as well let me go, because taking me against my will won't make me leave Mike. So you can get that shit out of your head right now."

I'd been ducking and dodging his calls since I realized that he wanted me to relapse on drugs. Python wanted to have mind control over me. He knew the only way he could do that would be to get me back hooked. I did get high with him twice, but once the feeling wore off I knew I never wanted to go back to that life.

Right after I got high that second time, I went home and told Mike. He forgave me and told me I needed to get my shit together or he was leaving my ass for good. The sound of his voice and the look in his eyes let me know that he wasn't playing with my ass. Mike had given me too many chances and I knew he was fed up with my shit. After all, I'd been cheating on him with Python from the moment he came back into my life.

My kids were so mad at me. I had to get my shit together before I lost everything that was near and dear to me. Python wasn't shit and I wasn't about to lose my family behind his demonic ass. This nigga had fooled all of us. He had me thinking that he was a good guy. He was, until he didn't get his way. This motherfucker had to be out of his mind if he thought Ta'Jay, Tahari, or Ta'Keesha were going to go against their husbands for his ass. The moment those girls turned down his offer, he started talking grimy about Sarge, Thug, and Quaadir.

That's where he had me completely fucked up, and where the problem came in. I refused to sit back and let him make idle threats against my fucking nephews. Not to mention talking about how he was going to kill Mike. That was the last and final straw for me. To this day,

I know it was Python who had shot him a while back. He was adamant that it wasn't him, but the more he ran off at the fucking mouth I knew he was the culprit. Mike was shot from behind, so he doesn't know where it came from.

Python stood up from the couch and walked over to where I was sitting. He grabbed me by my hair and yanked my head back hard as hell.

"What you won't do is question me or say shit to me about your motherfucking kids. They aren't mine so I don't give a fuck about them missing you. Your ass might as well get comfortable because this is where the fuck you live now. You can forget about your other life. That shit is a distant memory. Now what you're going to do is call that nigga Mike and tell him that whatever y'all had is over and you're never coming home."

"That crack pipe has fried your fucking brain, Python. You might as well do whatever the fuck you're going to do to me because I refuse to call my husband and tell him some shit like that. Your ass is crazy talking about forget my old life. Let my hair go, motherfucker!"

I yanked away from him but he grabbed me by my throat and begin to choke me to the point where I was seeing spots in my eyes and began to lose consciousness. He let me go and I started coughing and choking. I fell off of the couch and on my knees trying to catch my breath.

"Now, like the fuck I said, you're going to call him and let him know it's over."

"You might as well kill me because that shit ain't happening."

He started beating the fuck out of me like I was a nigga. I was trying my best to fight back, but he wasn't let ting me get a lick in. He delivered a vicious kick to the side of my head that caused me to black out immediately.

*****

I didn't know how long I had been out of it. I came to and was sitting up in his bedroom. I was completely naked. I didn't feel like I had been penetrated, so I didn't understand why he felt the need to remove my clothes. My head was hurting so bad that all I wanted to do was lay down and go to sleep. I was trying to figure out how in the fuck I could get out of here. Python had never been so cruel to me and I knew eventually he would kill me because I was never going to agree to do what he wanted. That shit was out of the question. I was prepared to die at his hands before I made Mike or my kids think I left them for Python's ass.

I got up from the bed and walked over to the bedroom door. I was surprised that it was actually unlocked. I peeked my head out and looked down the long hallway. I was familiar with the layout of his condo because I'd been there on several occasions. If I could make it down the stairs, I would be in the clear. I didn't hear anything so I slipped out and tiptoed to the top of the landing. It was then I overheard him talking. I peeped over the banister to see if I could get a good look at who he was talking to. That's when I realized he was talking on the phone.

"Yeah I have her. She upstairs knocked out cold," He said into the phone. He placed the phone down and flamed up a cigar. During that time a voice that I thought was familiar speak.

"She should be dead. Not out cold. This is what the fuck I be talking about. You're slacking on my fucking watch. You need to handle what the fuck I sent you to handle. Either you do that shit or give me back my ten million dollars."

I could've died when the realization of who the voice belonged to came to my mind.

"I'll handle it. All of that shit ain't necessary."

I immediately turned around and tiptoed back into the room that I was in. I went over to the window and surprisingly it was open. I pushed it open and peered out. I was only on the second level of the condo but it looked like a long ass fall if I jumped. I contemplated for a couple of seconds before I got the courage to jump.

"Where the fuck you going?"

I looked behind me and Python was coming towards me. I closed my eyes and I jumped out of the window. I heard a gunshot go off and I felt pain in my shoulder as I fell down inside the flower bed. It took me about a minute to gather myself before I was able to stand to my feet. My whole body was hurting from the fall and my shoulder was bleeding profusely. Despite being in pain, I knew that had to get the fuck out of dodge and at least make it home to my family to tell them the shit I'd heard.

I wanted to cry because I couldn't believe the shit. I was still naked as the day I was born as I limped down the street. It was late at night so there weren't that many cars out. God must have been on my side because my prayers were answered in the form of a police squad car that came up and helped me. This was the first time in my life I was sitting in the backseat and not in handcuffs. I didn't even care that I was naked I just want to get to wherever my sisters were.

Instead of me calling Mike or Markese, I called Peaches and Sherita. I made sure to tell them not to tell anyone that they had found me and to keep on the low about my whereabouts until after I spoke with them. My shoulder was in so much pain, but I didn't give a fuck. I signed myself out of the hospital and waited for them to come and get me.

*****

"What happened, bitch? Please tell us and be truthful. Did you go with Python willingly?"

I was sitting in the backseat of Peaches' car and I wanted to reach up and slap the shit out of Sherita. I'd only been in the car for like ten minutes and from the moment I stepped in, she'd been giving me the third degree like I had faked getting kidnapped or some shit.

"Come on out and say what you really want to say, Sherita. You think I faked this shit, but I didn't. I'm so sick of your stuck up ass passing judgment on everybody else."

"Don't get mad at me because Python got control over your dumb ass. Got you back smoking that pipe again and shit."

"God damn, Sherita! You talk too fucking much. Didn't I tell you not to repeat that shit?"

I just stared at Peaches and shook my head. She had no business telling this bitch my business. Especially since she was adamant about not fucking with us.

"Why would you tell her my business? Now bitch you would be mad if I told her ass how you be licking Quanie ass. Ooops! Did I spill that tea?"

"Now bitch you dead ass wrong for that. That's my personal business and I'll make sure to never tell your ass nothing else."

"Serves your booty licking ass right. If I wanted the world to know I slipped and smoked some crack, I would've let them know. Sherita's black ass can't hold water. I bet you'll think twice before you tell my motherfucking business again."

I sat back in the seat, very satisfied that I'd put that bitch out on front street.

"Damn sis! You do that shit for real? I wouldn't tell nobody that," Sherita said as she flamed up a Newport. I tapped her on the shoulder so she could hand me a cigarette.

"I'm not ashamed of anything I do in the bedroom with my husband, sis," Peaches said with much confidence.

"That's why you got that little boy running around here like he crazy."

"Shut the fuck up, Gail! Just tell us what the fuck happened so I can drop your worrisome as off to your husband and kids.

"I'm not saying shit until Sherita apologizes to us."

"What the fuck I got to apologize to you bitches for?"

"How about for acting like we personally did something to you? I sold drugs and Gail was strung out on them. Please help us to understand how that affected you."

"It affected me because y'all left me home alone. I needed my big sisters and you guys weren't there for me. All I had was Ma. You guys don't have an idea of what I went through to take care of her. I had no life because I had to deal with our Schizophrenic mother who heard voices and saw people that weren't there. Y'all was out living the life while I was stuck taking care of a woman who told me every day that she wasn't our mother. I never understood any of this because before she went crazy, she was always the best mother in the world to us.

"I had no one to talk to but Dino. I got sick and tired and I just left her and moved with him. To this day, I resent y'all because I didn't have my sisters there to help me deal with her. I vowed to just cut off all ties. I never thought I was better then y'all. I just felt alone because one day we were all together and then it was like I was an only child. I hated y'all for leaving me with her. Even on her death bed she was talking crazy about us not being her daughters and how we needed to take Quaadir from Aunt Ruth. I knew her ass was crazy then because she's the one who talked you into giving her your son. So, I thought she was just talking crazy. That's why I never said nothing."

I laid my head back on the head rest and the wheels in my head started to turn. Something wasn't right and we needed to get to the bottom of it.

"I hate that you felt like that and that you had to go through that. We love you and we're sorry for everything. Could you please find it in your heart to forgive us?" Peaches said as she wiped the tears from her face that had fallen. I wiped my little tears but they weren't all dramatic like Peaches' ass. I was still in my feelings about this bitch thinking I faked being kidnapped.

"Of course I forgive y'all."

We all hugged it out and that was the end of this silly ass beef we all had.

"Are you going to keep sitting back there smoking that motherfucking cigarette and not tell us what the fuck is going on?" Peaches yelled.

"Don't raise your voice at me, bitch. Anyway. Python had me at his house. For some reason it was like he kidnapped me but wasn't acting like I was really kidnapped. This damn fool didn't lock the doors, chain me up, or nothing. He kept demanding that I call Mike and my kids and tell them I was with him now and that I wasn't coming back. I refused to do it so he roughed my ass up.

"He ended up kicking me in my head and knocking me unconscious. When I woke up, I was in the guest room of his condo. I knew I had to get the fuck out of there some way. I saw a side of that nigga that let me know he had every intention on killing me if I didn't do what he wanted me to do. The door was open so I was able to get out into the hallway and that's when I heard him talking on the phone to someone about him having me. Y'all not going to believe who it was telling him that he should've been killed me."

"Who?" They said in unison.

"Aunt Ruth. That was her voice I heard. I've been knowing that woman all my life. Her raspy voice is distinct. That was her, I know it was. But what I don't understand is why she's dealing with Python and why does she want me dead. I ain't never did shit to that bitch."

"I got a bad feeling about this, y'all. Just thinking about how Ma used to tell me to talk to Aunt Ruth about who our mother was and now she wants you dead. Something ain't right, y'all," Sherita said as she flamed up another cigarette.

"There's only one way to find out. We board a private jet to Atlanta. It takes less than two hours to get there. We can go talk to this old bitch and be back before anybody knows it."

"But Peaches, don't you think we should at least tell everybody that Gail is okay."

"No because they won't let us go. I have to go and see what's really good. I gave that lady one of my most prized possessions. My son. My mother convinced me to give my baby to her. I was young and I didn't know any better. I thought my mother and Aunt Ruth knew what was best for me at the time. However, I'm sitting here listening to what y'all saying and that lets me know something ain't right and until we know what's what, I won't rest.

My son, my grandkids, and my daughter-in-law live out there and they love her. I was just out there with my babies sleeping under her roof and she made me feel welcome. But if this bitch got ulterior motives, I want to know about it before it's too late. I just lost a grandson and I'm devastated because I haven't had time to mourn him properly. I've been trying to put my kids and their families back together. If there's an unseen threat and she's it, I want to kill her ass myself. For fucking with my family, and that includes y'all.

"Say no more, sis. Let's take that ride," Sherita said and I was more down than ever. I wanted to know why this bitch wanted me dead.

Chapter 23- Ulterior Motives

Quaadir

Since the incident at the repast, I hadn't spoken to Thug and I wasn't really trying to. This nigga had broken my fucking nose on that jealous shit. He knows motherfucking well there is nothing going on between Ta-Baby and I. That just proves that the nigga still had ill feelings towards me from the shit that happened years ago. Yes, there was a point when I was in love with Tahari, but shit changed when I found out I was married to her sister and she was married to my brother. All of the lustful desires I had for her went out of the window.

I'm not going to lie or front, when we had sex that shit was like moving mountains for a nigga. But I also came to the realization that it wasn't that deep for her. She loves that nigga Thug and I don't know why he doesn't see that she's not checking for me. I wish Keesha would see that I'm not checking for her sister. I've loved Keesha forever and I'm going to be loving her until God calls me home. My wife is the total package, there ain't bitch out here that can hold a candle to her. Not even Tahari.

Keesha is beautiful and sexy as fuck. Going to sleep next to her every night and waking up to next to her is the highlight of my day, every day. A nigga couldn't ask for a better life than the one that Keesha has given to me. So the fact that she thinks she's not good enough for me because of my dealings with Tahari hurts me. I love my wife more than anything in this world. I know that I've been a dog ass nigga in the past but no matter what bitch I fucked or had dealings with, Keesha got my heart.

Since the death of our son, we've been distant with one another. She's sank into a depression and I'm worried about her. Keesha is living in her own existence as if my kids or me don't exist. I'm mourning as well, but I can't forget about my other kids and wife. They still need me to make sure we all get through this together as family. Fuck this street shit, all I want is for my kids and wife to at least get back normal. I know that we won't ever be the same with Quameer being gone, but we have to move forward and be there for each other. Keesha has completely shut down on me. I just need her to let me in so I can take care of her.

*****

"What the fuck!" I said as I walked in the room and observed Keesha laying on the floor with pills spread out in front of her. A fifth of Patrón was sitting on the side of her. I rushed over and I started stepping on all the pills, crushing them. I snatched the bottled up and threw it up against the wall, causing it to shatter.

"No Quaadir, just let me die. I want to be with my baby."

I picked her up off the floor and carried her into the bathroom. I cut on the water and I ran her a hot bubble bath. I removed her clothing and placed her inside of the tub. I've never in my life cried as hard as did when I looked at the shell that my wife had become. She was crying and I was crying even harder. Just knowing that she wanted to kill herself fucked me up in the head on so many levels.

"How you just gone leave us, Ma? What about me and the kids? We already lost Quameer. We can't lose you, too. I'm sorry about everything, Ma. If you don't want to be with me anymore that's fine, but please don't kill yourself. That will kill me, Keesh. Baby, I need you now more than ever. Why would you take those damn pills like that?" I grabbed a towel and poured some Olay body wash on it. I started to wash her body from head to toe.

"I never got a chance to take a pill. You came in before I could."

"Promise you won't do that shit again, man. What the fuck would I tell our daughter and our son if you checked out on me like that?"

"I promise I won't. I just miss my baby so much. I can hear his voice and it's driving me crazy. Just please be patient with me, Quaadir. This mourning period is harder for me than I thought. I'm sorry I've been blaming you and shutting you out. I was wrong on so many levels for that. I think this mourning process has been so hard on me because I've been trying to do it by myself. I know now that I won't get through this without you or the kids. I'm so sorry, babe. Please forgive me for everything."

I lifted her from the tub and dried her off.

"Stop apologizing. You were just hurt. I just want you to know that I'll never leave your side. I also want you to know that I need you in my life. I'm nothing without you. I'm sorry for all the hurt and pain that I caused you during the course of our relationship. I just want us to focus on the healing process."

"I love you so much."

"I love you, too."

I grabbed her around her waist and pull her in closer to me. She wrapped her arms around my neck and we engaged in a passionate kiss. I gently pushed her back on the bed and got down on my knees in front of her. I opened her legs and placed them on my shoulders. I dove in head first and started to feast on her pussy. It'd been so long since I tasted or penetrated her. So this shit was like air to me right now. The sweet smell of her nectar mixed with the Olay gave off an intoxicating scent. I applied pressure to her clit with my tongue as I slipped my fingers inside of her.

"I'm cumming, God!!!!"

Just hearing her call me that made me go harder until she was squirting full force. I had to jump back because that shit was gushing like a waterfall.

"Damn, Bae! You came hard as fuck. I ain't never made you squirt like that."

"That was just round one. Lay back."

I stood up, removed my clothes, and laid back on the bed. Keesha straddled me and I had to brace myself because I knew, without a doubt, I was going bust in a matter of seconds. Keesha and I had been going through so much that we hadn't had anytime to be intimate with one another. So being inside of her for the first time in a long time was like Heaven. That's exactly how her shit felt, too.

Her strokes were slow as she grinded her body into mine. She stared into my eyes as she sucked on each of my fingers. I grabbed onto her waist and tried to gain control because I knew I was about to explode. She knocked my hands away and she begin to bounce up and down wildly.

"Mmmmmmm!" She moaned as she dug her nails into my chest. I wasn't able to hold it any longer. We both came at the same time. If she hadn't got her tubes tied, she would most definitely be popped off.

Keesha hopped up and went into the bathroom. She came out with a hot towel and cleaned me up. Once she was finished, I sat up in the bed and grabbed a blunt from the dresser. Just then, my phone begin to ring. I jumped up and grabbed it from my pants. I looked at the screen and it was Thug calling. I immediately sent the nigga to voicemail. I'm not fucking with him period.

"How long are you going to ignore him? You know he didn't mean it. I'm sure he's just calling to apologize."

Keesha was standing at the foot of the bed putting on her underwear when her phone started to ring. She walked over to the dresser and grabbed it. She looked at the screen and answered it.

"What's up, sis?" I watched as her eyes got big as saucers. That made me step closer to her to see what was going on.

"What's going on?" I asked her and she put up her finger telling me to give her a minute.

"We'll be there shortly."

"Where in the hell are we going?"

"That was Ta-Baby. Aunt Gail is missing. That's why Thug was calling. Thug Inc. back in business. I'm about to pack us some clothes."

"We don't have time for that. We'll grab some shit when we get out there. Let's go now, but first I need to swing by and check on Aunt Ruth. She called and told me she needed to see me and that it was urgent. I don't know what's wrong with her, but lately she's been a little off to me."

"Maybe she's sick."

"No she's not sick. I just came from the doctor with her and she got a clean bill of health. Her doctor told her she was one of the healthiest sixty-five year old he ever seen."

"Are you sure he said that?"

"Yeah I'm sure. Do you know something that I don't know?"

"I need to tell you something but you got to promise that you won't get mad."

I looked at Keesha with a confused look on her face and wondered what in the hell she needed to tell me. I had too much going on already for her to be springing shit on me out of the blue.

"Tell me whatever it is, but I won't promise that I won't get mad."

"I'm confused right now. The day the incident happened with Quameer I had went to see her. She told me that she had Stage Four Lung cancer and didn't have long to live. She also told me not to tell you because she didn't want you to worry. Something is definitely wrong. You heard the doctor say she had a clean bill of health. Now either she lied to me about having cancer or she had the doctor lie because you were sitting there with her. Either way, something ain't right."

Now I was just as confused as Keesha was. Aunt Ruth would never lie about having cancer so she must've had the doctor do that because I was in the room.

"Let's get over there so we can get to the bottom of this." I ran my hand over my face in frustration because I just didn't understand what was going on with Aunt Ruth. If she did have cancer, it would break my heart. That woman raised me and taught me everything that I know. Life for me wouldn't be shit without her. Although Peaches is my birth mother, Aunt Ruth raised me and taught me all the things that a mother is supposed to teach you.

"Don't say anything to her when we get over there about what I told you. Let's just let her tell you everything okay," Keesha came over and wrapped her arms around me. If nobody in the world knew how I felt about Aunt Ruth, she did.

"I think it's better if I go and talk to her alone. I know how much you love her and don't think that I don't care about your relationship with her. I know that she's been the only parent that you've had as well. I just need to see where her head is at, okay." Keesha nodded her head yes.

"I'll just stay here and wait for you to come back. We can catch a flight out to Chicago later. I miss the kids anyway and I'm sure they miss us as well."

"You know what? I need to deal with this situation with Aunt Ruth first. I'll call Thug and let him know I'll be out there first thing in the morning. I want you to book me a flight and send me the flight information. Go on ahead of me so that you can see the kids. That will be good for you, Bae. I promise that I'm right behind you. Kiss the kids for me. I love you, Keesha."

"I love you too, Quaadir. Be careful."

"I'm good. I ain't going nowhere but to Aunt Ruth house."

We kissed each other and I left out of the house. I was anxious to get over to Aunt Ruth's house so I could find out what the fuck was going on with her. Once I found out what was good with her, I could get back to Chicago and make sure my family was straight.

*****

Aunt Ruth was sitting at the kitchen table smoking on cigarette with a bottle of Jack Daniels in front of her. I grabbed a chair and sat at the table with her. I looked and there were numerous black and white photos on the table. I picked a couple up and looked at them. I was shocked to see pictures of Thug at different times.

"What's all of this about?" I said as threw the pictures across the table.

"I've always had high hopes for you. That's why I gave you the drug game. It was my dream to make you the Boss of all Bosses. You have the streets out here in the A on lock, but not like you used to. You've failed me. I don't even feel right calling you God anymore. You let this motherfucker treat you like you're beneath him. He's too powerful. Little too powerful for my taste. Especially since you're supposed to be the chosen one.

"The moment I took you out of that bitch Peaches' arms, I had a plan for you. After I put all of my blood, sweat, and tears into molding you into the perfect Kingpin, you manage to fuck that up in one motherfucking visit to Chicago. The plan was for you to go down there and take that motherfucker out. Imagine my surprise when I get a call from Don Santerelli telling me you done fell in love with this nigga bitch. No, let me rewind that, you hit that motherfucker up and he didn't die."

"Hold the fuck up! I don't know what type of motherfucking drug you're own right now, but you sound crazy as fuck right now.

"What's so crazy about what I'm saying, Quaadir?"

"I don't know who you are right now. You're not the woman that raised me. I'm trying to wrap my mind around what the fuck you saying to me right now. I walk in and you have pictures of my brother on the table like you've had him under surveillance or some shit!"

I watched as she poured herself a shot and flamed up another cigarette. She gave off this devilish ass smirk. It was then I saw a side of her that I never seen. This woman was the devil. This woman, whom I've loved all my life, never had good intentions for me. There was always an ulterior motive behind it.

"You should feel ashamed of yourself sitting over there calling that motherfucker your brother. He doesn't give a fuck about you, that's why you sitting over there with a broke ass nose. I know you wondering why I feel this way towards Thug. No man should have that much power. It's time you do what the fuck you need to do and take over as Head Nigga in Charge. When I sent you out there to kill him, you failed. Now you're in deeper and closer to him and his family. Now is the time for you to get rid of him, once and for all. I raised you. Your loyalty is to me, not to them or that Thug Inc. shit you walking around here repping."

"Wait a minute, let me get this shit straight so that I can understand. You were the one who actually sent me out to Chicago to kill Thug and not Don Santerelli?"

I was now standing to me feet, looking down at her. She was sitting and speaking so nonchalantly. Like the shit she was saying to me was nothing.

"Exactly. Who do you think put them on the payroll? I've sent any and everybody at them that I could. All them motherfuckers failed and got themselves killed, including the bitch Tahari's family members. I go wayyy back with her grandmother Serpent. In case you don't know who Serpent is, that's Venom, Snake, and Python's mother. We were the best of friends growing up. We built the foundation for the Chicago faction. That shit was supposed to remain in our families only, not in the Kenneth family."

"I can't believe this shit. Did you ever love me? Was anything you ever done for me or my wife and kids genuine? You knew he was my brother and you sent me out there to kill him."

I swiped all of the pictures off of the table.

"It was genuine to a certain extent, but I took you from Peaches so that you could serve a purpose in my life and in my drug empire. The moment I laid eyes on you I knew that you would be destined for greatness. So all this shit with you letting Thug steal your shine is unacceptable. I've stood back in the shadows in the hopes that Thug would finally be taken out, but it hasn't happened. It's up to you to take that motherfucker out and take your rightful place as King of the Streets. I didn't lay the foundation for you to be a part of his crew. I laid it so you can run it. So like I said, you need to take that motherfucker out."

"Do you hear what you're saying right now? You want me to kill my brother. Not to mention your nephew."

"Technically, you and Thug are my grandsons."

"Oh really! I need you to enlighten me, because all my life I was raised believing you were my aunt."

I looked up to see my mother, Aunt Gail, and Aunt Sherita coming inside the back door. I was glad I'd left it unlocked. Peaches came over and kissed me on the forehead.

"Aww ain't that sweet," Aunt Ruth said as she acted like she was going to throw up.

"Cut the bullshit you, old ass bitch. Tell us what the fuck is going on. What the fuck have we ever did to you? I'm standing here with a hole in my shoulder because you want me dead. Why are you working with Python against us? From the revelation that we just heard, this shit is deeper than what we think."

Gail bent down and picked up the pictures and started looking through them. She shook her head and handed them to Peaches.

"You crazy old bitch!" Peaches reached across the table and started choking the shit out of her ass.

"Don't kill her yet. We need to find out what we came here for."

Sherita grabbed Peaches back. I was literally at a loss for words. I stared at her dead on, trying to figure out if there ever was a sign that she was against me, but there wasn't. How is it possible that this lady was doing a complete one eighty on me? I can't catch a break. I ran my hand over my face trying to keep the tears away. This shit was hurting me to the core. How was I ever going to get over this?

"Get to talking bitch. I ain't got all day to be dealing with your psychotic ass. I'm just hurt to know that you went out of your way to hurt us. What have we ever done to you?"

"You were born and I never wanted girls. So each time I gave birth to a girl, I gave it to one of my hoes that worked at my brothel. Which is who actually raised you and you believed was your mother. But she fucked up when she gave you my recipe for dope and that wasn't a part of the plan. I threatened to kill that bitch if she didn't give me something to make me feel better and she knew not to fucking play with me. So that's why she convinced you to give me Quaadir. He's always been the chosen one, not Thug. No need to worry, he had the best life a kid could have. I guess it's good he did come with me since you're not that much of a mother anyway."

"You are sick and demented. I'm happy as hell you gave me away. That's the best thing you could have ever done for me and my sisters. I'm not mad at you. I'm actually glad that you did because it made me who I am today. My only regret was giving you my son. He was nothing but a pawn in your sick ass game. Just knowing that you have all these surveillance photos of Thug and you dealing with Python's ass, I don't need to hear anymore. It's obvious who has been against my kids and me from the jump. I just hate it took us so long to figure it out."

I couldn't listen to this shit anymore. This bitch sitting across from me had caused too much pain. At this point, nothing she reveals or says will help me, my mother, or my aunts. She's hurt us enough. And knowing that I loved her with everything inside of me killed my soul. I didn't care whether she had cancer or not because that definitely wouldn't be her demise. I pulled my gun from my waist and let off as many rounds as I had in it in her ass.

"Thank God! I was tired of hearing her ass. Let's go home. You gone be okay, nephew. You're with your real family and we love you," Gail said.

"I think I'm going to be sick," Sherita said as she rushed over and vomited in the sink. Gail went over and helped her get cleaned up. The whole time I was sitting in the same spot, holding the smoking gun, trying to will myself from blowing my own fucking brains out. Everything I thought to be real was fake. Peaches walked over to me and removed the gun from my hand. She lifted my chin up so that she could talk directly into my eyes.

"Let me tell you something Quaadir Kenneth, you are my son and one of the best things that has ever happened to me. Had I known that this bitch was just using you as a pawn, I would have fought for you to the bitter end. I was young and I didn't know any better. I was raised to believe that Mona was our mother. No, she *was* my mother and she took damn good care of us. She's not here to defend herself or explain, so it doesn't matter and I don't even care. I have you in my life and that's all that matters.

There's nothing this bitch can do now to rip our family apart. She thought that she could pit us against each other and act like she was a godsend to us, but in the end we won baby. We found each other. You don't ever have to worry about shit again. I love you. We all love you. Come on, baby. Let me take you home to Chicago where you belong."

Peaches grabbed me by the hand and led me out of the house. The same house that I grew up in was the now the house that I hated. How could a house full of great memories turn into a house of horrors? I had no idea how I was going to get through this shit. At the same time, I was glad that I found out Ruth's true intentions. I would've ended up killing her ass anyway, because I was never going to kill Thug. Granted when I didn't know he was my brother and I wanted to kill him. That shit was business. I've built an unbreakable bond with not only Thug, but my entire family. Thug is my best friend outside of being my brother. I would never bring harm to him. He would give his life for me without hesitation, and I would do the same for him.

About an hour later, I'd boarded a flight back to the Chicago, still confused about the things that had transpired. I'd lost so much in a matter of months. I needed Keesha and my kids more than ever at this point. The chapter of what I thought was my life was now over and it was time to let that shit go and focus on my future with my family.

Chapter 24- When It's All Said and Done

Thug

The whole family had been out all day trying to find Gail with no luck. It was late at night and I'd told everyone to just head home and we could regroup in the morning. Markese and Mike were apprehensive, but I knew it was for the best. I had met up with Adonis because he had some information on where I could find the nigga Python. I didn't even tell the rest of the family how Adonis had been helping me. He was like my ace in the hole. So far all of the information that he'd brought me panned out. When he disappeared and then reappeared all of sudden, I was skeptical, but he's proven his loyalty to this family. I'm glad he did because he was on my list for people to murk. My list was no longer that long since I'd killed all of my enemies over the years. Just sitting back and thinking about the shit is giving me a hard on out of this world.

I knew in my gut this nigga Python is behind kidnapping Gail. All the evidence points to him. I also needed to get at him for playing with my wife's heart and wasting her time. I already had every intention on killing him from the jump. I was just waiting for a valid reason. Not that I needed one.

I just had to be able to show my wife that he wasn't shit and he'd proved me right. I knew when he made his surprise ass appearance there was going to be trouble. Anything remotely related to Venom or Snake I knew was no fucking good. I had to give it to him though, he did a hell of a job at playing the victim to his child molester ass Momma. I don't even believe that story now.

I was glad that Quanie no longer had dealings with Python. Quanie never elaborated to me as to why he hated his father these days, but I knew it had to be serious when he told me he didn't care if I killed him because he'd never been a father to him anyway. For some reason I thought it was so much more to it than that, but I didn't ask. I was happy he was onboard because I would've hated to leave my mother a widow and the twins fatherless. I have to kill any and all potential threats, but just seeing Quanie point his gun at his father and some of his men, I knew he didn't care about that nigga.

As I headed towards Python' condo I couldn't do shit but think of Quaadir. I felt bad as hell for fighting him and breaking his nose. That shit just showed me that I was a crazy ass nigga behind Tahari. I never meant to break my brother's nose. Just seeing my wife hugging him did something to me.

I'd been calling so that I could apologize but the nigga wasn't answering. He was sending my ass to the voicemail and leaving my texts messages unanswered. I wasn't mad at him, though. He had every right to be in his feelings. I just needed him to know that he was my brother and I was sorry. I pride myself on the love of my siblings, so the fact that he and I weren't on the best of terms was fucking me up in the head. I finally have all of my brothers and that shit meant everything to me. I've never in my life been the type of nigga to apologize for shit if it wasn't to my wife, and I hate to apologize to her ass because she takes that shit to the extreme.

However, Quaadir deserves the biggest apology ever. We've come too far in building our relationship and friendship to end it over my jealous ways. I just can't help it, though. My wife got the best pussy on the planet. I'm not trying to share that shit with anybody. In my head I'm her first, last, and her everything. In reality, the only nigga I knew that had it was dead and I liked it that way. My brother got a sample by default. Had it not been for Peaches, I probably would've killed him years back. That's my nigga though, and I wouldn't trade him for the world.

*****

All of the lights were off at Python's condo when I pulled up. I knew that his ass was most likely gone by now but I wanted to make sure I saw that shit for myself. I tightened the strings on my all-black hoodie and I checked the chamber of my gun. I hopped out my truck with my gun down to my side. I checked all of the doors and they were locked. I went around and saw that the patio door was shattered. I stepped inside and that's when I heard a man's voice and what sounded like moaning. I walked through the house trying to find out where the moaning was coming from.

I stepped into the kitchen and that's when I saw Python on the floor in a puddle of his own blood. Someone was standing over him aiming a gun at him. I couldn't see the full body of the person but I was able to see the black glove with the sparkle of diamonds shining on the wrist. It didn't take a rocket scientist to figure out who in the hell kills people iced the fuck out. I must say my money looks good on my wife. I stepped all the way into the kitchen and she locked eyes with me. She turned back around and let off a shot into Python's gut.

"Ahhhhhh!" He howled out in pain as he held his stomach.

"I thought I told you to go home and wait until I got there." I say in a low tone in her ear.

"If I was going to retire Boss Lady Inc., I needed to go out with a bang. Not to mention getting rid of the last of my bloodline that walked the Earth. I knew you could handle him, but it would be even better if we did it together. A Boss and his Boss Lady, what better way to end a dynasty than to do it with your better half?" Tahari reached back and pulled my head in so that we could kiss.

"That's real. Did he tell you anything about Gail?"

"Yeah. She got away from his ass."

Tahari let off another shot in his right leg. That shit made me jump because I didn't expect for her to let off that shot in mid-conversation.

"You sexy ass fuck when you torturing people. Feel that, got me rocked up."

I grabbed Tahari's hand so that she could feel my dick. She turned around and we started to kiss passionately. The whole time that we were engaged in the kiss, I had my gun pointed and one eye opened watching his ass.

"I'm ready to take you home and do that motherfucker the right way."

"Well you know we got a murder to commit first but before we do that. Let's find out why he was talking to Feds and why he never meant you or your sisters any good."

I felt Tahari needed to know so that she could have closure and move on from all of the years of hurt and pain that her family had caused her.

"After all that I've been through at the hands of these people, it doesn't even matter to me anymore. I already know the reason and I'm looking at him. Every enemy, friend, or foe that ever trespassed against me was mad at me for loving you. I chose you then and I choose you now. I'll do the shit all over again if it meant I could meet you, marry you, and give birth to all your babies.

"You're all the family and validation I need. Nobody can hurt me to the point where I give up or walk away from you. You've made me the happiest woman in the world. Which is more than I can say for my supposed-to-be family members. This beef started before we were ever born. Our parents started it and we get to finish it and live our happily ever after. You see, you met me at my lowest point and you loved me despite the black eyes and bruises. I met you, and if I can remember correctly, you said it was fate that brought us together. I used to think you were crazy, but after all of these years together. I know for a fact it was fate. It was meant for us to go through everything with each other.

"When I was younger, I dreamed of a Fairytale life with my Prince Charming, but that was just a dream. I had no idea my reality would be a nigga named Thug with Pussy Monster tatted across his chest. No matter what, you've always been here to save me. Right now you're here to defend my honor. Even when I'm hardheaded and I don't listen, you turn right around and go hard for me.

"I'll never love another man and another man could never replace you. You've been more than just a husband, my best friend, and the father of my children. You're my knight in shining armor and I don't know where I would be without you. From the beginning of our love affair you gave me that Thug Passion, you took me to Thug Paradise, and now can finally live our happily ever after in Thug's Mansion. Let's kill this motherfucker and go home to our babies."

Tahari turned around placed her hood back on her head and I did the same. We lifted our guns and aired Python's ass out. We held hands and walked out a stronger united front than we were before.

*****

I sat at the head of the massive dinner table dressed in an all-black tuxedo, smoking on a Cuban cigar. I took a puff and exhaled as I observed my family in all of our greatness. We'd all been on a journey of love and redemption together. I smile as I look at my mother and Quanie. This is the happiest she's been in a long time. Peaches deserves it though, she's been through a lot. Outside of my wife, she's the strongest person I know.

I look across the table at Ta'Jay and Sarge. It warms a thug nigga's heart to see her happy and able to live out the rest of her life with her first love. I laugh on the inside when I remember how we found out they'd been fucking around. She was willing to go against her family to be with that nigga. I wasn't mad at her then and I'm not mad at her now. I'm just glad they were able to fix things.

I raise my glass and salute my twin brother, Quaadir. he's been through some shit and I'm just glad we have him here with us where he belongs for good. I never in a million years would have thought that Aunt Ruth was behind all of the attempts on my life. That just goes to show you, no one is to be trusted, not even sweet old ladies who claim to love you. Quaadir and Keesha had been coping the best way they could with the death of their son. It was a long journey but as long as they had each other, they would be just fine.

Then there's crazy ass Malik and Barbie. I don't even have to go in-depth about them, because they are who they are and they will never change. Of course they're still arguing and fighting no matter where they are. That's just how they express their love for one another.

It made a nigga happy to finally see Remy happy and accepting the fact that we are indeed family. He never again would have to worry about betrayal of a loved one because all of us in this room were loyal to one another, without a doubt. Having him and Rosé as a part of our family was a beautiful thing. I was happy to have Aunt Sherita in our lives. It was always plenty of laughs when her, my mother, and Gail got together. They needed each other to heal their unknown and fucked up pasts.

I looked at Adonis and I was still surprised to see that he was married to Barbie's brother/sister Chrissy Poo. Yes, you heard me right. I don't know what that makes him, but that shit don't matter to me and I make sure to let everyone else know it doesn't matter. That's our brother and what he chooses is his decision. Although we all know that Malik has had a field day with the jokes about this shit, at the end of that day he's family. Nothing in this world means more to me than family. We've been through it all and survived successfully. I wouldn't change them for anything in the world.

I wink my eye at my wife who's sitting at the other end of the table dressed in an all-black Roberto Cavalli custom-made gown. Of course she rocking Red Bottoms and iced the fuck out. You already know Ta-Baby does no fucking around when it comes to her wardrobe. There was a point in time where she would try to match my fly, these days I match hers. I observe my children and I'm proud to say that they are a reflection of Tahari and me. I can't wait to see how their story plays out. We've laid the foundation, it's up to them to carry on the Legacy.

As I knock back a shot, I close my eyes and thank God for sparing me. Most niggas don't live to enjoy their wife, children, or the money. I'm just thankful to be in the land of the living, enjoying my family, and living off the fruits of my labor. With everything that has been stacked against me, I'm surprised I made it this far. I've been through it all and I finally get to rest, kick it, and smoke my Kush in peace, in the comfort of my chromed out paradise. There ain't no Heaven for a Thug like me. That's why we go to Thug's Mansion.

THE END

Introducing Thug Legacy
(I am My Father's Son)

Chapter 1- Ka'Jairea

Some odd years later

I cried my heart out as I sat in my bedroom listening to *4 page letter* by Aaliyah. I loved all the old school songs my momma listens to when she in her feelings about my Daddy. He could be lying in bed right with her and she would still be in her feelings about something. My mother is spoiled rotten and it's my dad's fault. That's why when she gets in her moods he pays her no attention because that's all she wants is some attention. I look at my father and mother and I could only wish that I would be so lucky to have a relationship like theirs. At one point I thought that was going to happen but now I'm not so sure.

As I sit here writing this letter to Lil Hassan I just don't know what to do. Since the age of thirteen I had been in love with him and I knew for a fact he loved me. I was so in love with him that I gave him my most prized possession. My virginity. He took it and ran with it. Things were good with us until he became what every girl dreads. A Dopeboy. I guess in a way I shouldn't be mad because I knew that was his destiny along with my brothers. I'm so scared for all of them because the streets aren't like they used to be when my father was in the streets wreaking havoc. Now there is no code in the streets or honor amongst men.

My brother is considered the Prince of the Chi. Even though my father is retired he still reigns Supreme. He still has the power to shut shit down and make niggas bleed if they breathe wrong.

Nowadays KJ is the go to nigga and Head Nigga In Charge of Legacy Inc. His crew consists of Kaine, Kash, Lil Markese, Lil Sarge, Lil Hassan, Lil Rahmeek, Lil Malik, and Khiandre. These niggas are some young money getting niggas and goons just like their fathers. They might just be worse. I've sat back and watched how my brother moves and I am amazed. My father should be so proud to see my brother carry on his Legacy.

As I sit here and go through my Instagram I want to cry. The sight of Hassan and his new girlfriend is killing my soul. We haven't been broken up a good week and he out with these bitches showboating. I should buss the windows out of his car like my momma told me to do. Then again I'm too fly for that shit. I'm gone just have to show him that two can play that game. I'm the daughter of a Boss Lady. So without a doubt my moves must be Bossy. At the same time I should have listened to my father when he told me niggas ain't shit and all they do is break your heart. My father ain't no saint but he knows what's best for his Babygirl.

*****

"I'm telling you don't do this?" I stood in the bathroom fixing my makeup with my best friend Hadiyah completely ignoring what the hell she was talking about. We were at my mother's boutique hardly working as usual. It was just something for us to do and to help out my mother because she was so busy with our other businesses. It had been a year since we graduated from high school. I wouldn't dare go away to college so I enrolled at the University of Illinois with a major in Nursing. Of course Hadiyah did the same as well. We had been best friends since Kindergarten. So there was no way we were going to different colleges or to other states. Plus, for some reason I think my parents didn't want me to leave anyway.

"Why shouldn't I do it? Your brother out here in these streets making a fool out of me. I refuse to keep sitting waiting for him to come back to me. Fuck that shit. I understand that 's your brother but fuck that nigga. I'm sick of him trying to treat me like I'm one of these random ass bitches he out here fucking with. He got me fucked up."

"Look I understand that you're mad and all in your feelings. At the same time you know this shit will cause a war if you go out with that nigga Kato. He a Southside ass nigga and you know they beefing with them niggas. This ain't about my brother this is about your brother and the drama that your ass is about to cause because you in your feelings." I rolled my eyes because that was the last thing I wanted to hear. Kato had been trying to get me to go out with him for the longest but I kept curving his ass because I wanted to be with Hassan.

"I ain't got shit to do with that Hadiyah." I grabbed my purse and I headed out of the door.

"Your ass hardheaded. Don't call me crying when KJ beat your ass."

"You must got me mixed up with you. I'll fuck KJ up with the quickness if he even thinks about it and he knows it. You are the only one scared of my brother sweetie. I love you though friend. I'll call you later and tell you how my date went." I kissed her on the cheek and rushed out of the door. I didn't want to hear her clap back from my statement. She hated when I threw KJ in her face. I loved my brother but he had her wrapped around his finger and he was so damn aggressive with her when he got mad. I hate how he treats her but if she like then I love it. I found out to mind my business a long time ago when it came to KJ and Hadiyah. He was gone do whatever he wanted to do and she was going to be sitting idly by until he came around and did right by her. I loved Lil Hassan but I refused to be a dummy for his ass.

******

When I walked outside Kato was standing outside his cocaine white Benz with a bouquet of beautiful red roses. This nigga was dark chocolate and sexy as fuck. He was rocking an all white Robin Jeans suit and the matching hat along with a pair of white and gold Giuseppe's to match. I blushed as I walked over towards him and he handed me the roses.

"These are for you beautiful. Thank you so much but you didn't have to do that." He said as he handed the roses to me and we engaged in a hug.

"The Princess of the Chi is going out on a date with the nigga the streets call Kato. I had to come correct Lil Ma." He said as he opened the passenger side for me and I slid in. I was so nervous because I had never dealt with any nigga outside of Hassan so this shit was new to me. As soon as we were about to pull off KJ swerved his Ferrari in front of Kato's car and hopped out. I was about to piss on myself when I see him walking towards the car with his gun out.

"Get the fuck out the car now!" He roared as he banged on the passenger side window with butt of the gun.

"I'm so sorry about this Kato."

"It's cool. You might want to do as your brother say. I promise we'll get our chance to kick it." He said with a grin on his face. I hurried up and stepped out of the car and immediately KJ yoked me up by the collar of my shirt.

"You trying to get this motherfucker murked huh?

"You ain't got to manhandle her like that my nigga." Kato said as he jumped out of the car.

"How the fuck I handle my sister ain't none of your concern. If you want to make it home back to yours I suggest you walk that shit off. Take your ass back to the Southside with your whack ass crew!" KJ cocked his gun and started walking towards the driver side where Kato was standing.

"Please KJ stop!" I screamed at him through tears as I tried to pull him back.

"Get your ass in the car Baby Girl!"

"You got this one my dude. I'll be seeing you around. Stay sexy Babygirl." Kato said as he licked his lips and hopped back in the car and blasted Chief Keef as he drove away. I looked up and watched as Hadiyah walked her simpleminded ass out of the boutique and got inside of his car. I just shook my head at her and walked over to my own car. I sped away and headed straight home. I knew it was about to be some shit when I got there. I was ready to hear my father's mouth. He hated the entire Southside with a passion. He was more of a Westside nigga and that's how we were all raised. I was so mad at Hadiyah because I keep all of her secrets. Just for that I'm about to tell my brother her ass pregnant by him and too afraid to tell it. That will teach her ass about running off at them big duck ass lips of hers.

Chapter 2- KJ

Stuntin Like My Daddy, I Ain't Nothing Like My Momma

It took everything inside of me not to knock this nigga Kato shit back. He knows motherfucking well not to ever grace the Westside if he wasn't ready for a gunfight. What my dumb ass sister didn't know was that me and that nigga was beefing big time over territory. Niggas in this city knows that I run shit on the West, South, East, and North side of Chicago. I just choose to stay on the Westside were the fuck I was born and raised. Any nigga from any other set knows they work through me. Kato wants to run his shit on the Southside. That's all fine and dandy. I want everybody to eat but of course them niggas got to pay me to do it and it ain't no way around it.

The niggas over East and Up North fell in line quick because of course they don't want no smoke from the kid. Kato and his crew insisted on thinking this shit is a game. He just don't know the only reason I didn't leave his brains on the side of him was because my sister and my girl was in close proximity to us. He lived another day but his time is almost up. I've let that nigga slide for the last time because apparently that nigga starting to think he can ice skate.

This is exactly why I didn't want her and Hassan to mess around in the first place. She was only doing that shit to get back at him not knowing the consequences that were sure to follow. My father insists that I keep my sisters and brothers out of harms way and that's what I intend to do. The last thing I want to do is let my father down. He's passed the torch on to me and I have every intention of running the city just the way he did and maybe even better.

I knew my sister was mad at me but I didn't give a fuck because she knew better than to be fucking with that Southside ass nigga. She hopped in her car and sped off almost hitting my shit. I knew she was trying to beat me there but it didn't matter because our Pops already knew. Who do you think told me to get my ass over to the boutique and get her ass? I slid inside my car and looked over at Hadiyah who was trying her best not to look at me and I knew her ass was fully aware of what the fuck was going down. So since she didn't tell me I'm gone punish her ass too.

"Where you want me to drop you off at?"

"What the fuck you mean where I want you to drop me off at? I thought we agreed that I was spending the rest of the day with you."

"I need to head over to the crib and handle this shit with my sister. So, again where do you want me to drop you off at?"

"You know what KJ you don't have to take me anywhere? Let me out. I'll call me a Uber or something. I don't have time for your wishy washy ass. You must think I'm stupid or some shit. Gone head over that bitch Trese house. I swear when ever I catch you and her together I'm fucking both of ya'll up." I couldn't do shit but laugh because Hadiyah was so quiet and mild mannered until a motherfucker made her mad. Hadiyah and I have history and I know that one day I'm going to settle down and make her my wife. Right now I'm married to the streets and I'm just not ready for the commitment that she wants.

"Calm your ass down and watch how the fuck you talk to me. Fuck Trese. I don't fuck with her like that so all that shit ain't necessary. You of all people know I'm not about to sugar coat my whereabouts. If I was going over to her house to fuck with her then I would tell you. I never lie to you about these hoes that I fuck with. I'm like that because you have my heart and it ain't a hoe out here that can come and tell you some shit about me that you don't already know. Plus, you know how this shit go when I'm with you, I'm with you and when I'm not, I'm not." I leaned over and grabbed her chin and kissed her passionately.

"That's just it you're never with me and I'm tired of waiting on you KJ. I know you have to handle your business but why must I get the short end of the stick. I deserve better than to sit back and wait for you to come around and be with me. So, I'm done with you. Going forward it's all me or nothing. You don't have any idea how many niggas I turn down out of respect for you but you won't do the same for me. Every time I turn around you fucking with these tired ass bitches. I'm mentally and physically exhausted. My hair is falling out from the stress KJ." Hadiyah put her head down in her hands and started to cry. Lately, she had been so emotional and the shit was driving a nigga crazy. I was starting to think her ass was Bi-Polar or something. "Stop crying man. You're upset for shit. Hadiyah you know you got my heart and one day I'm going to make you my wife. Them other bitches ain't nothing to me. Come on we can kick it the rest of the day. You need some of this dick in your life that's why you sitting over there all emotional and shit." I grabbed her hand and kissed the back of it and we headed over to my parents crib.

******

As soon as I pulled into the driveway my Pops was standing in the driveway washing his old school box Chevy. He had nothing but the latest luxury cars but he loved the first car he ever had. That car is his baby. Not even my mother is allowed inside. So you know that car got to mean something to him.

"What's up Pops?"

"Don't what's up Pops me. Where the fuck is Kaine and Kash? Go in the house Hadiyah let me holla at my son real quick."

"Yes Sir." I grabbed Hadiyah and kissed her on the cheek before she headed inside.

"I don't know I haven't talk to them since earlier when we made that pick up." I was fuming because they never did shit they were told. Little niggas is straight savages.

"Them little niggas gone make me fuck them up out here on that dumb shit. You need to get a handle on your motherfucking crew. Brothers or not put them in their place. What's this I hear about them running up on Ingleside and airing the fucking block out in broad daylight?"

"I don't know shit about that Pops." He threw the sponge he was washing his car with at me and I jumped back before the water could get on me.

"That's the problem. You need to make it your business to know what the fuck your crew doing as a matter of fact they don't make moves unless you tell them to. This my last time getting on you in regards to your fucking operation then I'm going to step in and regulate my way."

"I got it under control Pops."

"Fuck under control! I want that shit in order. " Before I could respond my mother appeared in the door looking mad as ever.

"KJ get your ass in here right now! You come too Ka'Jaire. It seems like our son is about to be a daddy and we don't know shit about it." She walked down the stairs and staring beating my ass with a broom stick.

"What are you talking about Ma? I don't got no kids on the way." I was dead ass serious. I had no idea what the hell she was talking about.

"Give me this damn broom! Get your ass in the house with them damn booty shorts on got these nosey ass neighbors looking at my shit. " My father said as snatched the broom from my mother and threw across the lawn.

"I'm in the prime of my life. I'm far too young to be somebody's grandma. How could you be so careless KJ? My mom said with tears in her eyes.

"I swear to you Ma. I don't know nothing about nobody being pregnant." I had to grab my mom and look in her eyes to let her know I was being truthful. Plus, I hate to see my mother cry about anything. When I was younger I wanted to murk my Daddy when he would hurt her. So, the last thing I would ever want to do is make my favorite girl in the world cry.

"Can we please take this shit in the house so that I can find out what the fuck is going on?" My father said and the veins in his head was sticking out so pissed wasn't even a word. He was mad as fuck and he wanted to kick my ass but I hadn't did anything wrong. I walked into the house followed by my parents and the first person I saw Hadiyah and she was crying.

"I'm sorry KJ. I've been trying to tell you but I just couldn't find the words."

"We were just in the car together you could have told me then. Why would you come in here and tell my mother some shit that you could have told me?"

"Watch your mouth!"

"I'm sorry Ma. I'm just saying that was foul on her part. If she supposed to be carrying my seed don't you think I should have been the first to know?"

"True she should have told you but she didn't even tell me. Ka'Jariea is the one who came in here airing shit because she mad at Hadiyah for telling KJ about messing up her date with some damn boy named Kato." My mother said as she turned her glass of wine up and drank it straight down. OG was stressing for real.

"Wait a minute. Let me get this straight you're mad at your brother about some fuck nigga you was about to go on a date with that you knew was against this family. Don't be mad at him be mad at me because I told him to go get your ass. You ain't no better than Yah-Yah walking around here telling people fucking business. Get out my sight Baby girl because that shit was dead ass wrong and you know it!"

"Why you cursing at me?" I knew them tears were coming and I could see that my father was about to get weak for her ass.

"Look Baby Girl I –" My father tried walking towards Ka'Jariea but my mother stepped in his path.

"Hell no! Ain't no fucking explaining she dead ass wrong. She can take her ass upstairs and sulk. While we handle this shit here. I've been telling you for years to stop walking around here letting these girls get away with murder Thug.

"Go on with that bullshit Ta-Baby! How I am with the girls ain't no different then how you are with the boys. While you worried about me and how I discipline the girls you need to talk to Kaine and Kash about the shit they out here doing before I break my foot off in their ass. You got this one here standing in front of us about to be a father. After all the talks and unlimited condoms that I supply him with. You would think he would have prevented this." My father grabbed a Newport from the pack and flamed it up.

"Wait a minute. What the hell are you doing with an unlimited amount of condoms?"

"Not right now Ta-Baby. This is not the time for you to make this about us."

"Yeah aaight! Don't make me come out of retirement. Ms.Pearlie all shined up and ready. You know how I roll." My father just started laughing and grabbed her around the waist and kissed her on the neck. Just that quick they forgot about the elephant in the room but I didn't needed to holla at Hadiyah alone. Her being pregnant had a nigga feeling some type of way. Especially since she claimed to be on Birth Control

Pills. I'm nineteen years old and the last thing on my mind is being a father.

"Can I please talk to Hadiyah alone first? Then I'll be able to talk to you guys after."

"Handle your shit KJ!"

"I got you Ma Dukes." I grabbed Hadiyah by the hand and led her upstairs to my old bedroom. I no longer lived at home but my room was still available if I ever wanted to sleep over or needed to come home. Once we were inside of the room Hadiyah looked like she was trembling and nervous.

"What you all nervous and shit for?"

"I'm not nervous KJ. I'm scared. I'm only nineteen. My daddy is going to kill me. This was the one thing he asked me not to do. He gave me permission to be in a relationship with you. Once he finds this out he's going to make me stop seeing you.

I just shook my head at her this was one of the things that made me not want to be exclusive with her. She had no mind of her own. She's grown and still answers to her parents. That shit so childish to me. I need my bitch available to make decisions for herself. The line of work that I'm in needs me to have a bitch that thinks on her toes. I'm not going to even respond to any of this other shit she talking about especially since she promised that she was taking her Birth Control faithfully.

"I thought you were on birth control? Let me find out."

"What the fuck you mean let you find out? What you trying to say? That I got pregnant on purpose?" Hadiyah was now crying again. No wonder her ass was crying and emotional all the damn time she was pregnant.

"I mean you keeping the shit a secret from me. You told me that you were taking your Birth Control Pills. I never would have dropped my seeds off in you had I known you were trying to trap a nigga. I can honestly say I'm not ready for kids. I have too much on my plate with running my father's empire. I think it's best for you to get an abortion." I handed her all of the money I had in my pocket. Hadiyah stared at me through hurt eyes. I felt bad that I was the reason for her tears. I fucked with Hadiyah the long way. She was a good girl in love with a street nigga. Right now I'm married to the streets and it comes first with a relationship coming second. She might not understand now but she will without a doubt thank me later.

"You know what KJ. Fuck you and your money. I'll pay for my own abortion." She threw the money and it hit me in my face and it all fell to the floor.

"Pick my motherfucking up!" I grabbed her by her hair and forced her down to the floor to get the shit up. Hitting me in my face with that dirty ass money was disrespectful. Hadiyah of all people know how I am when it comes to respect. She picked it all up and handed it back to me. I let her go and roughly pushed her ass away from me.

"I would never trap you KJ. I've been in love with you since I was thirteen. How could you ever think I would do something so foul? I agree that we're both young and right now isn't the time to have a baby. A part of me just wished that you would have shown an ounce of happiness for the life that we created. Then again I'm not surprised at your reaction. That's why I had been scared to tell you from the jump. In my heart I knew that you would have that negative ass reaction. After all you don't really love me. I'm the most loyal bitch on your team. Yet, you treat me like shit for all these random ass hoes. I'm going to walk out of here and I will schedule an abortion. I don't want anything from you and I don't want you either. Loving you is too hard and it hurts too much." She took off her Tiffany necklace and tennis bracelet and threw it on the bed. A part of me wanted to grab her as she walked out of the room but my pride wouldn't allow me to do it.

"What did you do to her?"

"Get the fuck away from this door. This shit is all of your fault anyway. You did this shit because you can't fuck with some square ass nigga. Instead of standing here questioning me you need to go and make sure Hadiyah straight." Ka'Jairea had a lot of fucking nerve after just exposing her best friend like that.

"Last time I checked you didn't live here. Don't take your anger out on me because you just lost the only girl who really loves you KJ. You need to go after her. I can't believe you treated her like that Bro. We all heard everything. That's how damn loud you were. Momma said bring your ass downstairs. Just to give you heads up she got her broom in her hand. I advise you to tuck and roll you know how them Boss Ladies do it." I needed to get the fuck out of this house before my momma put me in the hospital. I know for a fact she's about to wild out. As I got up and headed back downstairs to face the music with Ka'Jairea I could hear my parents arguing.

"I'm done discussing this shit. Her getting an abortion is what's best right now. KJ did the right thing by telling her to get an abortion. Business is what's more important right now. Having a family will knock him off of his square.

"Like father like son huh?"

"What the hell is that supposed to mean?"

"I know exactly how that girl feels right now. I know you like to suppress a lot of shit and act like it never happened but I don't forget shit. This reminds me of when I first got pregnant by you and you wanted me to get an abortion. That shit hurt me to my heart. Especially when I came back home to find out that you were the father of three year old twins. Don't even let me get started on the bitch Kelis."

"Who is Kelis?" Babygirl had took the words right out of my mouth. At the same time I was trying to see what three year old twins she was talking about. I looked at both my mother and my father trying to read their facial expressions.

"What three year old twins? We got some more siblings ya'll never told us about or something?" I asked in a joking manner but serious as hell. My mother looked at my father before she spoke.

"You and Ka'Jairea were those three year old twins. Kelis was the person that gave birth to you. From the day your Daddy bought you guys home I've loved you. You guys are my kids and I'm your mother." She tried to step toward me but I step back.

"So ya'll lied to us!" I yelled.

"Watch who the fuck you're hollering at!" My Pops said as he started walking towards me but my mother grabbed him back.

"Where is Kelis now?" Ka'Jariea asked. My mother got ready to respond my father but his hand up.

"She abandoned ya'll. This the last time we will ever have this conversation. Tahari took ya'll in and raised you as her own and she is your mother. Show her some fucking respect and stop asking about a bitch who didn't give a fuck about you." My father said as he walked away. My mother sat down on the couch and out her face I her hands.

"It's okay Ma. We love you. Don't be upset. I hate it when you cry. You have nothing to worry about you're our mother." I kissed her on her left cheek and Baby Girl kissed her on the right. I hurried up and left out because the shit had me fucked up in the head. Ka'Jariea and I both handled the situation accordingly because she is our mother but to know that she didn't birth us is like a dagger. I wonder do our brothers and sisters know?

As I drove home at every red light I tried to sit back and think if I could remember something. For some reason I remember getting pushed by a woman into the street and a car hit me. I was in such a deep thought that I snoozed and I didn't realize until the first bullet hit me in the stomach. I looked up and saw the nigga Kato hanging out of a passenger side window of a car shooting at my ass. I got hit up a couple of more times before I stepped on the gas and crashed head on into a truck. The last thing I remember was my car flipping several times.

Stay Tuned For More
Thug Legacy

CPSIA information can be obtained
at www.ICGtesting.com
Printed in the USA
LVOW04s1747021216
515533LV00010B/890/P